MAKE ROOM
FOR THE JESTER

LIBRARY OF WALES

Thomas Evan Jones was born in 1922 and brought up in Pwllheli, north Wales. He attended University College Bangor, where his studies were halted by World War Two and five years in the British Army. He found himself in France on D Day, and was later promoted from private to corporal and given a signal detachment in India and Burma. After demobilisation he completed his degree and teaching qualifications. In 1952 he took the position of lecturer in Liberal Studies at Leyland Motors Technical College in Lancashire, where he remained until his retirement. He married and was the father to two daughters.

His first novel, *Make Room for the Jester*, was published in 1964 in both the UK and the USA to much critical acclaim. It was followed in 1966 by *The Ballad of Oliver Powell* (published under the title *The Man with the Talents* in the USA), and in 1968 by his third and last novel, *The Lost Boy*. He published all his books under the name of Stead Jones. He died in 1985.

MAKE ROOM FOR THE JESTER

STEAD JONES

PARTHIAN
LIBRARY OF WALES

Parthian
The Old Surgery
Napier Street
Cardigan
SA43 1ED
www.parthianbooks.co.uk

The Library of Wales is a Welsh Assembly Government
initiative which highlights and celebrates Wales' literary
heritage in the English language.

Published with the financial support of
the Welsh Books Council.

www.libraryofwales.org

Series Editor: Dai Smith

Make Room for the Jester first published in 1964
© Stead Jones 1964

Library of Wales edition 2011
Foreword © Philip Pullman 2011
Publishing Editor: Penny Thomas
All Rights Reserved

ISBN 978-1-906998-27-1

Cover design: www.theundercard.co.uk

Printed and bound by Gwasg Gomer, Llandysul, Wales
Typeset by Lucy Llewellyn

British Library Cataloguing in Publication Data

A cataloguing record for this book is available from the British Library.

FOREWORD

Stead Jones and *Make Room for the Jester:* well, I'd never heard of it. But there are books that are unjustly forgotten, and I think this is one of them. When I read it for the first time a few months ago I was enchanted with it, not only for the memories of place and atmosphere it evoked so skilfully, not only for the light touch and the sympathetic voice of the narrator, but mainly for the brilliantly drawn portrait of an extraordinary individual, about whom I shall have more to say later on.

To deal with the biographical facts first: Stead Jones was born in Pwllheli in 1922, the youngest of a big family. He was actually christened Thomas Evan Jones: the Stead came, in a perfectly normal Welsh way, from the fact that his father once managed the local branch of the Stead and Simpson chain of shoe shops, and was himself known as Stead Jones. (When *Make Room for the Jester* was published Tony Richardson's film of *Tom Jones* was not long out, and very popular, and Tom Jones the singer was having his first hits. Jones' agent thought that the public would find it hard to cope with a surfeit of Tom Joneses; so the novelist became Stead like his father.) The young Tom was educated at Pwllheli Grammar School, and then at Bangor University, though his higher education was interrupted by service in the Royal Signals during the Second World War. He took part in the D-Day landings, an experience, he said, 'which seems more alarming now [1964] than it did then'.

After the war he returned to university, and then became a lecturer in Lancashire. There he remained until he retired. He died in 1985, leaving a wife and two daughters.

So much for the quotidian, salaried and pensioned, golf-playing, respectable outward life. But where did this novel come from? Within four years during his forties, he published *Make Room for the Jester* and two others – and then there were no more. No more published, at any rate, for he continued to write: but publishers felt that for one reason or another the sort of novel he wanted to write wasn't the sort the public wanted to read. Sometimes a writer's tone, or subject, or world view, is not to the prevailing taste. Sometimes, dare I say it, publishers are simply wrong. Jones wrote on till the day he died; I hope there is another novel as good as this among the papers he left.

One admirer of the book has called *Make Room for the Jester* 'the Welsh *Catcher in the Rye*', and it's certainly true that Jones' novel, like the infinitely more famous work by J.D. Salinger, contrasts the passionate authenticity of adolescence with the hypocrisy, the phoniness, of adulthood. But Stead Jones never had to deal with the sort of celebrity that came to Salinger. Perhaps his timing was unfortunate; if he too had published his novel in 1951, instead of 1964...

The novel is set in the little harbour town of Porthmawr. It's in North Wales: we're not in Dylan Thomas' Llareggub, with its fishing boat-bobbing sea, but in a harsher place where there's little point in having a boat at all because the fishing is dying. 'No competing with Fleetwood and Grimsby,' says one character. The year is 1936, and the narrator, Lew Morgan, is a scholarship boy at the County School. The events that begin the story take place during the summer holiday, when Lew and his friends the hard and daring Dewi, the agreeable blockhead Maxie, and the superbly inventive and eloquent Gladstone Williams become involved with an ancient feud between the Vaughan brothers Marius and Ashton. Marius Vaughan is rich and solitary and lives on the hill, and the feud involves the accidental death many years before of the youngest Vaughan brother, Jupiter. The plot begins when Ashton returns to Porthmawr from many drink-sodden years of wandering.

The events are farcical-tragical, and Lew is a good narrator; the story is safe in his hands. But one thing that lifts this book quite out of the common run is the character of Gladstone Williams. He's seventeen, older than the other boys in this little gang, and whereas Lew is the educated one, the one set on a scholarship track towards matriculation and whatever lies beyond, Gladstone – for all that he has the best vocabulary, English and Welsh, in all Porthmawr – is what would later be called a dropout. 'I found school very restrictive,' he says airily.

But here comes the originality of the book: Gladstone is no proto-beatnik or ur-hippy, absorbed only with his own unformed self. He has assumed the task of looking after his three little half-siblings, Dora, Mair, and Walter, his mother being a drunken slattern, and he does so superbly. The scenes with the children are funny and tender and full of Gladstone's boundless inventiveness, for his method of keeping the children quiet or tractable or happy is to tell them stories. The older boys listen too:

> He told us one none of us had heard before – about a fisherman who found pearls in the seaweed bubbles, and how he collected them for his sweetheart, and how the pearls all became tiny fish on her neck. I swear he made it up there and then.
>
> 'Don't understand,' Maxie said.
>
> 'Why did they turn to fish, then?' Dora asked. Dora was eight and wriggling with questions.
>
> 'I don't know,' said Gladstone. 'You should never ask a poet to explain...'
>
> 'Very good,' Walter croaked.
>
> 'Got a meaning,' Dewi agreed. 'Like a sermon in chapel.'

But Gladstone is not just a charming fantasist. He represents kindly, protective adulthood as well:

> Then the children upstairs began to cry, and before Gladstone had moved from his position under the light they had come tumbling downstairs and into the room, little old people in their nightshirts, faces puffed with sleep and tears.
>
> 'Now then,' he said as he crouched down to them. 'Now then, what's this?'
>
> 'Had nightmares,' Dora sobbed.
>
> 'Not *all* of you?' He was touching them and kissing them and smoothing back their hair. 'Not at the same time?'
>
> 'It was terrible,' Dora said.

Gladstone felt Walter's bottom. 'Not wet the bed, have you?'

'Never,' Walter said firmly.

'Tell me, then. What did you have nightmares about?'

'Chips,' Walter said.

'And cockroaches,' Mair added.

'That's a mixture, for sure,' Gladstone smiled, and Walter and Mair smiled with him. 'Recovered now?' They nodded.

'Then off to Lew by the fire, while I talk to Dora...'

And so on. The gentle teasing and warm reassurance continues beautifully for two more pages. What I find remarkable about this passage and others like it is the unaffected authority that Gladstone displays. He's in charge of these children, and he's neither embarrassed nor resentful about it. The author's touch with Gladstone and the children is masterly.

There's another aspect of Gladstone's manner that is so delicately handled it's only visible in the tiniest details. From time to time someone such as Harry Knock-Knees, the town bully, will call Gladstone a pansy or a nancy-boy; and someone else will say of him meaningfully 'He's a *great* friend of the Vaughans, that one', and there'll be a lot of laughter; or Ashton Vaughan will say in a spiteful tone (or *sbeitlyd*, as Lew thinks, the Welsh word having a wider range of meaning than the English) 'a proper little nursie boy, isn't he?' and this at a time when Gladstone, out of hearing for the moment, has been gently cleaning the vomit off Ashton's face; or someone else will say of Gladstone 'My opinion is that he isn't right – never was...'; and there is Lew's own observation that 'He had a voice like a girl's, not high, but with a girl's sound to it'; and then, most importantly, there is Gladstone's own general attitude to the world, which I can only call camp. One of his fantasies involves 'a master-plan to move the Azores (why *do* they have such vulgar names?)'

And his obsession with the Vaughans is due largely to his feeling that 'they've got *style*, don't you see?' as he says to Lew, gripping his shoulder tightly.

Is Gladstone gay? Certainly he's not like anyone else, and his sexual nature might easily be one marker of the difference. I think that if Stead Jones were writing today we'd know for certain, because he'd feel more able to allow a sexual dimension into the lives of his little gang. For the strange thing is that whereas these are boys of sixteen or so, with their hormones presumably fully functioning, their lives and speech are entirely chaste. The only one of them to express any sexual feeling is the animal-like Maxie, who watches a girl running down to the sea, her breasts bobbing inside her bathing costume.

> Maxie sat up, pointing. 'By God,' he cried, 'look at them headlamps...'

That's not to say that sexuality is absent from the novel. Sex is there, but mysterious, something for dreams and darkness. The consequences of sexual activity are only too evident, from the French letters washed up after every tide to the nightmare that poor little Dora whispers to Gladstone later on in the scene quoted above. And there is Eirlys Hampson, the glamorous woman with the ample breasts and the silk blouses, whose teasing makes Lew blush. It's just that the boys have other concerns for the moment, and Gladstone's fascination with the Vaughans is at the heart of them. Certainly his courage, in acting the way he does without equivocation or apology, resembles the courage of every gay young person who has to live in what he calls 'the primeval swamp of respectability'.

There are too many pleasures in this short novel to list in a very short introduction, but I must mention Jones' character-drawing. Everyone is clearly imagined and clearly described, and everyone has a function in the story. There is a terrifying religious zealot in Mrs Meirion-Pughe; there is a philosophical carpenter, Rowland Williams, who has a quiet voice that says quiet, sharp things. There is the generous, teasing, troubling Eirlys. There are Dewi and Maxie, and there is the bitter and troubled Ashton Vaughan.

And finally, not as a central theme but as something that sounds now and then like a bell from the future, and arouses harmonics in all sorts of other places, the big question for every teenager in a small town, whether it's Porthmawr or Pwllheli, Caernarfon or Porthmadog, or for that matter King's Lynn, or Weymouth, or any one of a hundred thousand small towns in every country in the atlas: will we have to leave our native place in order to live as fully and richly as we feel we need to? Gladstone's ambition is grand and clear and unequivocal: 'I want to be the finest man in the world,' he says.

But will that mean leaving Porthmawr behind and engaging with the larger neighbour to the east, whose language happens to be spread more widely around the world? One of the first questions Gladstone asks Lew after hearing of Lew's ambition to be a poet is 'Welsh or English, which do you write?' Lew's answer is already implicit in his name, which the headmaster of the County School is very scornful about: 'Lew? No such name as *Lew*, boy! Llywelyn is your name.' The language question is one, perhaps, that teenagers in King's Lynn or Weymouth don't have to consider. It's a delicate and complex one, and adults aren't much help: the ferociously pious Mrs Meirion-Pughe thinks the English Bible unsuitable for Christians, while Rowland Williams in his carpenter's workshop, talking to Lew about the Nationalists who've just burned an aerodrome in Pwllheli, expresses with his prophetical eloquence a passion that goes right through Nationalism and the language question, and deeply into something concerning the nature of humanity itself: 'It's a great fire we want that'll scorch away all the institutions of mediocrity...'

This short novel isn't perfect. But it expresses far more themes than many a weighty book five times the length, and it does so with a delicate precision that delights me more the more I read it. To this English lover of Welsh places, Welsh voices, Welsh weather (even), it brings back with a surprising intensity my own youth a quarter of a century later (at the very time Jones was writing this book, in fact) and a few miles down the coast from wherever Porthmawr is. And now that I know it, I'll treasure it. The company of Gladstone has the same effect on me as it has on 'the little ones', as he calls them: he makes me happy.

Philip Pullman

MAKE ROOM FOR THE JESTER

I

'Geography begins at home,' Evans Thomas announced. 'No doubt we are all in agreement with that?'

The class nodded, but very reluctantly. It was the last day before the summer holiday.

'Porthmawr the fair, then,' he went on, and paused for the laugh. 'Sunset metropolis by an Irish Sea. Other Eden, demi-paradise – *including* the Palace Cinema, of course, where so many of you worship at the shrine of Metro and Goldwyn and Mayer; where Clark has a Gable, where Mae goes West, twice nightly, best seats one and six...'

'Humour is the curse of the Welsh,' Goronwy whispered to me. 'Watch out for the catch...'

Evans Thomas' glasses flashed a warning as he searched the class. 'Population of Porthmawr, Goronwy Jones?' A whiplash question that killed the laughter. 'On your feet, boy! Up!'

Goronwy's desk went bang as he stood. 'Five thousand, Mr Thomas.' Goronwy was using his insulting voice. 'Main export – the unemployed.' And the brave ones laughed.

The colour left Evans Thomas' face, came back again bunched up and dark below his glasses. 'Insolence!' he thundered. A purple vein coiled itself across his forehead. 'Big lout! Buffoon! Think you can say what you like, don't you? Father on the Education Committee, so you think yourself privileged.... Let me tell you, boy...' But he never did. Suddenly he was swaying there in front of us, one hand clutching at his chest, the other searching for support. 'Sir!' one of the girls cried out. 'Sir!' said Goronwy at my side. The dinner bell rang. Evans Thomas seemed to lunge out for his tall desk. It went over with him, the bottle of red ink in the air, splintering against the wall.

The class rose. A silence that hid screaming, then there was a rush to the front. And I would have been with them had Goronwy, his face the colour of lard, not blocked my way. 'He's dead,' he was saying over and over again.... But now the staff were in, even Mr Penry, the Head, and they were saying 'dead, dead', too. Form VA were back in their seats, graveyard faces, a graveyard silence. 'Take them out,' the Head cried. 'Will *someone* take them out?' We filed past the prone body of Mr Evans Thomas. I never saw his face, never even tried to look.

The summer holiday began like that, with a sudden, public death. It was an omen, Meira said – would set off others, a thing like that. I'd got some of my colour back now, she said: it must have been a terrible shock. She licked the jam off her knife. 'Married, was he?'

4

'Bachelor,' I said. 'Used to call him "the Snake".'

'There you are, then,' she said, as she buttered another piece of bread. 'Get married is the motto. Single – and they go like that.' She gave me a cheeky smile. 'Not upset, are you?' She was all sympathy, but anxious for the details. 'Kept you in, did they?'

'That's the Head all over,' I said. 'Always getting to the bottom of things.' I remembered the hole in the seat of my flannels, and how a girl had giggled as I left the class. The Head and Super Edwards and Alderman Mrs Meirion-Pughe from the Governors were behind the table in the study. Mrs Meirion-Pughe's thick eyebrows made remarks as I entered.

'Name?' said the Head. Lew Morgan, sir. 'Lew? No such name as *Lew*, boy! Llywelyn is your name.' Lew, sir. 'Rubbish, boy. Where do these boys get their ideas from?' Smiles all round. 'Home address?' Number Twelve Lower Hill Road.

'Ffordd Allt Isaf,' said Mrs Meirion-Pughe, giving our street its Welsh name. Mrs Meirion-Pughe was so Welsh that she thought the English Bible unsuitable for Christians. She was very religious, too.

'What did they ask, then?' said Meira.

'Lot of nothing,' I said, remembering the agony of backing to the door, one hand clamped over my behind.

'Some cake,' Meira offered. 'Only workman's, though. Baked them this morning.'

Workman's – pastry and raisins – was fine, and so was sitting there in the kitchen of Number Twelve Lower Hill Road, Porthmawr, Wales, with Meira making things ordinary – even the sight of a man dying – with a cheeky word, a lick of the knife, a smile that came from the eyes.

She was my cousin – my only relative now that my mother was dead – a small, dark woman with dimples like stars in her cheeks. Living in Number Twelve with her and Owen was fine, even if they did act like lovebirds, even if she did talk about sex all the time. Meira was thirty-five in 1936, the year all this happened, and now and then there was mention of how she was getting past it, talk of the third month being bad, and how she'd lost them every time. Talk I had to pretend not to understand.

Owen was tall and fair and very thin. He was a handyman, Owen, capable of any work, except that economic conditions, as he said himself, were against him. Most of the year he was on the dole, but now, for the summer, he had a job up on the beach, minding the boats and deckchairs. He wanted a boat of his own but there wasn't much point because, just as the quarry had died in the hills at the back of the town, so the fishing was dying in the bay. 'No competing with Fleetwood and Grimsby,' he said through his bread and jam, 'so this boat I saw today might as well have been the old quinquireme of Nineveh herself. Know about that, do you?'

He was forever testing me – the penalty of having passed the scholarship to the County School. 'John Masefield,' I said.

Owen chuckled. 'Salvation through education,' he said. 'We'll have you down the library to read out the situations vacant for the proletariat...'

'A teacher died today,' I said. 'In class...'

Owen dropped his knife. 'Good God,' he said, 'is it possible to have too much education?' But by then, unaccountably, I was in tears, and they were both rushing

6

to comfort me. 'Tell me, Lew – get it out of your head.'
And after I had done so Owen, in a local preacher's voice,
went on about death and Mons and Vimy Ridge. 'Out of
our hands, see... Don't be upset.'

'A greater Power,' Meira joined in.

'Forget it,' Owen said. 'What d'you say – come to the
Palace with us? Second house? Pay-day today...'

Down Lower Hill Gladstone Williams would be
waiting, but I couldn't resist a chance to go to the
pictures, so it was the Palace that night, the visitors all
around, wet macs steaming, the air smoke-blue and
tropical hot, and the dying forgotten.

But, some time in the early hours, Evans Thomas was
there at the window, eyes burning, mouth twisted and
ready for the bite. I had the light on quick, and in a
shaking sweat was clawing for the curtains to keep him
out, for in my nightmare I had been convulsed with
laughter – standing on my desk, roaring – as he fell down
like Buster Keaton, fell down and got up, fell down and
got up again.... I clung to the curtain and in a while
managed to tell myself it was a dream. But once back on
the bed I was overcome by black remorse – a man dies in
front of you like that, and all you can do is laugh, make a
comic film out of it – and I became stiffened there, my
arms tight around my knees, unable to move, unable even
to cry out for Meira, as if paralysed, only my mind
thundering as the hours of night passed and the window
grew light.... If only I had gone to see Gladstone.... Then,
as if in a film again, I was in Gladstone's house and it was
two years ago and I was telling him about my mother,
about finding her like that, and how I had thought it

7

funny, had actually laughed: and how the shame of that was like a knife turning in me. 'Pushes on the comedian, something sad,' Gladstone was saying. 'Cap and bells and all.' And he was on his feet, arms waving, dancing, being the Jester for me in order to stem my tears. 'Never be afraid to open the door and ask the Jester in,' he cried, then stood still and grave, adding almost fiercely, 'Always, Lew. *Always.*'

My arms and legs were mine again. I stretched and lay back – let the Jester in, like a prayer, let the Jester in – and in a while, as the day climbed over Porthmawr, slept.

Impossible to predict, certainly at that moment, that it was going to be a summer for the Jester.

II

Gladstone was trying out various signatures on the sand.

Adolf Hitler Jones, he wrote. Then after it he added A. H. Jones, BA, BD. 'Well,' he said, 'it might have been Adolf Hitler if he'd been born in Berlin, or somewhere like that.'

The Rev A. H. Jones, BA, BD, was minister at Capel Mawr, and they didn't make them any bigger than that. A. H. stood for Alvared Hounsdow, as we all knew, but Gladstone liked playing around with names. 'Adolf Hitler Jones, BA, BD,' he went on. 'The famous Welsh-German, or German-Welshman... Lew, you never know, do you? It could be his real name. I mean, nobody calls him anything except A. H.'

We were sitting at the unfashionable end of the beach. It was the only place for us with our bathing gear. Dewi and Maxie had their sisters' knickers on, a bit modified, but with moth holes in the wrong places; I was wearing a pair of khaki shorts which Meira had picked up in Capel Mawr jumble; the little ones were in knickers and underpants – the ones they wore all the time – and they didn't hide much, especially when wet. But Gladstone, of course, had a proper pair of bathing trunks, Marks and Spencer, blue, with a white stripe down the leg and a white belt with a chrome buckle. Gladstone always managed things right.

'Clarke Brentford,' he wrote with his stick. 'That's a nice one. Clarke with an e – for distinction and affectation.' He had a voice like a girl's, not high, but with a girl's sound to it. 'Mussolini Morgan,' he wrote. 'I like that, too. It sounds like an Italian tenor who does juggling as well. Anything's nice when you've been launched as Gladstone Williams.'

'Chief Lord of the Navy, Gladstone was,' Maxie said.

'Prime Minister,' Gladstone hissed.

Maxie was the thickest going. He had been in the same class for years. His real name was Will, but he had a boxer's face so he was Maxie to everyone, even his mother.

'Beethoven Jones,' Gladstone wrote. 'Is that how you spell Beethoven, Lew?'

'Ask me another,' I said.

'Composed the "Messiah",' said Maxie.

We threw sand at him.

'You're the smartest, Lew,' Gladstone said. 'Scholarship and everything. I wish I had brains.' He wrote William Shakespeare Hughes on the sand. Gladstone was seventeen, the oldest among us, and he was, as he said, practically a non-starter in the Porthmawr Education Stakes. 'I didn't go to school much, you know,' he said. 'I'm not really sorry,

10

but it might have helped me to concentrate. Of course, I'd have gone more often, only Mam kept on having the babies there. She had to have someone to give her a hand, after all. Besides, I found school very restrictive.' He wrote Tennyson Keats Cadwaladr on the sand, and with a flourish added Professor of Comparative Alcohology, Bangor University.

Gladstone had the best vocabulary, English and Welsh, in all Porthmawr. But Dewi was all for swearing. 'Too bloody right it's restrictive,' he said. 'School puts bloody years on you.'

'Language,' Gladstone said.

Dewi was my age, and until I had got the scholarship we had shared the same desk. As well as being an artist at swearing, he carried more scars than anyone in the town – on his knees, hands, face, even through the close-cropped hair on his scalp you could see them – and they were all the result of doing things the hard and daring way.

'I don't like dirty language,' Gladstone went on. 'The world's plagued with dirty talk.'

We all nodded, even Dewi, because Gladstone was the leader. Not because he was older, though, not even because he was very tall and slim and handsome, but because he had authority. Gladstone could tell you he put peroxide on his hair, and waved it now and then, but you didn't start thinking he was soft or anything like that. He had this girl's sound to his voice, but you were held by it just the same.

'William Wordsworth Williams,' he wrote. 'A lovely old poet.'

'It was the schooner *Hesperus*,' Maxie began.

'Wrong poet,' Gladstone said gently, but firmly.

11

We lay back on the warm sand then, the four of us, while the children fought and played. I was with my friends and the sun was back in the sky, and I had almost forgotten that they were burying poor Mr Evans Thomas that day. Behind us Porthmawr looked warmer, gentler – not the way it did in winter, or when it rained. The sun was crimson and amber and gold through my closed eyes, and the wind tasted of salt. Poor Evans Thomas had died of natural causes years ago. All I wanted now was for the clocks of the world to stop so that it could stay like that for ever.

'When you leave school,' Gladstone was saying, 'what are you going to be, Lew?'

'Gangster, me,' Dewi broke in. 'Going to have a mob and live in Hollywood.' Dewi saw nearly all the pictures that came to Porthmawr's three cinemas. 'A mob and molls,' he added.

'Nobody asked you,' Gladstone said.

I kept my eyes closed and said, 'I'm going to be a poet.'

Maxie tried again: 'It was the schooner *Hesperus*...'

'Shut up,' Gladstone said. 'A poet? Seriously?'

'Yes,' I said.

I felt the fine sand falling on my face and knew they had sat up.

'Tell us a poem, then,' Maxie said. 'Tell us one of them...'

Gladstone yelled at the children because they had buried little Walter. Then he said, 'Got a poem handy, Lew?'

I kept my eyes closed and said, 'Thousands'.

They all considered that. 'Like the National Eisteddfod?' Dewi asked.

'All singing that,' Maxie said scornfully. 'Singing and sopranos...'

12

'Oh – imagine Lew winning at the Eisteddfod,' Gladstone said. 'Going to the front in his nightie. I'll lend you mine, Lew.'

I sat up. 'I wouldn't try for the National. I wouldn't try for anything.'

'Because of the nightie, Lew?'

I had been working on this for some months. 'Because that isn't a poem,' I said. 'Writing to order isn't a poem.'

Gladstone nodded. 'Quite right,' he said approvingly.

'Shouldn't do it, that's all,' I said. I'd nearly sorted this out a few nights before, but now the idea escaped me – like trying to remember what happened next in a dream. 'A poet shouldn't do that.'

Gladstone smiled and gripped my arm, but the other two looked at me with blank wonder. 'What's he to do, then?' Maxie demanded.

'Shouldn't do anything,' I said heatedly. The stuff about being a poet had slipped out. I'd never told anyone else. 'Just write it down, that's all,' I said.

Both Dewi and Maxie nodded, but blankly.

'I wandered lonely as a cloud,' Gladstone said, as if to explain it all.

'Wyt Ionawr yn oer,' Dewi put in.

'Welsh or English, which do you write?' Gladstone asked.

'English,' I said, and that was another lie. I hadn't written anything yet.

They all nodded approval. 'Wales is the best country in the world,' Dewi said, 'but the language is old-fashioned.'

Gladstone considered that carefully. 'It's the best language all round,' he said firmly, 'but there's too much talk about good Welsh and poor Welsh; and good Welsh is too stiff altogether.' He held up a fistful of sand and let it trickle out slowly. 'The poems are nice, though. But we're all half and half here, aren't we? English and Welsh all mixed up. Maybe...'

'There's no pictures in Welsh,' Maxie said.

'Know why that is, don't you?' Dewi put in. 'That's because Hollywood isn't in Wales.' He turned to me. 'Lew – say a poem. Go on.'

Gladstone clapped his hands. 'Come and listen, children. Lew is going to tell us a poem.' Dora and Mair and Walter scrambled across and crouched facing me. They all stared at me, except Walter who had cross-eyes – but probably he was staring too, in his way.

'All right, Lew?' Gladstone asked gently.

I was in a panic now. Cornered. I didn't have a poem ready, and I knew I could never remember one which Gladstone, at least, didn't know.

'Can't do it,' I mumbled. 'They're not ready yet – my poems.'

They all looked disappointed, but Gladstone took over smoothly for me. 'Don't force him,' he said. 'Lew's not ready to tell us – and he's quite right. You can't force flowers to grow, can you?' I knew then that Gladstone had seen through me, knew that relief was at hand, too. 'Tell you what,' he went on, 'I'll give you one of mine. Not a real poem, Lew – just a bit of an entertainment.'

He told one none of us had heard before – about a fisherman who found pearls in the seaweed bubbles, and how he collected them for his sweetheart, and how the pearls all became tiny fish on her neck. I swear he made it up there and then.

14

'Don't understand,' Maxie said.

'Why did they turn to fish, then?' Dora asked. Dora was eight and wriggling with questions.

'I don't know,' Gladstone said. 'You should never ask a poet to explain...'

'Very good,' Walter croaked.

'Got a meaning,' Dewi agreed. 'Like a sermon in chapel.'

'It's not a sermon,' said Maxie. 'Just a poem...'

'Just a po-em,' a new voice echoed behind us. 'Just a bloody pansy po-em!'

We were on our feet in a flash, hustling the children to shelter, picking up our clothes and making for the nearest sand dune.

'Harry Knock-Knees!' the children screamed, but we didn't need telling. Harry Knock-Knees and Wil Fawr and the rest of them, and they had been sitting there above us on the sea wall, listening to every word.

We pulled on our clothes and stuffed the children into theirs whilst Dewi and Maxie began to reply to the stones which were already zipping through the sand above our heads.

'You children stay down,' Gladstone ordered. 'Anyone up and off goes his head!' The children huddled down.

'They're six to our four,' he went on, 'but we're all right for stones.'

Stones and insults came over in showers, but we were used to both. Once a week, regular as the rain, we fought it out with Harry Knock-Knees and his gang. They were rougher than us, the harbour crowd, but we usually held our own so long as we had stones. Man to man, fist to

15

fist, we wouldn't have stood a chance.... But every time they attacked us like this, I had the feeling it was only Gladstone they were after. 'Bloody old Pansy,' they roared now. 'How's your knickers then, Pansy?' They always left me alone whenever I saw them: Gladstone was the target. 'Big cowards,' he shouted back. 'Attacking little children.' 'And big girls,' they jeered, 'don't forget the big girl!' Gladstone rushed forward in a frenzy, picking up and hurling stones as he went. Maxie and Dewi and I, moved by his example, heaved more furiously, following in his wake. And, as on previous occasions, Harry Knock-Knees and his gang broke and ran for it. We followed them to the foot of the sea wall, whooping like Apaches, the stones still flying. Only the crash of broken glass somewhere beyond the wall halted us, and without even waiting to find whose glass had gone, and where, we were back to the sand dune in a flash, and on from there, the children flying in front of us like the Israelites when the Red Sea nearly got them.

'Make for the boat,' Gladstone cried as we charged through the visitors. 'Must have been Davies Ice cream.'

During another fight, one of the windows in the ice-cream cart which Davies wheeled along the narrow road behind the sea wall had been smashed. It seemed logical to suppose that the same thing had happened again.

We stopped running once we were clear of the beach just in case the police were around. We were by the harbour now and could afford to stroll. The tide was out, the white yachts and fishing boats sitting on the mud, their masts slanting. Up on the mudbank that no tide ever reached was the *Moonbeam*, which was, for the time being at least, our headquarters.

She was a scarred and battered old has-been, mastless, peeling, warped and leaking. It was a good job the tides never reached her because she would never sail again. She had been a fishing boat and she still smelt like it; she hadn't an owner, so far as anyone knew, but now and then one of the boozers from the town occupied her and slept the night under newspapers in her cabin. We had taken her over at the beginning of summer and Gladstone had set us to work on that cabin. We had scrubbed and patched and fixed a broken porthole and reassembled the stove. One night, I knew, the *Moonbeam* would fall apart in a high wind, but that cabin would hold firm.

We walked to her across the mud. Like the *Moonbeam*, the harbour had seen better days too when the small coasters called every week. But now it was mud criss-crossed by rotting ropes and rusty chains. One day those ropes would snap, I used to think, and the walls and storehouses along the quay would crumble and fall into the water. The decay had set in, all right.

'We had them running,' Dewi said. He had a new cut above his left eye – only a small one, but he let it bleed.

'Trouble over Davies Ice cream,' Maxie said gloomily.

'Only for Harry Knock-Knees,' Dewi said, and we walked on laughing, as the gulls wheeled and called, until we came to the planks which gave us a fairly dry way to the *Moonbeam*.

Gladstone waited with me until the children had followed Maxie and Dewi along the planks, then he took my arm and said, 'Do you really want to be a poet, Lew?'

'Only talking,' I said, not looking at him.

'Oh, but you must be one,' he said. 'You look like

17

one.' He prodded the mud with the toe of his shoe. 'D'you know what I want to be, then?'

I shook my head.

'I want to be the finest man in the world,' he said.

III

We sat around in the cabin of the *Moonbeam* and discussed the fight and planned repairs.

'We'll get little curtains on the portholes,' Gladstone said. 'And some paint. Woolworth's have cheap paint...'

'I know where we can get some paint,' Dewi said.

'Stealing?'

Dewi winked. 'There for the taking. Back of Williams Painters. Easy.'

'Thou shalt not steal,' Maxie said. We told him to shut up.

'Seen the tins,' Dewi went on. 'Easy. Only a bit of glass on the wall.'

Gladstone nodded. 'Well – we'll have to think about it. We need some paint and that's a fact...'

'I'll go now,' Dewi said.

That was the trouble with Dewi. Pinching in broad daylight was better than pinching after dark. The risk was everything. Dewi was always the last to leave a raided orchard, and afterwards he would push apple cores through the police station letterbox. We had to control Dewi.

'We'll talk about it later,' Gladstone said, indicating the listening children. Gladstone was more careful than a woman with them: we hadn't to swear in front of them, and they weren't to hear anything bad. 'Best to give them a nice, clean start,' he used to say.

We sprawled around on the cabin floor. The harbour smelled like a corporation tip through the scrubbed boards. I was smoking one of Dewi's Woodbines and feeling pleasantly drunk.

'We could make a real little home here,' Gladstone was saying. He'd stretched himself out on the bunk and had little Walter crouching on his chest. 'We could be safe and snug here, winter and summer. I'd like to stay here forever. I would really.'

'All of us, too?' Maxie asked.

'All of us, if you like,' Gladstone agreed. 'We could catch fish from the harbour and pick up plenty of wood for the stove there. Go after rabbits now and then, too – just for a change of diet...'

'Chips, too?' Maxie, I'd heard, even had chips for breakfast.

'All the time,' Gladstone said. 'Potatoes are cheap enough.'

The children had all gathered to him now, their eyes full of pictures – even Walter's, only God knew where he was looking.

'We could all live here. Like that, would you?'

'Yes,' the children said in unison.

'No rent to find, like at Lower Hill.'

'No,' they agreed.

'It would be lovely. Big fire in the old stove, and candles on winter's nights, and the wind howling outside. Could soon fix little bunks for you children.' They all nodded eagerly, especially Walter. 'We could get the food going on that old stove there. And there'd be nobody to interfere.' We were all nodding in agreement now. 'Nice by ourselves. Separate bunks. Not like now – all of you in that old bed.' Gladstone's mother had married again after his father died. Dora and Mair and Walter were from the second marriage. The second husband had packed his bags and left soon after Walter's birth. 'Think of it, will you? We could make some money fishing, and sell firewood, and go after the lobsters for the pubs. Then there's blackberries and mushrooms. Oh, we'd make enough to keep the lot of us...'

Dewi sighed. 'My mam would never let me.'

'Mine neither,' said Maxie.

'It's a great idea, though,' I said.

'None of you coming?' Gladstone asked with a smile. 'Ah, well, it'll just have to be me and the little ones, then. We'll keep visitors, shall we? Like Mam used to. And Mair can be chief bottle-washer, Walter waiting on, and Dora can be the maid.'

'Maidth of honour,' Dora said. She was very affected and had a lisping spell now and then.

'And what shall I be?' Gladstone asked them. 'Go on – tell me.'

'The Prince of Wales,' Mair whispered shyly.

Maxie, made restless by all this talk, had got up and was pacing the cabin. He had the stump of his Woodbine

21

on a pin, getting the most out of it, but it was about finished, and since Gladstone had told us nothing was to be thrown on the floor he carried it over to the stove.

Gladstone was saying, 'Shall I tell you about Llywelyn, the last Prince of Wales?' when Maxie cried out.

'Jesus, there's a fire in the stove!'

We were crowding around him in an instant. He'd dropped the lid on the floor, and had had his ear pulled by Gladstone for doing so, but he was right all the same. There, in the dark depths of the stove, was the last glowing piece of wood. I could smell it now, brackish yet sweet, and full of mystery.

'Some bugger's been in,' Dewi said.

'A tramp,' Maxie said. 'It'll be a tramp...'

'Last night,' Gladstone agreed. 'An old fire...'

We were grouped around the stove, looking at one another uneasily. This was disturbing.

'A tramp,' Maxie suggested again.

'Just passing through, maybe...'

We all looked at Gladstone for his verdict. 'That'll be it,' he said. 'Can't see any other signs around the place. Mind you...'

There was a crash on the sagging deck above our heads.

'My God, what's there?' Dewi said.

Loud swearing came clear through the thin planking. Then heavy footsteps and the sound of something being dragged.

'A ghost!' Maxie's whisper broke the terrible silence that had fallen over us.

'A bloody good swearer, too,' Dewi said.

'No ghosts in the afternoon,' Gladstone said grimly.

'Might be Harry Knock-Knees. Quick, children, behind the stove there.' They scuttled to the dark forward part of the cabin. 'We'll stand here,' he went on. 'Ready for him.'

My heart was pounding against my chest. 'Might be more than one,' I said in a voice that sounded strange.

'Twin ghosts,' Dewi said. His eyes were shining. He had that top of the telegraph pole look.

Gladstone held my arm. He stood shoulder and head above us, his waved blond hair shining. He looked like the Greek statues in the history books. I stopped trembling.

The footsteps stopped and started again. A thud, as the man came down into the well, followed by more swearing. The man, whoever he was, stood outside the cabin door now, breathing heavily. Suddenly he began to sing in a high, quavering voice. It was a hymn – Yn y dyfroedd mawr a'r tonnau – and he was slurring note and word. We smiled at each other with relief. A boozer! Someone full of drink and music come to sleep it off. And he was Welsh, too.

The cabin door crashed open. I saw a pair of brown trousers, brown shoes caked with harbour mud, a big brown suitcase. Then the man stooped to come in through the low doorway. He saw us, and remained stock still, his mouth sagging with shock. He came in slowly and made himself tall. He was breathing hard, one shoulder hanging lower than the other, a wreck of a man. He dropped the case to the floor with a thump. The children came running silently to Gladstone.

'Gentle Jesus!' the man said. 'How many more of you on a gentleman's yacht?' He had a deep furry voice now.

No one answered him. My tongue was starched tight to the roof of my mouth.

23

'What's this – a Sunday-school trip?' He removed a green hat and threw it on the bunk. 'My yacht, and half the children of Porthmawr aboard!' He was thick-tongued all right, and we could smell the drink clear across the cabin. 'Trespassing...'

'Excuse me,' Gladstone said, 'but this boat doesn't belong to anybody...'

The man had very pale blue eyes which fixed themselves on Gladstone. They had a staring match.

'You the leader?' he asked.

'Naturally,' Gladstone replied.

'By God,' the man said, shaking his head. 'By God, I'll have to sit down. Puffed. Puffed.' He took a cigar end from his pocket and stuck it in the corner of his mouth. He had a long, haggard face, the lines deep enough for scars. The skin was peeling across his temples. He had the remains of red hair.

After a few minutes' sitting on the bunk he was on his feet again, pointing at Gladstone. 'Name?'

'That's my business,' Gladstone said.

The man sat down heavily. 'Good God – all Wales is a secret society.' He pointed at Maxie. 'Your name, then?'

'Mussolini,' Maxie said. The children tittered.

'Cheeky,' the man commented calmly.

'And mine's Charlie Chaplin,' Dewi said, 'and we're four against one.'

'Gentle Jesus,' the man said, 'you in the South Wales Borderers, then?'

'This is our boat,' Gladstone said firmly. 'You've no right...'

The man stopped him with a wave of his hand. 'That's

where you're wrong, kid. This boat is mine. My yacht...'

'Prove it, then,' Gladstone said. 'Go on – prove it. Nobody's owned this boat for years.'

The man took a swig from a dark green bottle and showed yellowed teeth in a smile. 'Take you to see my solicitors, shall I? The honourable Messrs Jones, Jones, Jones and Jones.'

We didn't know what to say to that, not even Gladstone. We knew all about the power of solicitors, though.

'Got you, haven't I? Can show you papers. You been having a den here, haven't you? Trespassing on a gentleman's yacht.'

'We cleaned it up,' Gladstone said. 'We did a lot of jobs on it. We fixed the roof...'

The man looked upwards. 'I'm very grateful. Looks as if I'll have a dry berth tonight.' He broke wind very loudly.

'You're not going to *live* here?' I said.

'Where else? What's your name, then? Mickey Mouse?'

'Lew Morgan,' I said.

'If it's any of your business,' Gladstone added quickly.

The man took no offence. 'Lew Morgan? There always was plenty of Morgans in Porthmawr. Morgans Butchers, Morgans Post Office, Morgans Dairy, Morgans Fish and Chips. Oh, hell, aye – some of the *elite* of the place was Morgans. There was a Morgans Big Spit once, if I remember.'

We smiled in spite of ourselves.

'A Morgans Come-to-Jesus, too.'

'Not in front of the children,' Gladstone said sharply.

The man's heavy eyebrows went up. 'Got to be careful, have I? What did you say your name was?'

'No right to ask,' Gladstone replied. 'Only with a warrant – that's when you've a right...'

'Well up in legal matters, I see. All right' – he banged his hand against his knee – 'tell you what I'll do. This is my boat. The nearest thing I have to home in Porthmawr and the land of my fathers. But I'll tell you what – you can go on using it as your den. I'll only be needing the place at night, anyway...'

We looked at each other wonderingly. This wasn't the kind of agreement we were used to. Most people, if they didn't chase us away, generally began to talk about the police. Dewi's face said there's a catch in it, but Gladstone was smiling.

'On what terms?' he asked with dignity.

'Terms? Don't ask me to talk about terms. Just come along when you want.' He held out his hand. 'You can shake on it, can't you?' None of us stepped forward, except Walter, who was mad keen on the handshaking business, but Gladstone yanked him back. 'By God, suspicious sons of Wales you lot are, all right.'

Then Gladstone stepped forward. 'My name is Gladstone Williams,' he said. 'What's yours?'

'Gladstone Williams? Bet you don't like that, do you...'

'That's got nothing to do with,' Gladstone snapped.

'Fair enough, kid. Got to admit it's better than Lloyd George Brown. Knew a feller called that, once...'

'Was it you lit the fire?' Dewi asked.

'It was cold in here in the early hours,' the man said.

26

'Came over just as I was. But I've brought my kit now, see...'

That seemed to settle it. He was moving in. I felt my resentment rise. He had no right to barge in like this, even if he really was the owner. I turned to Dewi for support, but Gladstone was speaking again.

'May we know your name, sir?'

I was surprised at Gladstone, angry too. There was no need to be so polite to a broken-down old boozer like this. No need for adding sir, either.

'Certainly you may know my name. It's Ashton Vaughan.'

'Ah,' Gladstone said, nodding his head. Ashton Vaughan, I thought: one of the Vaughans, the one who had gone away a long time ago. I'd heard about him too – it was something bad, everything about the Vaughans was bad, but I couldn't remember at all clearly.

'A bit before your time,' the man went on as he stretched himself out on the bunk. 'You weren't around, I'd say, and that means we can start with a moderately clean slate. Gladstone – you and your gang here can come along any time you like. That clear? But now it's time I had a siesta, so I'll grant the lot of you shore leave.' With a wave of his hand in the direction of the door he dismissed us.

This isn't right, I thought, and I could see Dewi felt the same, but there was Gladstone hustling us out, tiptoeing even, holding his finger up to his lips.

On the peeling deck I said, 'He can't do that. Do you realise he's just taken over our boat?'

'Too bloody true,' Dewi said.

But Gladstone insisted we get off the *Moonbeam* before there could be any discussion. He had a small mutiny on his hands by the time we were on dry land.

'Listen,' Dewi said, 'he's pinched our boat.'

'He's Ashton Vaughan...'

'What's that got to do with it?' I said. 'It isn't his boat...'

'Just climbed aboard and kicked us off. We ought to go back and have it out with him...'

'It might *be* his boat,' Gladstone said soothingly. 'He's Ashton Vaughan. They're rich people...'

'Not any more,' Dewi said. 'Used to be rich. Now they're just as poor as we are...'

'Shouldn't have come off,' Maxie said.

'What should we have done, then?' Gladstone asked, his temper rising. 'Think we should have *thrown* him off, do you?'

'Why not?' Dewi said. 'He's just a bloody Vaughan...'

'What are you talking about?' Gladstone asked. 'What do you know about the Vaughans, anyway?' The afternoon degenerated into a long semi-quarrel all the way home. 'He's Marius Vaughan's brother, come back,' Gladstone kept on saying, as if it were a great event. 'Put the bloody flags up, shall we?' Dewi asked. And I was with Dewi all the way. We'd lost our boat – just walked off, quiet as mice – lost it to Ashton Vaughan of all people. I couldn't understand Gladstone at all. I'd never heard anyone say a good word for the Vaughans in Porthmawr.

IV

But it was an important thing, the return of Ashton Vaughan. I knew that as soon as I told Owen and Meira. They made mouths as big as sparrow chicks, although Owen had to spoil it by saying he had heard something.... That was one of the troubles with Owen – you couldn't tell him anything, especially if you were in the County School.

'Trade should be up in the pubs,' Meira commented in her best acid-drop manner. 'Should be some fighting too, I shouldn't wonder.'

We had the Vaughans all through tea. Owen said, 'I wonder if that one on the Point knows?' Marius Vaughan had his big house right at the tip of Graig Lwyd, with the ocean on his doorstep. 'Bet the bastard hasn't heard.'

Meira gave him a row for using dirty language in front of me, but all the boys in Porthmawr called Marius Vaughan a bastard. A word with a lot of meaning, I thought.

I took the news to Polly who lived next door, and by the time she had finished I knew that Ashton Vaughan's return was one of the most interesting things that had happened all summer in Porthmawr.

'Well,' she said, 'you *do* interest me, Lew. How terribly interesting. I wonder if brother Marius knows?'

Polly always spoke English to me, and it was always high-class English for a few sentences at the beginning. Later on it became less so, more homely, more like the English everyone else spoke in Porthmawr. She had been my Auntie Polly when I was small, but now she insisted that I call her Polly, 'Auntie is so old sounding,' she'd say. 'Call me Polly – not pretty Polly, of course.' She said it without a laugh; she never went farther than a grin.

Polly had her father living with her – the Captain – and he was stone deaf and silent as a planet and eighty odd, so she was always glad of a bit of company and someone to talk to. I always liked going there, too, because Polly's special interest was murder. In her black dresses with her hair high in a bun and her pale, oval face with the great hooked nose in the middle, she had the look which spelt the law and courtrooms and cross-examinations for me. Besides, her living room was full of the sea – pictures of ships riding seasick storms, pieces of quartz from Brazil, the skin of an Indian snake in a glass jar, trim ships snug in green bottles, a dried fish big as a football from Madagascar, Chinese plates on the wall, and surf breaking in the big shells on either side of the blackleaded fireplace. It was fine there on winter nights with the old man snoring in the rocking chair and Polly talking about the great murderers.

'So Ashton Vaughan is back at last.' Her black eyebrows,

thick as a man's, swept up. 'Are you quite certain, Lew?'

'That's who he said he was.' I tried a description. 'He'd been drinking,' I said.

'That'll be him! My word, won't this cause a stir in the old town...'

'Why, then?' I said. 'Why should it?'

Polly went mysterious – the way she did when sex came up. 'Events of the past,' she whispered. 'The wheel going full circle.'

I'd realised at tea, as Owen spoke, that I had heard a great deal about the Vaughan brothers. Polly, however, brought it all into sharper focus. In 1920, she said, Marius and Ashton Vaughan had fought it out, with knives, down there by the harbour. It had taken all the policemen in Porthmawr to part them; that scar on Marius Vaughan's cheek was a relic of that night.

'Then Ashton vanished from sight. Hardly a word of him until today...'

'But why did they fight?' I asked.

'Brothers born to hate,' Polly replied, and left me hanging on for more. It was a fatal mistake to cross-examine her. I had to wait until she was ready to tell me.

'Their father,' she continued, 'went to sea with Tada there. As a matter of fact, Marius Vaughan always has a word to say to Tada.'

Polly said it as if it was an honour or something – just as Owen had admitted that the Vaughans were better than that crowd of shopkeepers up on Hillside: the Vaughans had fought it out brother against brother, but they were somebody and it was an honour when they spoke to you. It didn't make sense.

31

'Poor as a church mouse, their father's family was, but my word he picked up some money from somewhere, that man did. Robbing poor sailors, I shouldn't wonder. Serving bad food on those ships of his.' She touched the Captain's hand to see if he was still warm. 'More money than I'd care to mention in coasters in those days. That's what Tada used to say. And he used to wonder how William Vaughan made it, I can tell you. Born in those old houses used to be by the gasworks there – the ones they took down in 1930. Those old slums. Made all that money. Built that big house on the Point. Bought up all that property from the old Estate.' She lowered her eyebrows so that I could no longer see her eyes. 'Ways and means, dear. There must have been ways and means.'

She jumped up suddenly and put the ear trumpet to the Captain's ear. 'Do we want to wee-wee?' she roared, so that the Chinese plates did a dance on the wall. The Captain shook his head, opened one small blue eye and gave me a wink, then closed it again.

'*He* never made money,' Polly said, 'and he was a master mariner, Tada. Ways and means, dear.'

'Stealing?' I said.

Polly sniffed the air. 'Who knows, dear? But he made it all right.'

I risked the question. 'But why did they fight?'

Polly's reply told me I had been too early with it. 'They fought all the time,' she said. 'They even fought in Capel Mawr.'

'Did they go to Capel Mawr?' I said. We went to Capel Mawr, too – well, we went to the Mission by the harbour which belonged to Capel Mawr. We didn't have clothes

32

good enough for the big building itself. The shopkeepers on Hillside set the standard.

'They went when they were small.' Polly gave one of her shudders. 'Marius Vaughan doesn't go anywhere. He doesn't fear God. He doesn't even fear the Devil, that man.'

'An atheist?'

'Well – he threw the Rev A. H. Jones out of his house. Threw him down the steps, they say – put him in bed for a week. That should make him an atheist...'

And that was something else I'd heard, of course. Hadn't someone – Meira probably – said the Rev A. H. Jones had been too much of a Christian to bring a case against Marius Vaughan? And hadn't Owen said the Rev A. H. Jones had been too scared of Marius to do so? Owen never went to Capel Mawr or anywhere else. Religion, he used to say, was the dope of the masses.

'Why did he throw him out?' I asked.

Polly curled her mouth in the way she did when she wanted to give something full force. 'Because the minister went to ask him, as a man of God, to mend his evil ways.'

I thought about that for a moment. 'Do you like the Rev A. H. Jones, Polly?'

'A snob's man in a snob's chapel,' she said sharply, and without thinking.

'The kingdom of Heaven is reserved for exclusive draper's models,' I said.

Polly was still with shock. 'Who told you to say things like that?' she asked, very slowly.

Owen had said it, but I said it was one of the boys at school.

'The County School!' she said. 'Talking like that!' She

looked at me carefully, lowering her eyebrows again. 'Lew
– the Rev A. H. Jones is a man of God. Don't you ever
forget that.'

I'd made a mistake, I realised. I'd shocked her. There
would be no hope of getting any more details about the
Vaughans from her now. And in any case the Captain was
awake and making noises which meant he wanted to go
out to the back. I told Polly I had an errand to do, and
went out quickly.

Porthmawr was the colour of lead, and wet. It sprawled
up Hillside as if shrinking away from the sea, as if it was
afraid that a heavy shower might wash it right into the
ocean. Everyone was moving back, moving inland –
especially the ones with money up there in their big
houses on Hillside. The old town near the harbour had
been left to the rats, whole streets pulled down. No one
wanted the sea, not even the retired sea captains who
were inland too, each with a flagpole in his garden. Only
Marius Vaughan wanted the waters on his doorsteps.

By now my head was brimming with the Vaughans,
although Marius had been there all the time in his big
house on the Point. I hadn't bothered much about him
before, except to hate him with rest. But now he was
nearer, somehow – like the close-ups at the pictures. I
looked across the harbour following the line of the road
which ran to his house – a road riddled with Private and
Trespassers will be Prosecuted – along the foot of the great
bulk of Graig Lwyd. I'd never taken my chance along that
road. Dewi said he had – but we didn't really believe him.

I'd seen Marius Vaughan, of course, many times.

34

Usually at the wheel of his car, very rarely on foot and in the town. I'd seen his house too. From the town there was just a part of it showing, a corner and a chimney, but one day up on Graig Lwyd I'd looked down on the slate roofs and seen a courtyard and a white wall between the house and the sea. There had been a car on the courtyard and a man had limped out of the house to it, and he'd looked up, and Dewi had nearly fallen off the rock where we were perched. 'Old bastard Vaughan,' he'd said, and to prove he hadn't been near to losing his nerve he'd suggested we heave some stones down straight away. But Gladstone had stopped him. 'The dogs will come,' he'd warned. All the boys in Porthmawr had heard of Marius Vaughan's dogs.... The limping man, so stiff and straight, his head of white hair shining in the sun, had carried on to the car and driven off towards the town.

I turned away from the Point and looked across the old fishermen's hards to where the *Moonbeam* lay. The tide was in, but it wouldn't touch the *Moonbeam*, wouldn't cause the other Vaughan any trouble. Was he aboard now? There were no lights showing. Why had he come back after so many years, and why had he taken over the *Moonbeam* as a place to live? Couldn't he have gone along that road to the Point? But they had fought like savages, that was it. Perhaps on this very spot where I stood, in a heavy shadow which the gaslight made, the knives had slashed the air.... I looked around suddenly, but there was only a couple of visitors, a man and a woman in macs, arm in arm, wishing they were back in Manchester.

The lights were coming on now, all over the town – the lights outside the Palace Cinema brightest of all. Once a week at least, Gladstone and I took a walk along the harbour and through the town, taking in the side streets as well. Gladstone made it an adventure, somehow. Walking the town, he called it, and we would make things out of the names over shops, imagine what was going on behind the squares of lighted windows, wonder what would appear suddenly from the darkness around the next corner. In no time I would feel all my senses suddenly more acute, and our talk was rapid and high and excited. Walking the town after dark. I liked it best of all in winter when there was no one about and the wind was strong and the sea smelled everywhere, and the signs above the shops creaked and groaned, and the town cats went skidding and screeching ahead of you from doorstep to doorstep. We would stand and talk softly in the darkness, talking but half listening for a footfall, a sudden cough, the creak of a shoe, something said somewhere on the wind; and watching all the time for a shadow, the spurt of a match, a sudden light.... We were building it up, making it an adventure, moving towards the point where something was going to happen.... Gladstone said it was like the time when you were young, and you had in your hands the first page of *Treasure Island* by Robert Louis Stevenson, and that was the best page, he said, because you didn't want to turn over, because you knew that whatever was to come wouldn't be, couldn't possibly be, as good as that feeling of being on the edge of something, of not knowing. 'I hope nothing happens,' he used to say. 'It might spoil everything.' I watched the lights come on and remembered the sound of his voice, the way he'd looked.... There was a newness about everything that night, and everything had a meaning.

But I kept on turning back to the *Moonbeam*, and after a while I was walking quickly down the alleyways between the old storage sheds, then along the edge of the harbour towards the hards. I wondered, as I walked, if I'd have the courage to climb aboard and speak to him.

The light was going rapidly and I found it difficult to keep my feet clear of the old ropes and chains that were strung along the hards. It didn't seem to be such a good idea now. What would I say to Ashton Vaughan, anyway? Did you have a fight with your brother, Mr Vaughan? With knives? Did you win? I stood there and asked myself questions and knew I wouldn't dare take a step farther.

Then I heard the crunch of feet on the gravel. Someone running towards me, coming from the direction of the *Moonbeam*. I crouched quickly, screwing my eyes up against the darkness. The runner came into sight, and I knew straight away it was Gladstone. Nobody else ran with his shoulders raised high like that. I stood up and called to him. He halted almost in mid-stride.

'Lew,' he cried. 'Lew the last prince! How did you know I'd gone to see him?'

'Just out for a walk, that's all...'

He threw back his head and laughed. 'Funny place for a walk. Looks as if you had the same idea.' He gripped my arm briefly. 'Come on. Martha's out as usual and I had to leave the children. Come on...'

I ran by his side. 'See him, then?'

'Oh, yes – he was glad I'd come.' We reached the quay. Gladstone stopped to try the drawer of the new cigarette machine they'd put up on the corner of Harbour View Road. 'Are you *the* Ashton Vaughan? I said. And he said in person... of course, I knew all the time who he was.' I tried a cigarette machine farther up, near Market Street, then doubled speed to catch up with Gladstone.

'Was he – all right?' I asked.

'Who's that? The Emperor of Abyssinia?'

'Abyssinia to you too,' I said. 'Was he nice, then?'

'Ask the League of Nations,' Gladstone replied. He increased his pace, so that by the time we got to Lower Hill I was puffed and blown. 'Wants us to help him,' Gladstone said.

'Doing what?'

We reached Gladstone's door. 'Blow up Capel Mawr,' he said.

V

For Martha Davies, Gladstone's mother, living on Lower Hill was the end of the line. Once, when her first husband was alive, she had lived in a bigger house by the beach and taken in visitors. With her second husband she had gone in for businesses as well, a lot of businesses. But the boarding house had gone to pot, the businesses had all failed, and the second husband had caught the 7.10 one morning. So there was nowhere for Martha except Lower Hill. 'Such a comedown,' she would tell us sadly, but Meira said she'd asked for it. 'I was made for better things,' Martha would complain, but most people were agreed that she was too fond, by far, of a drop and more of gin.... Martha Davies had big breasts and a very big behind, and a top lip that was only lipstick. She dyed her hair all the time, and there was always a cigarette going, and she was forever cuddling you and kissing. With

Martha it had to be either a screech of laughter or a howl of anguish. 'It's a bit pathetic, really,' Gladstone used to say. 'Her emotions aren't properly balanced, you see.'

Martha's house was identical to ours, except that it was never as polished, never as tidy. That night when we walked in, it looked as if a hurricane had struck it. And the children were all up, too – standing in front of the fire in their nightshirts. They were the kind of children who look windblown on a summer's calm; they could make the finest clothes look like oddments from a jumble sale without any effort at all.

Gladstone ran to them. 'Naughty! Naughty! All of you,' he cried. They rushed to him and had him on the floor in no time. 'Why are you out of bed? Didn't I tell you Mam wouldn't be long?'

Martha went out every night, usually to the Harp where she waited on. 'What have I got to stay in for?' she used to say.

Gladstone struggled to his feet. 'No playing about,' he cried, trying to be stern. 'What are you doing up, all of you?'

'Walter wet the bed,' Dora said.

'Had to get out, quick,' Mair added.

'Nearly had to swim,' Walter croaked.

'We pulled the mattress off the bed,' Dora explained, 'but it got stuck on the stairs.' She remembered her lisp and added, 'thstuck on the thstairs.'

'You were going to put it in front of the fire?' Gladstone groaned. 'Oh, what have I told you about that? What have I said?' He did his enraged act, falling on his knees, banging his fists on the floor. The children howled with laughter. 'Haven't I told you never to go near the fire?' he cried, and

40

their faces were suddenly stilled, except for Walter who kept on laughing and pulling up his shirt to show all. 'Lew,' Gladstone ordered, 'bring the mattress down.'

I went up the stairs and dragged the mattress to the fire. Martha had one of the bedrooms in the house, the children the other. Gladstone always slept on the sofa in the living room. He never slept much, he used to say. Most of the night he spent reading.

'It'll be dry in no time,' he announced, 'but never again, mind.' He took Walter on his knee. 'Now, everybody sit down – not on the tiles or you'll have cold bums. Right – now we'll have a little concert until the mattress is dry. Everybody's got to do something. All right?'

The children squatted down eagerly.

'Now then – who's first?'

There was the usual dead silence. I broke it by saying, 'What does he want us to do?'

'Later,' Gladstone said. 'Tell you later. Now – who's first? Dora?'

'First last time,' Dora said sharply.

'Walter then.'

Walter was always a volunteer. He got up and gave us a hymn – which one it was impossible to tell – in a voice like a crow.

'Lovely,' Gladstone said. 'Sings like a beautiful bird. Now – Dora.'

Dora recited 'Y Sipsiwn' by Eifion Wyn. It went very well too, so she followed it with 'I wandered lonely as a cloud' – only the first three lines, though, because she got it mixed up with the 'Lake Isle of Innisfree'.

Then Mair tried 'Calon Lân', but had to give up

41

because her emotions got the better of her. So we had Walter again, whistling the 'Hallelujah Chorus', on one note all the way through, but his rhythm was very good.

'Your turn now Gladstone,' the children cried. 'Another poem like on the beach.'

He gave us an old one – a favourite – about Buck Jones riding off the screen at the Palace, and sending the dust flying down Porthmawr Market Street, and all the children cheering, and all the deacons scowling, and how he finished up picking a fight with the man on the war memorial in the Square, and how they had to get a posse out to get him back to the Palace in time for the second house.

As he finished it, Dewi and Maxie came in fresh and whooping from the pictures. They'd been thrown out, as usual.

'Wasn't much of a picture, anyway,' Dewi said. He wanted to swear, I knew, but didn't dare do so in front of the children, not with Gladstone there.

We persuaded Maxie to tell us about the picture. 'In China it was,' he began.

'Arabia,' Dewi said wearily.

'About this man who loved this girl only she was a gypsy, or something.'

'A narab,' Dewi said.

'Anyway, it was slow.' Maxie scratched his square nose for a moment, thinking deeply. 'All licking and stuff.'

'A love story,' Gladstone explained to the children.

'Would have been better if they'd had the man tunnel through the sand like a mole,' Maxie went on.

'Oh, dear God,' Dewi said.

'Get down in the sand and tunnel through like a mole,

42

and come up the other side, and catch them when they weren't looking...'

'That never happened, you old fool,' Dewi said.

'I know,' Maxie replied. 'I was wishing it would, though. Wishing that all through the picture.'

Maxie always wanted the hero to become a human mole. There had been a serial in the Saturday matinee about that once, and he'd never forgotten.

'Just tunnel through,' he said. 'Not choke or anything with the sand. Then come up in the dark and get his knife out and catch them...'

'Lovely,' Gladstone said to stop him. He felt the mattress carefully. 'Now – it won't be long. Who's going to be next?'

'You again,' the children chorused, so Gladstone settled back with little Walter on his knee to tell us the story of *Wuthering Heights of Wales* by Emily Brontë. He had books everywhere, Gladstone – used to comb the jumble sales for them. Only rarely did he come to the pictures with the rest of us.

'*Wuthering Heights of Wales*, by Emily Brontë,' he began – and it all happened in the hills at the back of Porthmawr. Heathcliff was Lloyd the gypsy, Catherine was Rhian, Edgar Linton was Lord Caradog Snell (Snell was a favourite villain's name for Gladstone), and Hindley Earnshaw was Trefor Baring (another villainous name). Gladstone altered the story too. Heathcliff was a great violinist that night – 'potentially the world's greatest, perhaps' – and Rhian was an operatic soprano who could hit the highest note in the world. At the end he had Heathcliff playing a violin *obbligato* while Rhian sang 'Oh, for the wings of a dove' (Gladstone sang it for us, all the way through) in a concert hall before five thousand people who rose, at the end, in a frenzy of applause. The concert hall was in Bond Street, London, not in heaven or anywhere final like that. In most of Gladstone's versions the good ones never died.

When it was over they all wanted an encore. Mair wanted the story of Montagu Hughes and Capulet Williams, by William Shakespeare. I liked this one, too – especially towards the end when Romeo captured all of Juliet's family and took them to the dungeons under Caernarfon Castle, and injected them one by one with a serum called common sense. Once that was done they all realised that, as Romeo explained, he couldn't marry Juliet because she was under age, and even a bit young for her age too. The ending came with Romeo and the nurse eloping to the South of France, which seemed to me more satisfactory than the version we had just pawed through for the Senior.

Maxie said, 'What about having the *Fall of the House of Cadwallon*?' This was a comic one. If you made *everything* happen to people, like Edgar Allen Poe did, Gladstone used to say, then it was bound to be comic.

Gladstone shook his head firmly.

'Can we have *Silas Morfa* by George Eliot?' Dora pleaded, but again Gladstone was firm.

'No more tonight,' he said, and sent Dewi up with the mattress.

'Not even *Llywelyn Macbeth Williams*?'

No. Not even that. The children had a small mutiny straight away, and we had to have a couple of dragging, missionary hymns to get them into the right mood for sleep.

Finally they were marched off, and after a while

Gladstone came downstairs, a smile on his face. 'If I had a Woodbine,' he said, 'I'd give it to anybody.' Dewi gave him a Woodbine. 'What a struggle,' he went on. 'Listen to them laughing up there.' He stood with his back to the blackleaded fireplace, the cigarette dangling from his lips. 'Nice though. In about half an hour sleep will have collared them all, and they'll be lying there like new puppies close together...'

'Tell us, for heaven's sake,' I said.

'Tell us what, then?' Dewi asked.

'He went to see the man on the boat,' I said.

'Oh, yes – Ashton Vaughan,' Gladstone said lightly. 'I paid him a call this evening.'

'What did he say?' I asked. 'Tell us...'

Gladstone sat down. 'I had a word with Martha after tea,' he said, brushing his hair clear of his forehead. I asked her about Ashton Vaughan. She told me a lot...'

'They fought with daggers,' I said, getting it in quickly. 'Him and his brother.'

Dewi whistled, high pitched. 'Daggers? Never...'

'It's true,' Gladstone said. 'They had this fight, then Ashton vanished into thin air. Never been back till today.'

'Where'd he go?' Maxie asked.

'Oh – everywhere. Australia. America. All over. He can speak six languages – fluently...'

'Did he say so?'

Gladstone nodded. We all considered this.

'Including Welsh?' Maxie asked.

'He's been a sailor and a rancher...'

I envied Gladstone now, having heard this before any of us.

'A gold prospector, too...'

'Did he find the lost mine?' Maxie asked.

We ignored the question.

'Went away in 1920, and this is his first time back.'

'Fought his own brother?' Dewi said. 'With daggers – seriously?'

'By the harbour,' I said.

'And he's going to live on the old *Moonbeam*, too?'

Gladstone's face softened. '"Only the old *Moonbeam* for me", he said. Never said a word about his brother in that big house...'

'Marius Vaughan's a big bastard,' Dewi put in. 'Our Tada worked for him once. Hard, our Tada said. Hard like iron.'

'Won't take his own brother back?' I asked.

'Ashton hasn't asked him,' Gladstone said. 'He told me he wasn't going to lick any man's boots. Said he wasn't a pauper.' He thought about that for a moment, then he added, 'Ashton Vaughan's a sick man, though. You can tell by his eyes...'

'Has he got malaria, then?' Maxie asked.

We ignored that as well.

'Years and years wandering away from his native land. "Funny what a grip the old place has on you," he said to me. He had to come back, you see.' The electric went out as Gladstone said this. There was no more money in the house for the meter so we stirred up the fire and made do with that. 'He was sitting alone in the cabin there – looking at the stove. I put a fire in for him. He didn't seem to have anything, except bottles...'

'Glad to see you, then?'

'Oh – *very* pleased. I took him half a loaf, but I don't suppose he'll eat it. Said he'd lost the taste for solid food. Then he said he'd been to a public school. Just like that. I didn't ask him or anything...'

'What's a public school?' Maxie asked. 'Where they send you if you're bad?'

'A boarding school,' Gladstone explained. 'In England. Cost his father a fortune, he said, and gave him the manners of a gentleman and the brain of a Chinese sea-cook. That's what he said.'

'That's a good one,' Dewi commented. 'Son of a bloody Chinese sea-cook.'

'No need to swear,' said Gladstone.

'What else, then?' I asked.

Gladstone brushed back his long hair. 'He asked a lot of questions about people who used to live in the town. I didn't know half of them. He said, "I don't know why I've come back, kid" – he called me "kid" all the time. "I don't know why I've come back – there's nothing for me here..."'

'What did you say?'

'I told him this was his native town, like. I didn't know what to say. "Is that reason enough, kid?" he said. I said I thought it was. I was only talking, like.' Gladstone jabbed away at the dying fire. 'Martha told me I didn't want to have anything to do with the Vaughans. Said she remembered Ashton Vaughan. He was rough, she said. Wicked. But – I'll tell you this now – *I* don't think he's rough.' He turned to me. 'Lew – I thought he was a man with a bit of *style* to him, somehow. Know what I mean?'

I wasn't sure what he meant, but I nodded. The man aboard the *Moonbeam* was important now, and exciting.

47

'What does he want us to do, though?' I said.

Gladstone stared reflectively at the fire for a moment. '"This bloody little town, God damn it" – that's what he said.'

'Said that?' Dewi too had forgotten we'd had our boat pinched by one of the Vaughans.

'"If I'll be needing friends anywhere," he said, "I'll need them here." He wants us,' Gladstone ended, 'to be his friends.'

We crouched on the hearth and held our hands out to the fire, suddenly cold all of us with the news. Gladstone looked very pale and very serious.

'He's right, isn't he? Bloody little town. He meant they're all hypocrites here. That's what he meant...'

'All lick my ass and money,' Dewi said fiercely.

'What did he say about his brother?' I asked.

'Not a word.'

'The fight, then?'

'Nothing.'

'With knives?' Maxie said. 'That right, Lew?'

'Polly told me. She'd know...'

Gladstone broke in, 'Martha said there was another brother. Had a funny name, she said. You know Martha – every name that's not Gwen and Mair and Elin is real comic. Maybe that's why she gave me Gladstone.' He stirred the fire up. 'You know what she said? She said that one on the Point – Marius Vaughan – shot this other brother dead!'

The plain words stunned us all.

'A bloody murderer,' Dewi managed to say at last. 'But – why didn't they hang him, then?'

'An accident,' Gladstone said grimly. 'They said it was an accident.'

48

'A bloody murderer, though,' Dewi said again.

'Suppose,' Maxie said, 'the one on the boat wants us to help him kill the one on the Point?'

'Don't be bloody daft,' Dewi replied. 'That would make us assessors before the fact...'

'Bloody hell,' Maxie said, 'would it?'

Martha came in at that point. We went home. But I didn't get much sleep that night for thinking of the man lying there alone aboard the *Moonbeam*, one of the Vaughans of Porthmawr, the man who had come back, the man who had asked us to be his friends. It was exciting, all of it, but sad too, like the sounds the curlews made in the harbour at dusk.

VI

I woke up in the morning, full of sadness and pity for
Ashton Vaughan, and went down to Meira in the kitchen.

'Well,' she said, 'it's started.' And before I could knock
the top off my boiled egg I was hearing how Ashton Vaughan
hadn't been lying there all alone on the damp boards of the
old *Moonbeam* while the heedless town snored. He'd been
taken to the police station instead because he'd fallen into
the harbour and been fished out, like a cod, with a boathook.
'Drunk as a monkey,' Meira added. 'Wet as a conger eel.'

'Is he all right?' I said, but not anxiously. I was less
sad about him all of a sudden.

We went down to the *Moonbeam* later that morning.
We didn't expect to find him there, but he was, looking
more ravaged than ever, the furrows deeper in his face. He
was trying, with trembling fingers, to heat up some water
for a shave.

Gladstone led us in and took over straight away.

'Are you all right?' he asked anxiously.

'Not so loud,' Ashton Vaughan said. 'By God, are you all in hobnailers or what?'

'Do you feel all right, Mr Vaughan?'

'Damp,' he replied, 'but undismayed. Fell like a brick into the harbour.'

'We heard,' Gladstone said. The children were chattering away so he ordered them up on deck after warning them against falling over the side.

'Thanks, kid,' Ashton said. 'You're a very considerate young man.'

'Did you have too much to drink?' Gladstone asked.

'Considerate and inquisitive,' Ashton replied. He pulled at his long, red nose and looked intently at each of us in turn.

'Bet you've heard some words spilt about drink in your time, eh? The evils of demon alcohol.' He held up trembling hands. 'When in doubt blame the old red beer...'

He was sniping at us, I knew, but he did it quite gently. We were Sons of Temperance to a man, after all – practically experts on the Evils of Drink.

'Any long service medals in the Band of Hope? Thought so. One sip, boys bach, and you're a goner...'

'I've had a drink,' Dewi bragged.

Ashton began to lather his face. 'Get thee from me, Satan,' he said through the soap.

'I was drunk as a lord one afternoon...'

Ashton winked at Gladstone and me. 'What on – wine gums?' Dewi had asked for that with his boasting, I thought.

51

'It was whisky,' he replied, giving us a side glance because he was lying. 'Nearly a bottle full...'

'Jesus!' Ashton said, 'you're for the high jump straight off.' He pointed the razor at me. 'What about you, Lew Morgan?'

I didn't answer. It was something that worried me – this drinking business. Everywhere you went they were always on about it. Even Meira and Owen, though I'd smelt drink on Owen many a time. I didn't think there was anything wrong in having a pint or two – but if anybody'd asked me what sin smelled like, I'd have said Owen's breath when he was straight in from the Harp. I looked at Ashton Vaughan, and tried a smile, but my mouth was stiff with embarrassment.

'I've had a barrel full,' Maxie said, and I was glad to see those pale blue eyes switch away from me.

'A big barrel or a little barrel?' Ashton asked with a grin.

'Biggest they had in the Harp,' Maxie said.

'And full of lemonade,' Dewi put in.

Ashton was suddenly serious. 'No joke, though,' he said. 'You lads want to steer clear of the drink, or you'll be tumbling like a brick into the harbour too. Mind you – with having been away a long time like this, I forgot my way. Been away from my old home town so long, see. Sp – LASH – that's how I went. Took me so much by surprise I even forgot to swim.' He looked along his trembling fingers. 'Shook me up, though, mind. See my hands this morning? Know what's done that? Shock. That's what the doctors call it – shock.'

One of the Vaughans, I found myself thinking, and

52

he's talking like one of the town drunks – same voice, everything.

Gladstone took over. 'Have you had anything to eat?'

'Had a cup of police station slops, kid.'

'Could you eat anything, then? I mean – sometimes people can't face food in the morning after...'

'What kind of food, kid? Mussels from the harbour?'

Gladstone dipped into the carrier bag he'd brought and produced two eggs, a piece of fatty bacon and a sliver of lard.

'By God,' Ashton said, 'a banquet.'

Gladstone went behind the stove and brought out the old frying pan we'd rescued from the harbour. In no time at all he had the fire going properly, and the fat was singing in the pan.

'I struck a good day,' Ashton said as he rinsed his face, 'when I came across you lads.'

As we watched him eat he plied us with questions about Porthmawr, and laughed at our answers. He never said a word about his brother. It wasn't like talking to a grown man at all – a Vaughan, too, I thought – oh, no, he was one of the boys in no time, easy and amiable. It was as if he was a bit simple, somehow – a bit simple and all broken down.

Every afternoon that week we spent in his company. Until six, that is: at six he was off like a flash. After two nights aboard the *Moonbeam* he decided the trips back from the pubs were too risky. It was better he found a dry berth, he said, and quickly fixed himself up with a room over an empty shop on Harbour View. It had an old iron cot and a gas ring. We cleaned the place out for him, and moved his kit over from the boat.

'Stay around with me, lads bach,' he said. 'You're the only friends I've got.'

He came with us to the beach, and joined us when we had a spell fishing. But he wasn't really with us at all – hunched up inside that brown jacket most of the time, even on the warmest days. He was silent and withdrawn, and I had the feeling he was waiting for something all the time, but whether it was for the pubs opening or for something else it was impossible to say. He bought us bags of sweets and seemed to really enjoy watching the children snap them up. Towards the end of the week, however, we began to notice that his speech was going – not only when he was fresh from the nearest bar, but late in the afternoons as well. 'The poor man's nothing but a sponge,' Gladstone remarked. 'I wonder if he's been without a drink for a long time before he came here?'

'He's bloody well made up for it since,' Dewi said. Gladstone gave him a dirty look for saying it. None of us took Ashton as seriously as he did.

Owen came up with his own ideas. 'That Ashton Vaughan,' he started on me one night.

I was on the defensive straight away. 'He's all right – why?'

'He's a Vaughan, that's what. With you lads all the time, isn't he? What does he talk about, then?'

'Nothing much. Just talks.'

'About his brother?'

'No,' I said. 'Never mentions him.'

Owen nodded gravely. 'Look, Lew – I've been meaning to have a word with you, like. You – you've heard about these funny men, haven't you? You know – queer lot?'

'Nancy boys?' I said, and was pleased to hear Owen draw his breath in sharply.

'Well – that's right, aye. Who told you about them?'

'In school,' I said. 'The boys talk. Why do they do it, then?'

'I don't know,' Owen replied quickly. 'Got a kink, see. But you listen a minute – you keep clear of that sort, understand? And if Mr Ashton Vaughan tries anything funny you let me know straight off...'

'He's harmless,' I said.

Owen didn't look convinced. 'That's what you say – but keep your eyes open and let me know...'

'What'll you do, Owen?'

'I'll flatten him,' Owen said harshly. 'Wouldn't mind the excuse, either. Nobody likes that Vaughan lot, Lew. Neither that old soak, nor that brother of his on the Point. They're dangerous, mate – so you watch out. And if he tries anything let me know...'

I was all out to defend Ashton immediately. 'He's all right. Just a soak...'

'You let me know, though. And keep clear of him. And if he offers you money don't take it, see. All right?'

'All right,' I said.

'So you've been warned off too,' Gladstone said. 'You know what, Lew – this town doesn't hate the Vaughans, it's just scared stiff of them.'

'But why?' I said.

'Because they dare to be different,' Gladstone replied.

We were in Ashton's room. It was evening and Ashton was touring the pubs.

'I wish I had this room,' Gladstone said. 'Just me and the children. We could really make something of it if we had a place like this. I could look after them properly. I'll get a place one day too – nicer than this. You wait...'

'Why did he come back?' I broke in. 'What's he doing here?'

'Why shouldn't he be here? This is where he started. It's where you started that counts, Lew.' He flicked away some dust off the window sill. 'I mean – imagine you having to leave Porthmawr. Where would you go?'

'Plenty of places,' I said. 'Liverpool, London...'

Gladstone looked at me in wonder. 'Would you go, though? Would you really go to all those places? Leave here? Leave Wales?'

'Maybe,' I said. 'I don't know.'

'But you'd come back, though. You'd be glad to come back. I went on that Sunday-school trip to Rhyl, and I wasn't happy all day. Not until I was back on Porthmawr station. This is the place that counts, see. That's why Ashton came back...'

'Maxie says he's planning to kill his brother...'

Gladstone laughed scornfully. 'Maxie's just a child – mentally, I mean. Not sophisticated at all.'

Sophisticated was new to me: I stored it up for the dictionary.

'Do you suppose the one on the Point knows he's here?'

'All Porthmawr knows it,' Gladstone replied. 'It's a seven-day wonder.'

56

I sat on the edge of the bed and watched Gladstone tack an old piece of lace he'd found as a curtain. Outside, the narrow street was in shadow although it was not yet dark. Gladstone stepped back to look at his work.

'That should stop the nosy ones – that lot across the way always looking in... God, it depresses me. It really does. All these people watching and waiting. Why can't they leave him alone? I bet they're glad enough of the drinks he buys them, but behind his back it's talk, talk, talk...'

'Where does the money come from?' I asked.

Gladstone turned on me sharply. 'You asking questions too?'

'Just wondering,' I said.

'Well – what does it matter? He's an allowance from what his mother left him, as a matter of fact...'

'Is it a lot?' I couldn't help asking.

He went to the door. 'Come on. Let's go.'

I followed him uneasily, knowing that I'd offended him.

'Why do people get like this?' he was saying. 'Always watching and asking questions, always waiting for something terrible to happen...'

'I wasn't...' I began.

'Why can't they leave him alone?' Gladstone went on. 'Leave him alone and look to their own things. They've all got something to hide, but they spend all their lives searching for the dirt on other people.' He stood with his back to the door. 'All that chapel crowd with their smart rig-outs on Sunday morning, and their Sunday morning faces too. That's all part of the same fraud.' He gripped my arm tightly. 'You know what, Lew? I once asked old Jenkins shoe-shop what you were

57

supposed to say when you walk into chapel first of all. You know – when you're supposed to sit there after you've gone in and lower your head and that. What should you say – that's what I asked him. And d'you know what he said? Count up to twenty, that's what I do. That's what he said – honest! A grown man like that! Count up to twenty – and if you feel very pious make it thirty, or even forty! Lew – what kind of thinking is that? It's a fraud, isn't it? You haven't got a chance against thinking like that. Ashton hasn't. None of us have...'

I'd started him off, brought that ring into his voice which came only when he felt deeply about something, and now I didn't know what to say. I was glad to see the photograph under the bed.

'What's that?' I said.

Gladstone knelt by the bed and picked up the photo. I looked over his shoulder. It was a picture of a boy, taken in a studio, a shadowy castle behind him. He had dark hair brushed across his forehead, and his eyes were fixed steadily on the camera. He looked special, somehow. One hand was raised so that his finger touched the top of his chin. It was an old face, and he must have made a witty remark to someone who was watching. Yet he was only a little boy in a sailor suit.

'Look at the writing,' Gladstone whispered. 'Jupiter Vaughan,' he read in an unsteady voice. 'Jupiter Vaughan, 1904–1920.'

He held the photo up for a second or two longer, then hurriedly pushed it back on top of the suitcase. 'Come on,' he said, 'we shouldn't have looked.'

He let me go out first, then closed the door very

gently, as you do when you are leaving a sickroom, as I imagined you did when leaving a room where someone lay dead.

VII

Saturday evening, Porthmawr crouching under open skies, and only the visitors out. They had spilled out of the trains all afternoon, and since they had come so far they had to see something, rain or no rain. So they padded the brimming streets in dripping macs and squelching pumps, and looked into windows of closed shops, and stomped into the pubs and the fish and chips and the pictures. Porthmawr in the wet on a Saturday night waved no welcome sign. It seemed to be hanging on, waiting, like the chapels, for Sunday.

I was at home, the house to myself with Meira and Owen at the pictures, passing time on with another Zane Grey but thinking of Ashton Vaughan. I had been warned not to have the wireless on because the wet battery was down and Meira would want the service in the morning. Meira always had the service on while the Sunday dinner was cooking – better than chapel itself, she said. So there was only the hiss of the fire, and the rain against the window, and the tick of the clock on the mantelpiece: quiet sounds that send the mind spinning.

How was the party going? The biggest yet. It had started at opening time that morning and had been raging ever since. By mid-afternoon Ashton and his crowd had been thrown out of the Bells. There had been a fight, Gladstone said, in the yard behind the pub, but the police hadn't been called or anything like that. Just an honest fight, then back to Ashton's room the whole lot went with a couple of crates. Gladstone had taken some laundry over at teatime and reported that it was wetter in that room than outside. 'All the town spongers, Lew,' he said. 'All singing hymns and swearing.'

At opening time in the evening they had all gone off to the Fishers, which was rough and the only pub that would have them. We had watched them go, the four of us. I think we all wanted to pull Ashton away from them and get him back to his room. He'd seen us too, standing there in the shop doorway, but he'd turned away and lurched past. I looked at the clock. Half past nine: they'd be out on the streets now, and so would the police. Zane Grey had all the pull of the *Three Bears* that night.

I was at the door almost before the sound of the knocker had stopped echoing in the empty house. It was Gladstone and the other two, huddled under an old umbrella with a hole in it.

'Get your coat,' Gladstone ordered. 'Ashton's down by the harbour somewhere. It's a matter of life and death.'

I had my coat on in no time, and was running after

them along the shining streets. I caught them up by Harbour View. They were looking up at Ashton's room.

'Sure he isn't up there?' I said.

'No light,' Gladstone replied. 'Dewi saw him leave the Fishers, then Maxie lost him because he stopped to see this fight.'

'Two men from the country,' Maxie said. 'Great fight. Teeth everywhere.'

'Should have stayed with him,' Gladstone snapped. 'Not safe for him near all that water. Now – spread out. Take a street each and we'll meet by the Lifeboat Hut. Right? Let's go, then.'

We took a street each. I saw nobody down mine, except a couple kissing in a doorway. The rain never stopped. Already my feet were wet.

We came together by the Lifeboat Hut on the quay. There was no sign of Ashton. We stared out across the dark of the harbour. The tide was in too. God knew where he had got to.

'Try the *Moonbeam*, shall we?' I said.

'A light,' Dewi broke in. 'Out there...'

We looked along the line of his pointing arm, and three of us saw it suddenly – a brief glow, then the black again. Maxie never saw it. He always had difficulty in seeing anything in the dark.

'By God,' Dewi said, 'someone striking a match out in the harbour!'

It had to be Ashton. We ran down the slippery jetty and pulled at one of the mooring ropes. It was so dark we only knew the boat had reached the side of the jetty when we heard its bow thud against stone.

62

'Quickly,' Gladstone said. 'Is there an oar?'

Dewi, who was already aboard said, 'One,' and we clambered in after him. We slipped the mooring rope and pushed the boat out then stumbled to the bow. Dewi was the best stern sculler going: we left him to it and crouched there, arms held out in case we rammed one of the moored craft. The night around us was soot black.

'You look out for the boats,' Gladstone said in my ear. 'I'll watch for the light...'

He had no sooner said it than the harbour was suddenly brighter than any day. Dewi had time to cry 'Flare' before the light went out and the dark moved in again.

Gladstone, Maxie and I huddled together in the bow of the boat, not speaking, not even moving, as if stunned by what had happened. Dewi in the stern had his oar out of the water, and I knew he was standing there, not believing there had been a light, like the rest of us.

'Dear God,' Gladstone cried out, 'it came from Marius Vaughan's boat! It was a rocket! It's Ashton...'

As if to prove him right another one went up, and this one held its light. We could see the rain now, and through it the *Cambrian Cloud* – Marius Vaughan's boat – the biggest and the slowest in Porthmawr regatta.

'To port,' Gladstone ordered.

'Which bloody way is port?' Dewi replied.

'Left,' Gladstone barked. 'Left and straight ahead. I can see him!'

Ahead of us was the *Cambrian Cloud*, white and shining like a ghost ship, and there was Ashton standing in the steering-well.

'There he is!' Gladstone cried.

63

'Must think he's bloody Guy Fawkes,' Dewi shouted back.

I felt Gladstone stiffen, but he didn't say anything. Before the light from the flare had gone we were close enough to grab the anchor chain, then we pulled ourselves slowly alongside the yacht. 'Hold her tight,' Gladstone said as he heaved himself aboard. Maxie and I hung on as our boat bobbed and swung away, then we drew it close to the yacht's side.

'Ashton,' I heard Gladstone shout on the deck above us. 'Mr Vaughan. Where are you?'

Ashton's voice came back. 'Here, kid. All tangled in the flaming rigging. Pissed as a coot and tangled up...'

Gladstone came back. 'Blacker than hell up here. Any matches going?'

'I've got a torch,' Maxie said.

'Well hand it up then.'

Maxie switched his torch on and tested the beam, then held it up to Gladstone. Dewi and I asked him what the hell he was playing at, not telling us he had a torch all the time.

'Got a new battery,' Maxie said.

'New battery, my ass,' Dewi replied, and went in for a spell of swearing. I couldn't blame him. The water was running down my sleeves and I felt like swearing too. I looked over their heads shorewards. There were lights all around the Lifeboat Hut. 'They're coming for us,' I said. We wouldn't have to worry about a light going back.

'Gladstone had better hurry up,' Maxie grumbled. 'It'll be the police station for us...'

'Lew,' Gladstone called above me, 'take the torch.

64

Shine it this way. We're coming down.'

He jumped into our boat and began shouting instructions to Ashton who stood above us, holding on to the rigging.

'Sit down, Mr Vaughan. Legs over.'

Ashton crouched down and pushed one leg over the side of the yacht, and there he stuck. 'Boys bach,' he howled, 'can't find the other bloody leg! It's dropped off!'

'You're sitting on it,' Gladstone cried. 'Try to get up, Mr Vaughan.'

Ashton just sat there tapping the deck, searching for his missing leg and rocking with laughter. 'By God, what a dirty night to lose your leg and all...'

'Hold tight,' Gladstone said, 'I'll come up and help you.'

He heaved himself aboard the yacht again, and after what looked like a wrestling match managed to get Ashton to put his legs over the side. But that was as far as Ashton would go. 'Don't wanna ger in the bloody boat,' he was saying. 'I'm all ri' here. Leave me alone. This is my yacht...' His head was lolling about on his shoulders. He was making strange noises which sounded like singing. 'Just leave me alone, lads bach. Leave me be...'

Gladstone tried to lift him, but he was a big man, and dead weight. 'Bring the boat closer,' he ordered. 'Closer still. Hold it there now. I'll shove him in. Ready, Mr Vaughan? I'll push him in – you break his fall down there...'

'What with?' Dewi said. 'He'll have the bloody lot over...'

Ashton Vaughan's head was sagging on his chest. If he didn't stop rolling about like that he'd be falling into the

65

boat of his own accord. Gladstone crouched behind him, arms under his armpits. He heaved, and we all let go of the *Cambrian Cloud* as Ashton was promptly sick. I dropped the torch into the bottom of the boat and it went out straight away. We were rocking and stamping and cursing there in the streaming dark. Especially Dewi: he was using every word he knew.

'Who's that swearing out there?' the voice behind us barked out – a foghorn of a voice, and we turned to face it at the same time as they switched on the searchlight. We heard the soft, powerful throb of the lifeboat's motor now. The light pinned us there, blinded us, came out of the night straight for us and we were locked there between the lifeboat and the *Cambrian Cloud*.

'Get them aboard,' a voice ordered. 'Mind that boat of mine, now. Young b—. Get them aboard. Oh – by God – will you look at that lot on the *Cloud*?'

We were hauled aboard the lifeboat as the men roared laughing. The dinghy was pulled clear and the lifeboat edged closer to the *Cambrian Cloud*.

'What's going on, then?' the Coxswain asked Gladstone. 'What are you mucking about at?'

'We came out after Mr Vaughan,' Gladstone replied.

'Silly young b—,' the Coxswain said. 'You must be stupid daft. Daft as the bloody visitors.' The Cox's name was Solomon Davies, and he was all right: even now he didn't talk really rough.

'Get aboard, Gladstone Williams,' he said. 'We'll have to rig up a winch for your friend there.'

'Bloody Vaughan,' someone said near me in the darkness. 'Let's leave him till he drops in.'

66

'You'd have the breweries after you, man. Think of the profit they'd lose.'

'Remember the bastard coming home in his officer's kit...'

'Remember the bastard telling me I was to salute him. Said he'd report me to my commanding officer, he did...'

'What did you tell him, Will?'

'Told him I'd put him in the harbour, sharp, uniform and all. Jesus bach! There was me just back from the Somme.'

'All right, boys,' the Cox ordered, 'get him in.'

'I'm not touching the drunken bastard,' the man at my elbow said. 'Leave the b—. Might have got these lads drowned...'

'Get him in!

'What's the matter, Solomon – does his brother pass a cheque over on lifeboat collection?'

'Marius Vaughan wouldn't pass water,' someone else said.

Gladstone was by my side, gripping my arm tightly. 'The poor man,' he said softly. 'They hate him...'

Two of the crew, gleaming like whales in their oilskins, heaved Ashton roughly into the lifeboat.

'Wonder what he was doing on his brother's boat, then?' someone said. 'Oh, by Christ, watch out – he's sick all over.'

Gladstone left my side and went to where Ashton lay. I stayed where I was. I felt sick myself by then.

'Let's take a look for the boat he used to get out here,' the Cox'n said. 'Turn the light around. It'll be Harri Thomas' more than likely...'

'Over there,' someone called. 'Pass us the boathook.'

They secured the dinghy quickly and the lifeboat

turned towards the town. 'By damn,' the Cox'n chuckled, 'that was the shortest trip for a few years and no mistake. Firing off rockets in the bloody harbour. Worse than the bloody visitors...'

'You want to make the bastard clean up this deck,' a voice grumbled.

We chugged softly back to the slipway, Dewi by my side now saying bloody good, bloody good, over and over again.

Maxie said, 'Never had a ride on the lifeboat before.'

Half the town and all the visitors seemed to be waiting for us on the slipway. Superintendent Edwards was there too, looking like the day of judgement. We were put ashore one by one, Ashton, who had come to, staggering last.

'Mr Vaughan can tell you all about it, Super,' the Cox'n called.

The Super bore down upon us. We were standing around Ashton like a bodyguard. 'Let's have a fight,' Dewi said, but Gladstone hushed him quiet.

'All right,' the Super said, 'you boys into the hut there. You too, Mr Vaughan.'

Two policemen broke up the crowd for us. Ashton led us, looking like the Ancient Mariner himself, and Maxie came last, muttering, 'Our Tada's there! Seen me!'

At the far end of the Lifeboat Hut, the Super lined us up. He drew himself up to his full height – a big man, sergeant-major moustache and all.

'Right,' he said, in a voice too loud to listen to, 'what's been going on, then?'

We all waited for Ashton to speak, but Ashton was

looking at someone standing in the shadow by the door of the Hut. A short, very stiff man with white hair and a white moustache, but I only recognised him properly when he stepped into the light. He swung one leg stiffly, and that made him Marius Vaughan. We all knew he'd lost a leg in France.

The Super saw him too, and immediately went over and gave him a salute. They stood close together talking, then Marius Vaughan turned away and limped off into the crowd. The Super came back.

'Right,' he said, 'that was Mr Vaughan. Just had a word with him. On his yacht you were...'

'No charges, of course?' Ashton kept his eyes lowered. 'I take it we are free to go...'

'Not so fast,' the Super said. 'I could charge you – know that, don't you? Drunk and disorderly...'

Ashton stuck out his fists. 'Handcuffs then. Do your duty. Lock me up...'

The Super gave a snort. 'Get yourself off home, man. Stop playing around like a big lad. Give over causing people embarrassment...'

Ashton laughed. 'So that's it? I'm causing my brother embarrassment, am I? Is that what he said?'

'Use your head,' the Super said. 'Act your age. Can't keep on like this...'

Ashton found a cigar butt somewhere and lit it. 'Now these young heroes,' he said. 'Came to my rescue. No charges for me, no charges for them? Right, Super?'

The Super glared at him. 'I'll deal with these boys after you've gone. Now – clear off and think yourself lucky I haven't mentioned that dinghy you took out...'

69

'Superintendent,' said Ashton, 'do you realise I might have drowned if these boys hadn't come out after me?'

The Super didn't seem very impressed. 'Very likely. Now – I'm telling you this, Mr Vaughan, don't chance your luck. I'm letting you go. I'd act on that if I were you.'

Ashton examined the cigar in his hand with elaborate care, then shook his head. 'No go, Super,' he said. 'You're not charging me, so you're not charging these boys...'

Superintendent Edwards' face was normally red, but now the colour deepened. He was chewing a bit at the sergeant-major moustache too, and his great fists were clenched tight.

Gladstone turned to Ashton. 'Please go home. We'll be all right.'

But Ashton refused to move. He stood there with a half smile on his face, looking down all the time at the cigar in his hand. The Super turned his back on him and arranged us in front for the talking to which we knew was bound to come. He made a big thing of it too, but that night there was no cutting edge to his words. Behind him, a dripping wreck of a man, Ashton stood, head cocked a little to one side, listening. And the Super knew it.

'Names, addresses, schools... you are all liable to a charge of larceny of one dinghy, you know that.... Next time you see a light in the harbour inform the authorities.... I don't think you realise the seriousness.... You can't take a man's boat....' The Super tried his best, but he was off form, and he didn't take as long as usual, either. He had the reputation of being able to reduce the roughest boy to tears – just by talking to him – but that night he wasn't at his best. 'It's a caution this time. I hope

70

I can leave your parents to deal with your fool-hardiness....' And he went on to his peroration before he ordered us all out of the Hut.

We went to the door, Ashton and Gladstone leading, Maxie and Dewi trailing after me because their fathers were waiting for them in the crowd.

'Gangway, if you please,' Ashton cried, waving his cigar, and he was laughing and joking and walking quite steadily. But by the time we reached Harbour View we were supporting him, and he was sick again. 'Comes over me in waves,' he said.

'We'll take him up,' Gladstone said, but it was easier said than done on that narrow stairway. At the top he suddenly flung his arms out and nearly knocked us both down the stairs. 'Jupiter!' he cried, in a strange, choked voice. 'Little Jupy. I see your face!' Then he fell forward to the floor.

We dragged him into his room and propped him up on the bed. After a struggle we got the sodden overcoat off him, and then his boots. Gladstone slackened off his tie, and I wondered how he could do it. With all that sick down his front I knew I couldn't have touched him.

'Is he dead?' I whispered.

Gladstone shook his head. 'Be all right. I'll have to clean him up a bit.' He found the towel and dipped it into the big jug on the washstand, then he dabbed away at the creased face of the man on the bed. 'He'll feel better waking up clean, poor man,' he said. He was as gentle and as careful as a woman bathing her child.

He turned away from the bed and went to the washstand to clean the towel. I looked down and saw that

Ashton Vaughan's eyes were open. I saw his lips move and bent over him. 'Your pal,' he said, 'is a proper little nursie boy, isn't he?' It was a sneer, the way he said it. My head came up as if he'd slapped me.

Gladstone came back with a glass of water which he put beside the bed. 'Did he say something?' he whispered.

'Not a word,' I said.

I was glad to get out, glad to be running home, my wet coat flapping noisily around me. Outside the door of Gladstone's house we stopped and looked at each other.

'An exciting night,' Gladstone said with a grin.

'Be trouble,' I said.

He gripped my arm. 'We did right, though, Lew. Only us on his side, remember, and he's a broken man. Got a big scar inside him.'

'Jupiter,' I said automatically, but I was remembering the sneer in Ashton's voice. 'I'll go or there'll be trouble,' I said, and although I was in the house a full three minutes before Owen and Meira came there was trouble all the same. The news had practically stopped the pictures.

VIII

There was trouble next day, too – all day.

'Good people go to chapel,' Meira said, and although it was the hottest day yet, I was sent to the ten o'clock service at the Mission, and back again at two for Sunday school. Chapel was a punishment where Meira was concerned: that was the only thing we agreed on that day.

At ten on the Mission benches, the hardest they ever made, we had a local preacher and a deacon warning us off things. That was the trouble with the Mission – it was always what we shouldn't do. 'Don't' they cried, and 'Beware', and everywhere you turned there were pitfalls and dangers. We were living on a tightrope suspended over burning fires – and everything, of course, had a moral.

'Take this fountain pen, made in Britain,' the local preacher was saying. He held up the pen for all to see. 'Is this pen not like a righteous man? Think of it – so much ink

73

it takes in – *enough* ink. It is not a *greedy* pen. *Beware* of the evil of *greed*. The pen takes in enough – and *no more*. And then I write with it, and it lets the ink out again. *Enough* ink. But it doesn't *blot*! It does not make a mess of a clean, white page. It does not let ink out in a great *blot*. So let us, friends, be like this pen. Let us take enough from life – enough and no more. And let us leave no *blots*.'

Rowland Williams, who was sitting next to me on the back bench, leaned closer and whispered, 'Better to buy some *blotting* paper, Lew. Quick.' Then he reached under the seat for his hat, got up, and walked out. The local preacher only managed fifteen minutes more after that.

At two I was back on the hard benches again, and so was Rowland Williams. He was in his fifties, Rowland, with a quiet voice that said quiet, sharp things. By trade he was a carpenter, working alone in an old workshop at the top end of Lower Hill. He didn't do much work, though, because he had more books than anyone I knew, and he must have subscribed to all the periodicals they ever printed. His sister, with whom he lived, wouldn't allow him to keep books in the house, so he had them up there with him at the workshop. They used to say that he had been found once sitting in an unfinished coffin reading Plato's *Republic*.... He had been in the war, and as he said himself he had a glass eye to prove it. Every evening, except Sundays, he spent on Porthmawr station watching the trains go by, and although he brought up his reading all the time at Sunday school he never said a word about the trains.

That day he was talking about Elijah, the prophet, and H. G. Wells, also a prophet, and Bernard Shaw, another one. But I wasn't in the discussion at all, and neither was

Dewi. Our eyes were on the door and the clock. At five to three the Rev A. H. Jones, BA, BD, always did his rounds and we both knew who he would be looking for.

He was ten minutes early that day, followed closely by Alderman Mrs Meirion-Pughe and Abraham Evans and Dr Gwynn. The Minister bounced in, roaring with laughter as usual; Mrs Meirion-Pughe walked as if on ice, her noble chin uplifted; Abraham Evans stopped to pat every little head he came to; Dr Gwynn walked like a Chicago gangster at the pictures, and with his dark jowls looked like one too. They swept past our class to the front and gathered around Mr Caradoc Probert who was in charge of the Sunday school. Start counting, I said to myself. I hadn't reached ten before the Minister was there in the aisle, his black stomach touching my cheek.

He spoke over my head. 'Afterwards, if you please. Dewi Price and Lew Morgan, stay behind.' Mrs Meirion-Pughe was by his side, watching him say it. She was everywhere, that woman. Rowland Williams always said there was no point in going to heaven because they were bound to have her on the committee.

'Now then,' the Minister said, tapping Elin Parri on the shoulder, 'let me hear a verse from this pretty girl.'

Elin wasn't pretty, and had a bad stammer. She was nearly eighteen, but simple. She looked up, startled, red-faced. 'G-god s-save the k-king!' she said. The Rev A. H. Jones let rip with one of his falsetto laughs, and all the Sunday school laughed with him, except for Dewi and me and Elin, and Rowland Williams.

We were collected after the last Amen, and ushered through to the small vestry. Sitting there, almost in a trance, guarded by Mrs Meirion-Pughe, was Gladstone. He didn't even look up when we joined him on the seat.

'Let us pray,' said the Rev A. H. Jones after Maxie had stumbled in. We lowered our heads as he knelt, but I kept my eyes open and took a good look at Mrs Meirion-Pughe, who was also kneeling. Her face looked harder, more like a man's than ever. She was wearing a wool dress, and she was sweating. It was Welsh wool, though – that's what she told everybody. She only wore clothes made from Welsh wool. I had once heard Meira ask Owen, 'Wonder how she'd go on, then, if she could only get French knickers?'

'Amen,' said the Minister.

Mrs Meirion-Pughe got to her feet and gave us a long, hard look. 'I'll leave them in your hands, A. H.,' she said.

The Minister had one of his laughing spells, 'Of course, my dear. Thank you. Thank you for everything.'

I wondered why they had to wring each other's hands like that. Come six o'clock they would be meeting again for the evening service. They seemed to overdo everything, even a handshake.

The door closed behind her. The Minister placed himself directly in front of us. He was a very short man, but round and soft like a suet pudding. You had the feeling, without touching him, that he was soft all over. His neck, I always thought, once he removed that white, tight collar, would bulge slowly out, like rising bread, to the same width as the rest of him. Everybody said he wore wigs – that he had some short and some long ones, too, so that people would think he had just been for a haircut. Everybody said he was an elegant dresser, with his white cuffs and his white handkerchiefs. Everybody said that he had a fine speaking voice, and that he would have made a wonderful actor.

'How shall I begin?' he said. 'Should I say boys will be boys and leave it at that?' He pointed to Dewi. 'What would you say, my boy? What is your name, first of all?'

'Dewi Price.'

The Minister nodded. 'I was a boy once, you know. In fact I was rather a naughty boy. A very naughty boy.' He ripped off one of his famous laughs. 'What do you think of that?'

We didn't say anything. I was studying the map of Paul's journeys on the opposite wall.

'Right,' he went on. 'Now – which is Gladstone...' He squinted at us until his eyes rested on Gladstone. 'Of course,' he murmured. 'Of course.' Only last winter he had asked Gladstone to say a prayer in front of the Sunday school, and Gladstone had said, 'Please God be patient, and make us as good as we think we are.'

'Of course. Gladstone Williams. Now – Dewi Price?'

Dewi raised his hand.

'And Lew Morgan?' I said me, sir. 'A mistake, surely? That should be Llew Morgan, shouldn't it?' No, sir. 'Were you christened Lew?' Sir. 'Are you sure?' Sir. 'Well, well.... And Maxie Roberts? Your name isn't *Maxie*, my boy, is it?'

'Sir.'

'Are you sure?'

'Sir. My mam calls me Maxie.'

The Rev A. H. Jones shifted his false teeth. 'I see. And you all live on Lower Hill Road?'

'That's right,' Dewi said, 'and if we lived up there on the Hill with the nobs you wouldn't have to ask our names.'

The Minister for a moment looked as if he'd been punched in the stomach. But he recovered quickly. 'Watch your tongue, my lad! Watch what you say. These names were given to me by Superintendent Edwards. Do you expect me to remember the name of every boy in my flock?'

He wasn't a hard man, I saw. He even had a staring match with Dewi and lost it, too. And all this asking names business was just killing time because he didn't know what to say to us.

He pointed to Gladstone. 'What school do you attend, Gladstone?'

'No school,' Gladstone said. 'Too old.'

The Minister looked disappointed. 'Where does your father work, then?'

'No father.'

He hesitated. Probably he had remembered who Gladstone's mother was. Martha was very well known. 'But you're the leader,' he went on. 'You can't deny that.'

'The leader of what?' Gladstone replied. 'We're not a gang...'

'Superintendent Edwards – on the phone – he said you were the ringleader...'

'We're not a ring, either,' Gladstone said flatly.

'But' – the Minister gathered himself – 'you can't sit there and deny that it was you who led these boys to risk their lives last night? To risk their lives in a foolish escapade in the course of which you all might have been drowned...'

'There's not much risk in the harbour,' Dewi said.

'In pitch darkness, boy. In a leaking boat...'

'Wasn't leaking,' Maxie said, then added 'Sir.' The Rev

78

A. H. Jones wasn't really getting a chance to go off on a spell of oratory, I thought.

He pointed a stubby finger at Gladstone. 'How old are you, boy?'

'Seventeen,' Gladstone replied.

'Seventeen – that's what the Superintendent said. Old enough to know better. Old enough to know...'

'The poor man was out there on the boat. We saw a light and went out to rescue him...'

'The poor man, as you call him, was hopelessly drunk. He should have been left out there. People who make a God of Alcohol get their just rewards...'

'Just a minute,' Gladstone broke in, 'are you saying we should have left him out there? Left him to drown?'

'Not at all,' the Minister replied. 'Over-simplification. Very much over-simplification.' Gladstone had let him in, given him something to talk about. 'Let us try to see the problem straight, shall we? Now – I agree you acted with the best of intentions all of you. I agree your motives were sound – generous in fact...' He was off now, on a tide of words, using his fine voice to best effect. 'All this I grant, boys. But – consider the facts. This man you went out to rescue last night is a hopeless drunkard. A sot.' Gladstone shifted his feet impatiently. 'Ever since he left this town many years ago – before most of you were born – he has been the slave of drink. Did you know that? Every morning, year in, year out, he was woken up, this man, filled with a vile craving for drink. He must have a drink, he must have a drink... Ashton Vaughan is an *addict*. And what has he done? Has he fought it off like a man? Oh, no – he has gone out, every day, to some dingy bar and

79

soaked himself anew in the evil stuff.' The Minister licked his lips. 'Day after day. An addict. Did you know, any of you, that this man has been in and out of hospitals where they treat people who cast themselves on the seas of oblivion with drink?' He came closer. 'What,' he asked, 'do you think of that?'

None of us had anything to say. These were facts. There was no argument to make.

'This man,' the Minister went on, his voice rising, 'in whose company – don't deny it! – you have been seen so often, is a bad man.'

'Not true,' Gladstone cried.

'A bad man,' the Minister insisted. 'I'm warning you now: the Vaughans are a law unto themselves.' He glanced over his shoulder and lowered his voice. 'They have placed themselves beyond – beyond everything. One a drunkard, the other an atheist. Both of them baptised in Capel Mawr; both of them forsaken the ways and the House of God. A law unto themselves heeding neither man nor God... I shudder inside myself when I think of them.' He closed his eyes and lowered his head, and being so near to him we knew it was an act. A chapel's length away it would have passed off, but this was point-blank range. 'Shall I tell you something, boys? Look – I know how you feel. I understand. When I was a boy...' It was time for a story – the story of his boyhood in the hills of Merioneth, on a tiny farm, his father an illiterate labourer, his mother saving every penny so that he could become a minister and go to Aberystwyth. He had never forgotten his background. He had been born poor, and was proud of it... his mother's face, the little cottage.... It was a good story, except that

80

Polly had told me it wasn't true. Polly had said that his father, for a start, had been a gardener to some rich family in the south, and his mother had been the parlourmaid. 'Servants,' Polly had declared scornfully. 'Doesn't want us to know his parents were in service. It was the people who had this house put him through college.'

The Minister was coming to an end. 'A small, poor farm on a mountain. But we were rich in one thing – we knew the right road and we followed it. We lived clean lives. We put our trust in God – and God knows his servants.'

The silence followed, the actor's pause to let the words strike home. Maxie ruined some of the effect by saying 'Amen', but the Rev A. H. Jones was a man who picked up anything and threw it back at you.

'Well said, my boy,' he whispered. 'Well said. Amen indeed.' He gave us a dazzling smile, mouth only. 'I'll tell you boys something, shall I? In confidence. There are many people in Capel Mawr whose one wish it is to see every public house in this town brought tumbling to the ground. Oh, yes – it's true. Burn them down, they tell me. Houses of the Devil…. And they are right. Public houses *are* places of the Devil, but do you know what I think? I think we should leave them open. Every one! Yes – every single one.' He came closer still. 'Some people, you know, consider I hold *advanced* ideas. I suppose they are right. My ideas *are* unusual. Modern – shall we say? Leave them open, that's my answer. Leave them open and be strong, and march past! We must be strong enough to walk past their open doors, head held high, all temptation cast aside. We must stand up and say – this is not for a Christian…. Oh, I know that's daring – *modern* – but that's what I believe. We

81

mustn't be like Ashton Vaughan. We mustn't give in to every weakness.' He belched softly and looked at his watch. 'Boys – I want you to do something for me. I'll let you into another of my secrets: I don't like telling boys off. Told you I was *unusual*, didn't I? But – do this one thing for me. Steer clear of Ashton Vaughan. Don't let him drag you down the slippery slopes. Stay away from him.' He had the watch out again. He licked his lips: you could almost see him working out what there would be for tea. 'I didn't ask you in here to give you a lengthy telling off. Don't think that....' He was hurrying now. It was near teatime, and probably he knew he wasn't making much of an impression, anyway. 'I want you to think things over – talk things over very carefully.' He gave us an uncertain smile. 'All right?'

Then he said the Lord's Prayer in double time, and we were out in the sunshine.

'Tell you what,' Dewi said, 'I'm beginning to like the Vaughans...'

'What was he talking about, then?' Maxie said.

We held up the station wall and watched the Sunday parade as Gladstone told us how two deacons had come for him, and he in the middle of washing, too.

'The trouble is,' Dewi said, 'we're not worth saving. Now – if we lived up there on the Hill...'

'He'd been told to give us a row,' Gladstone said, 'but he didn't know how...'

'Our Tada said we were no good,' Maxie said.

'He tried his best,' Gladstone went on, 'but he was out of his depth.'

'Are we steering clear, then?' I said.

82

Gladstone shook his head.

'My Tada will kill me,' Maxie said. 'Got the belt last night.'

'So did I,' Dewi said. 'My ass is red raw.'

'I took him some food this morning,' Gladstone said, then stopped suddenly as a big black car went slowly by. There was a woman in the front and she turned right round and pointed towards us and said something to the driver. The car drew into the kerb a little way down Station Road and the woman's blonde head appeared through the window. She was smiling and waving at us. We were so startled we even had a look to see if there was anyone behind us. 'Wants us,' Gladstone said, and ran forward to the car.

Dewi held Maxie and me back. 'That's Marius Vaughan's car,' he said softly.

Gladstone had his head in at the window now, talking. Then he stepped back and the car moved off up Station Road. He watched it go all the way to the corner before he came back to us.

'Marius Vaughan,' he said a little breathlessly. 'Said he hoped we hadn't got into trouble because of last night.' He laughed nervously. 'He – he was very nice.' He laughed again. 'Said thanks very much!'

There were two red marks high on Gladstone's cheeks. His eyes were shining.

IX

Polly spent nearly all of Sunday with the *News of the World*. She read it through a Woolworth's magnifying glass, aloud to herself, very slowly, the paper flat on the table under the lamp. In this way she had become an expert on the great murderers. She knew them as well as she knew her neighbours – Thompson and Bywaters, Rouse, Norman Thorne, Buck Ruxton, Dr Crippen – and she spoke of them as if she had been with them before the killing, during the trial, in the condemned cell. 'Such a high forehead he had,' she used to say. 'You'd never have dreamt there was murder in his heart.' The poison and the pistol, the hacksaw going in the cellar at dead of night, the fire stoked up, the sodden packages surfacing in the canal – these were images she brought out before the spitting fire while the Captain slept and dreamt of the sea. But Polly was an expert on local dying, too – especially on the white bodies which sometimes came ashore on Porthmawr beach after a great storm. The wheeling seagulls near the water's edge, seaweed and long hair, cold fingers on wet sand – pictures conjured out of the air for me.... All I had to do, I reckoned, was wait for the right time and work her round to the Vaughans.

'The Vaughans?' She folded the *News of the World* as if it was precious and returned the magnifying glass to the mantelpiece. 'You and your Vaughans. Never hear anything else out of you. There'll be trouble yet...'

'I don't know anything about them,' I said. 'That Marius Vaughan – I'd never seen him properly till last night.'

'Oh? Come down, did he? Well, well – you want to have a look at Station Road some night. He's always around there, they say. Has his lady friend living there. A very fancy lady friend, too...'

'Yellow hair?' I said.

'Blonde,' Polly replied, making it sound like a disease. 'Eirlys Hampson she's called now. Has a shop. Spoilt herself that girl has. Marius Vaughan won't marry her. And after what he did to his wife, I shouldn't think anyone in her right mind would want to take him on...'

'Did his wife die, then?'

'Divorce, dear.' It was worse than murder, the way Polly said it. 'She was a very refined person. English. Much too refined for the Vaughans. She divorced him – let's see, in 1928, was it?' Polly was very good on dates. '1928, that's right. Oh, she was very tall and slim. Had her hair bobbed. Used to smoke in the street – *that* raised a few eyebrows, I can tell you. And she used to go with him to the Red Dragon and stand with him at the bar.'

Polly held her hand up as if there was a glass in it, her little finger raised. 'This fancy one he has now does that, too – but she's a local...'

She considered this intently for a moment. I was trying to think of something to spur her on but I couldn't decide on anything. It was very difficult getting Polly settled down to a story.

'Ashton and Marius Vaughan?' she went on, and my spirits rose. 'Oh, yes, I could tell you a lot about them. Marius is the eldest, then Ashton, then Jupiter. Did you ever hear such names for Welsh boys? Trying to be different, that's all. They used to come to Capel Mawr in a carriage – tie the horse to the chapel rail. Aping the gentry. They liked to think they were gentry, but they weren't. You can always tell gentry – they own land, for one thing. Not just houses, but land. The Vaughans were never in that class. Property's not the same as land...'

'Jupiter died,' I prompted her gently.

Polly nodded sadly. 'Too beautiful to live...'

'I saw his picture,' I said.

Polly's eyebrows went up. 'Oh? Ashton had it? Well – fancy.' She glanced across at the Captain and touched his hand. The old man opened one eye. Polly, reassured, smiled. 'They were away at school most of the time, but they were here for holidays, lording it over everybody. Oh, but they were rough – not Jupiter – the other two. No, not rough – *vicious*...'

'What did they do?' I asked.

She shrugged, bringing her shoulders up high. 'Oh – they had everything. Guns, dogs, bikes – they ran wild, really now. And they talked like the English – you know, all ladida.' Nothing vicious in that, I thought. 'Both of them Welsh, mind, but it was English with them all the time.' Polly always spoke English too, I thought. 'And there was that bike they had...'

'Motorbike?' I asked hopefully.

'A cycle, Lew. Used to fly along Market Street there, knocking people down. Oh – they were rough...'

Nothing to bite on there, I thought. 'Jupiter was different, though, you said?'

'Oh – different altogether. Quiet and smiling all the time, not bragging like the others. He had this look about him – as if he had the stars in his shoes. He was smaller, see. Not old enough to go to the war with them. A lot round here said the army would make men out of them, but they were worse afterwards. That one on the Point – lost his leg in Flanders fields, but he comes home just the same as ever. And Ashton – making the boys round here salute him.... Oh, I remember a fight there was...' I moved to the edge of my seat. 'Big Huw – you wouldn't know him – been dead a good ten years. He was nearly seven feet tall, but when they buried him everyone said his coffin was no bigger than a child's...'

I nearly came off the chair. 'Did they kill him?'

'TB,' Polly said curtly.

I knew about TB. There were more cases than that in Porthmawr.

'This Big Huw had been in the war, too,' Polly went on. 'Had shellshock. You've heard of that, haven't you?'

I nodded. There were men in Porthmawr who had shellshock, men who couldn't stand still, men in wheelchairs.

'That's what made him terrible in drink, this Big Huw. Well – this night – down there at the old Fishers – they give him a lot of drink and pushes him into fighting the Vaughans. 1918, that was. The one on the Point there had just come home without his leg, and Ashton was on leave too...'

'What happened?' I asked.

'Well – the Vaughans come in, and by now Big Huw is like a raging tiger, crazy with drink. He goes up to Ashton Vaughan and he hits him clean through the door of the Fishers. Right out into the street...'

'Dear God,' I said.

'Then he starts on Marius Vaughan.'

'Only one leg.'

'That's right,' Polly snapped, 'one leg. But they say he had a bottle in his hand, and he threw it at Big Huw, and it catches him on the side of the head...'

'Knocked him out?'

'Oh, no. Never,' Polly went on. 'It wasn't a human head, Big Huw's. Someone said there was a metal plate in it. All the bottle did was shock him, made him fall to his knees.' Polly got up and went through the mime for me. 'It was deathly quiet, the way I heard, then Marius Vaughan goes right up to Huw and hits him one fearful blow across the neck – here – and Huw fell with a crash in the spit and sawdust. Marius Vaughan looks around the room. "Any more of you local trash?" he asks. Not a man moved. Then he goes up to the barman and asks for a pint of beer. The men haven't moved, standing there like statues. He takes the pint to the door, kicks it open and goes out to his brother lying there on the pavement. Then he pours

88

the beer over his brother's face. Some of the men said he even *kicked* him, even called him dirty names, never even helped him when he staggers to his feet. His own brother, Lew.' Polly was back in her chair but looking beyond me now, seeing it all for herself. 'Hard as granite, that Marius. His brother was just a no-good, but Marius was hard – is hard still. He didn't have to have a drink to make him do the things he did. You can excuse a drunken man sometimes.' Polly looked at me intently. 'Lew – they're not like us. That Eirlys Hampson has a husband, they say. If I were her I'd get back to him quick. *She'll* never make a man of him.' The intent look again. 'You won't understand this, Lew, but Marius Vaughan's an appetite for women.'

I wanted to smile, but Polly's face was dark and forbidding.

'Immoral,' she said harshly. 'In everything....'

I sat there and blinked and said nothing. I was hoping that Polly might go into detail. After all, we knew all about it. Didn't we sneak up on the couples locked together on the beach? Weren't there enough French letters to be seen among the rubbish left by each tide? But Polly was very careful with me. No details. 'Living in sin,' was the nearest she ever came to it.

We sat in silence and watched the fire. Polly had switched off the electric, which, she said, ran away with the money.

'The Vaughans,' she sighed, and the coal in the grate sighed with her. 'They had to be different. Their names tell you that. Marius and Ashton and Jupiter...'

'Jupiter died,' I prompted her.

'A beautiful boy. Makes you wonder if he was from the

same bed, that one.' Polly had a look of high tragedy on her face now – her Lady Macbeth look – and I knew then that she was in the mood to tell me more. That was the look she had when she got going on the great murderers.

'November, 1920. Just after Guy Fawkes. They'd set off for Traeth Hir, shooting.' Traeth Hir was up the coast, beyond Graig Lwyd, five miles off – all marshland. You could be cut off by the tide there, easy as wink. 'They always had guns, the Vaughans. Always dogs with them, too. Always shooting, as if there hadn't been enough in the war. But they were trying to act the gentry, see.... The people up at the Hall in those days never accepted them, though.' She gave a superior smile. 'Anyway, they went that morning, the three of them. A grey, misty morning, clouds down, cold. Can you see them, Lew? The three of them in knickerbockers and big boots and hats on their heads, guns under their arms? A couple of dogs following on. Hard to their dogs even, they say. They disappear into the mists that lie heavy over Traeth Hir, and from a distance you can hear the explosions of their guns.' Five miles away! I thought. 'Then – about eleven o'clock, with the turn of the tide comes the rain. People say there's never been such rain as fell in that hour – not in the whole history of Porthmawr, and God knows that's saying plenty. It was like a second flood, and out of it, Lew, over Graig Lwyd there, come the Vaughans – two of them only, Lew, and one of them carrying the dead boy in his arms. They walked slow because of Marius' leg, see – walked right through the town – did you know that? Right past the police station, right past everything, wet like some creatures of the sea. And this boy was there, lifeless, in

90

Marius Vaughan's arms, and there was blood everywhere. Edwards Llywn House – he was Chairman of the council then – saw them and ran out of his shop. He nearly fainted at the dreadful sight. Marius Vaughan, he said at the inquest, was *bathed* in his brother's blood. "Man, what happened?" Edwards asked them. "My brother is dead," Marius tells him. "An accident. I shot him. Get out of the way, old fool." They marched on, the dogs howling at their heels. "The doctor," Edwards cried. "Let the doctors see him." Marius Vaughan keeps on walking. "Can the doctors resurrect the dead?" he asks over his shoulder. "Mr Evans Capel Mawr, then?" cries Edwards. Mr Evans was minister at the time. Marius Vaughan turns around. There's a crowd on the street now. "To hell with Evans Capel Mawr," he says. "The age of miracles is past!" Oh – it was shocking, shocking! Then the police come, but the Vaughans wouldn't stop, wouldn't even listen. "Come to the house, if you must," Marius tells them, and they walk on in all that terrible rain, down past the harbour and along to the Point, Marius leading, Ashton behind him, and those dogs.... Someone said Ashton smelled of drink, but perhaps they were only saying that to make it sound worse. People in Porthmawr like doing that, you know." Polly, hands tightly clasped in her lap, shook her head slowly from side to side. "What a day that was. A terrible crime had been done. We all felt that. They say the town never slept for a week. They say that seeing it caused Edwards Llywn House to have the stroke that killed him two hours after that inquest. The whole town was for going after Marius Vaughan, I heard – but of course that was just public house talk. Nothing was done. They buried Jupiter, and that was that.'"

'Then he fought with Ashton?' I said eagerly. 'Killed his own brother, then they had this fight?'

'It was an accident,' Polly said sharply. 'Everybody knew that. It was his *attitude* people didn't like.' She shivered. 'Someone walking over my grave,' she added.

'They fought with knives, though,' I insisted, feeling her drifting away from me.

'A terrible family,' she said. 'Brother fighting brother...'

The performance was over, I knew, and Polly was spent with the telling of it.

'Tell me why they fought, then,' I said, but not very hopefully.

'Always fighting...'

'But why?' I'd never had a brother. It didn't make sense. 'What happened, then?'

Polly didn't answer. She had the absorbed, indrawn look which spelt the end. She had given a performance; now she had to go over it critically, like an actor when the play is over. I was a nuisance now. The audience had no right to be asking for more. But I stayed on with her for a while, just in case she might come to. Gladstone would have to hear this story before the night was out.

So I sat by the spitting fire and saw in it again that terrible, drowned, November day, and the two of them coming through the town, Marius carrying the dead boy, blood everywhere, Ashton following with the guns, and the dogs behind them, cowering and yelping like beasts out of a nightmare. It was very still there in Polly's room, and I felt as if someone was walking over my grave, too.

X

August came and brought good weather, except for Bank Holiday Monday when it poured. The visitors were everywhere. Normally you heard a lot of English spoken in Porthmawr, but that first week in August seemed to be all English. We even gave up Welsh ourselves just to be in fashion.

Most of the time we were on the beach criticising the visitors as they wore themselves out chasing after beach balls and jumping about in the sea and eating ice cream and drinking lemonade. They were from the big factories and had money to burn. They were English, from a different world, sharp and cocky with high, strident voices, of a higher class than us altogether. So we sat around and felt sorry for them because they weren't Welsh, because they were so pale, because their talk was so comic. Porthmawr in August made you realise what it was like being a native.

We had Ashton with us all the time. 'My gang,' he called us whenever he was able to get any words out. Most of the time he was a brimming barrel of drink and his speech was all over the place. But, sometimes, when he hit a sober patch, he tried to tell us stories about his adventures. They were so obviously untrue that even the children gave up listening. In any case, halfway through, his words would get all tangled up, and what the rest of the story was about was anybody's guess. I felt sorry for him in a way: he was all broken down, just skin and bone, as if corroded by some dreadful acid.

Gladstone watched over his every move, even going to the trouble of finishing some of his stories when his speech gave out, explaining afterwards that Ashton had told them to him in private. He carried and fetched for him more than any of us. He got the children to sing and recite for him. He made sure Ashton got home safely every night. With all the visitors about, and the town so busy, no one said a word to us, no one warned us off. The Rev A. H. Jones was away on holiday, anyway, and Super Edwards was too occupied arresting all the drunks from Birmingham. We didn't mention Ashton's visit to his brother's yacht, and neither did Ashton himself. In fact he never said a word about his brother, one way or the other.

But, although Gladstone tried his best to make me like him, I kept on thinking about him lying there, stinking on that bed, saying 'Nursie boy'. It wasn't just that, though: it was sometimes a look, a gesture, the way his mouth twisted when he spoke to Gladstone. We had an English word that we had made Welsh to cover what I felt. The word was *sbeitlyd*, but it meant much more than spiteful:

it meant cynical and mean and cruel, and somehow fraud. We were the only ones who bothered about Ashton Vaughan, but I felt that if he had a better offer from someone else we would very soon be given the push.... That's how I felt about him, but what bothered me more was whether I was the only one of us who sensed this. I watched Gladstone's face very carefully but could find no hint of it there. Often I caught him looking across the bay towards the Point, but he never said what he was thinking. As for Dewi and Maxie, I reckoned they took everything as it came: Ashton was one of our company because Gladstone ordered it so.

That was the week we went to Gwynfor Roberts' house for tea. The way I felt about Ashton was the way I felt about Gwynfor Roberts, and Gwynfor Roberts' mother, and Gwynfor Roberts' father too. If Gwynfor, who was harmless as milk and sat with me in Form VA, had had any more family I'd have felt the same way about them as well. Gwynfor was all right, I suppose, but he wasn't any one thing: not dull, not clever, not vulgar, not polite, not daring, not timid, not even dirty-minded. I was always forgetting what he looked like, but most days he came and sat next to me, and every time he met me I was asked up their big house on the Hill. I didn't understand why, had never really tried to understand, but sometimes I went up to his house for tea, especially if his mother had issued the invitation. It wasn't an invitation when Mrs Roberts asked, though: it was an order.

'You'll come to tea,' she'd say, and then she'd touch me pityingly on the shoulder, and I felt suddenly undernourished and about to go down with malnutrition or something. The Roberts had a big grocer's shop, and eating was their hobby. It was always a good tea, I'll say that for them.

Towards the end of that Bank Holiday week I was standing with Gladstone near the slot machine on the Square. I'd been trying to get some cigarettes out of it with a washer but without any luck. Then, out of the crowd, came Gwynfor Roberts, and sharp as a flash he put a coin in the machine, a real coin – Gwynfor always had money on him – and slipped a packet of Player's into his pocket. Then he saw us. He didn't blush exactly, but he looked as if he was going to blush. He handed round some chocolate straight away – he always carried a few bars with him – and said something about giving us a fag only his mother was on the way.

'Lew,' he said, 'will you come up this afternoon?'

'Well,' I said.

'Got a new Meccano,' he said.

I hated the sight of his Meccano, and his Hornby train too – but because he wasn't anything I said that's nice.

I heard his mother before I saw her. Practically everybody on the Square must have heard her. 'Gwynfor – is that your friend, then? Bring him to tea!' Mrs Roberts had her hand on my shoulder, checking if I'd fattened up a bit. 'Bring him along! Now! And his friend!'

Gladstone nearly fell over. 'Madam,' he said, 'are you serious?'

Mrs Roberts hitched up her enormous bosom, fixed her glasses on her podgy little nose and gave a great roar of laughter. 'Of course I am, cariad,' she cried. 'Come and have a good tea!'

She swung around and marched off into the crowd, charging them aside like Boadicea with the Romans.

'Better come,' Gwynfor said. 'It'll be all right for Gladstone.'

The three of us followed in Mrs Roberts' wake, Gladstone wide-eyed with shock. 'Haven't been out to tea since the Sunday school trip in 1933,' he whispered to me.

At the end of the street was the car. We piled in the back and Mrs Roberts drove off at her usual speed, which was the speed of Royalty. Gladstone, always quick to sense an occasion, sat bolt upright by the window, chin held high, and graciously waved to the crowds.

Meira had once done a bit of cleaning for Mrs Roberts and had always come home saying the house was a palace. All I knew was that it wasn't a house where you could wear tar on your shirt, and have a hole in the seat of your trousers. Not without feeling like a cat dragged in out of the storm, anyway.

'God,' Gladstone said, as we sat on the big couch in the big front room, 'it's very nice, but I feel like a flea-circus attendant.'

He didn't show it, though. He had Gwynfor showing him his things, and he was saying very nice, charming, how interesting, fascinating. 'I must get one of those,' he remarked, looking at an expensive building outfit.

By the door there was a grand piano – a German make which I'd heard was the best. When the boys bragged at school it was often about the make of their pianos.

'I suppose you can play it?' Gladstone said.

'Not much,' Gwynfor replied.

'Of course he does,' Mrs Roberts said as she stormed

in. She spoke Welsh to us all that afternoon, and English to Gwynfor. That was one of those things that made me have this feeling about her.

'Gwynfor – play for the boys,' she ordered.

'Oh – Mam!'

'Now then,' Gladstone said, finger raised, 'we mustn't make him play if he doesn't want to. Very bad, you know. Could so very easily turn him away from his music.'

Mrs Roberts' glasses slid down her nose as her eyebrows went up. She was so surprised she had to sit down – opposite us, her legs wide apart so that you could see the skin above her stockings. She looked like a chair we had at home.

'What did you say your name was?' she asked Gladstone.

'Gladstone Williams,' he replied, 'after the famous Greek politician.'

'Oh,' Mrs Roberts said.

'Not a politician I really care for,' Gladstone went on. 'Did you know he used to chew each mouthful of food eighty-six times?'

'Really?' Mrs Roberts breathed.

'And what I said just then about the piano is right, you know. I mean – you'll excuse me saying this to a lady, to a mother, like yourself – but you should never force a child into making an exhibition of himself. You might be spoiling a genius...'

'Well,' Mrs Roberts said, 'Gwynfor plays hymns very nice...'

'Exactly,' Gladstone replied, crossing his legs and showing her for the first time that he wasn't wearing socks. 'We all must start somewhere – but the great danger is that

98

we might drown a talent with too much insistence. But of course this is old-fashioned stuff to you, Mrs Roberts, isn't it? I'm sure you'll have thought like this.'

'Well – yes,' Mrs Roberts said, but vaguely.

'You need practice, of course,' he went on. 'Practise for as long as possible, but at the early stages like this it is so easy, so very easy to make a genius hate his instrument.'

'You must be right, I'm sure,' Mrs Roberts said, her glasses still at the end of her nose. 'Do you play, then?'

I kept my eyes on the *Boy's Own Annual* but I wasn't doing any reading.

'Well,' Gladstone said, 'I don't actually *play*. Let's say I merely amuse myself occasionally.' He swept the long hair clear of his forehead. 'A few notes sometimes, here and there.' He got up and walked over to the piano and ran his hand gently along the top as if he expected to find dust there. 'Beautiful,' he said softly, 'a lovely instrument...'

'Walnut,' Mrs Roberts explained quickly. 'Polished.'

Gladstone looked down at the keyboard – I was all attention now – then sat on the stool and stared at the music that was propped up on the stand. 'Handel's *Largo*,' he announced.

'Oh – beautiful,' Mrs Roberts said, clapping her hands. 'A lovely piece, that. Can you play it, then?'

Gladstone flexed his long fingers. 'I *have* played it, of course, Mrs Roberts. A popular piece...'

'Makes *me* think of Heaven,' Mrs Roberts said. Her voice sounded very spitty.

Gladstone began to hum the opening bars. Mrs Roberts joined in, conducting as well. 'Dah, dah, dah, daah, da, da, da-hah,' they sang. 'Lovely,' Mrs Roberts said. 'Oh – lovely.' I was wondering why she hadn't noticed that Gladstone's shirt was threadbare around the collar, and that his trousers looked as if he'd slept the week in them. She had always been very observant where my clothes were concerned. Once, she had even given me an old pair of trousers to take home, and I had thrown them into the harbour.... Perhaps she would pay more attention once Gladstone was forced to play.

He stopped singing. 'The *Largo*,' he said. 'You'll know it used to be the Chinese national anthem, I suppose?'

Something went in the pit of my stomach.

'Really?' Mrs Roberts breathed. She was sitting forward on her chair, eyes intently fixed on him. And now his hands were up, poised over the keyboard. Oh, God, I thought, perhaps he's carried away, perhaps he thinks he really can.... His eyes were closed. A strand of hair had fallen across his forehead.

'Handel's *Largo*,' he whispered, and his eyes snapped open, and he brought his hands down gently on the keys without striking a note. 'To be or not to be?'

'Oh – yes,' Mrs Roberts said.

'That – is the question,' Gladstone went on.

'Shakespeare, Mam,' Gwynfor explained. He was still crouched on the carpet, trying to straighten out a bent Meccano girder.

'I know,' Mrs Roberts said sharply. 'Been to school.' Her eyes pleaded with Gladstone. 'Go on, then – please.'

Gladstone sighed. He was looking at the ornaments on the top of the piano. Mrs Roberts believed in hiding nothing. There were a dozen and more of them – toy dogs, milkmaids, egg-timers with Present from Llandudno on them, and a pot monkey sitting on a spring, and a bird with a yellow beak that couldn't possibly have been a blackbird, and Humpty Dumpty sitting on a wall.... 'I had an uncle named Erasmus,' Gladstone began softly, 'who was a major pianist. Mind you – he only had two fingers on his left hand. Used to make up the chords with his right. Got into trouble at the Royal Academy of Music about that. He was a genius, of course – had to oil his hands every night and wear silk gloves in bed in case the damp got at them. He used to play concertos...'

'Really?' Mrs Roberts was bolt upright, sensing a story. 'And symphonies?'

Gladstone gave me a frozen-faced look. 'Only concertos – or, to be more exact, concerti. He played the Birmingham Concerti of John Sebastian...'

'Bach?' Mrs Roberts cried joyfully.

'Exactly,' Gladstone replied. 'A Welshman, thank God...'

You're taking a chance, I thought. Any minute now and it'll be the way out for us.

'Then there was the "Unfurnished" by Franz Sherbert, of course. Who *hasn't* played that? And "Hiding",' he went on, speeding up so as to get away with it, 'the "Machynlleth March", naturally. And Olga's "Circumcision", and the "List Post" by Lost. You've no idea – it was a musical education just to be near him. He practically *lived* at the Albert Hall....'

'On the wireless, too?' Mrs Roberts begged.

'Never,' Gladstone replied firmly. 'All that electric, you know – the currents might affect his *diminuendo*. He was always afraid of that. And he was right, of course. Doctors know they play havoc with the *diminuendo*...'

'Really?' Mrs Roberts breathed, and the maid came in and said tea was ready.

Gladstone hit one note on the piano, said 'Beautiful', and came away quickly. He held the door open for us, as if he was the host, and we went through to the kitchen where the table sagged with food.

During tea Gladstone kept it up. He was sitting next to me so I gave him a kick now and then, but he took no notice.

'I have always considered Henry Wadsworth Shortman a mediocre poet,' he remarked as he stuffed a couple of ham sandwiches into his pockets for the children. 'Mind you – the "Lay of the last Ministerial" wasn't bad...'

'Really?' said Mrs Roberts. 'Well – I never...'

'"Paradise Lost" by Muldoon,' he went on, '"When I consider how my light is spent", and so on,' he cried, lowering his voice. 'That's what I call my Chapel voice, Mrs Roberts. Have you noticed how people have one voice for work and one voice for Chapel?'

Mrs Roberts' bosom heaved as she giggled. She couldn't laugh because her mouth was full of food.

'Oh, yes – it's got to be a hollow voice for Chapel – no reverence unless it's mournful.' He did some more of his imitation for her. Any minute now, I thought, and it will all go sour, and we'll be out in the yard clutching a ham sandwich apiece. 'I wonder why there has to be a different voice for praying, too? A praying voice with a bit of a cringe to it. Chapel...'

'Now then, who's talking about Chapel?' And there was Mr Roberts by the door.

'Dada bach,' Mrs Roberts cried, 'you look tired out. Come and sit down then, cariad.'

Mr Roberts was about eighteen stone, but short. He looked as if he'd been blown up with a bicycle pump – blown up so hard that all the hair had popped out of his head. He sat down, breathing heavily, and began to reach for the bread and the pickles and the boiled ham and the mustard, not saying anything, just filling his plate until it overflowed.

'Having a tea party,' Mrs Roberts explained.

Mr Roberts looked hard at Gladstone. 'So I see...'

'Having a lovely chat we were, about poetry and music...'

'Chapel, too? Didn't I hear someone say Chapel?'

'We did mention it,' Gladstone said in a cold voice. He knew Mr Roberts, had been refused tick in his shop more times than he cared to mention.

Mr Roberts grunted. 'Didn't know you were a Chapel man, Gladstone?'

'Oh,' Mrs Roberts cried, 'you know him, cariad! A lovely pianist! Played the *Largo*...'

Her husband looked up sharply. 'Play the piano, do you, Gladstone? Never knew that. We'll have to get you on the harmonium at the Mission.' He wiped his mouth with his napkin. 'Been keeping company with the drunkards lately, haven't you?'

'I don't know what you're talking about,' said Gladstone.

'Ashton Vaughan,' Mr Roberts said flatly. 'That's who I'm talking about. I hear you've been helping him to drink himself to death.'

Mr Roberts prided himself on always speaking his mind. It wasn't really a matter for pride, Rowland

103

Williams said, because there was nothing in Mr Roberts' mind that was worth hearing.

'It's true, isn't it?' he went on. 'Been seen with him all the time. Rescued him from the harbour, didn't you?'

'Did we?' said Gladstone very calmly, but before he could go on Mrs Roberts had jumped up crying, 'Oh – here's Eirlys come!' She ran across to open the back door, talking all the time. 'Oh – now then, Eirlys come with my dress.' She opened the door. 'Come in, then – come in, Eirlys fech.' The woman who walked in was the woman who had been in the car with Marius Vaughan.

She was blonde and she was like a doll, all colour and warmth, wide-eyed and smiling. She made the rest of the room look grey. 'Tradesman's entrance,' she said. 'Oo, got a tea party going, Marian?' Her voice was husky, with laughter in it. She winked at Gladstone and me across the table.

'Come in,' Mr Roberts said without turning round, 'we were just discussing the Vaughans. Not the one you're interested in, though.'

'Dada!' Mrs Roberts cried reproachfully. 'Come and sit down, Eirlys fech. Sit here.'

'Only staying a minute, Marian,' Eirlys said, taking no notice of Mr Roberts. 'I only wanted to tell you those dress lengths won't be in till next week.'

'Sit down,' Mr Roberts ordered. 'This is Gladstone Williams, bosom pal of the other Vaughan.'

Eirlys didn't sit down. She stood there holding her handbag in front of her, calm and relaxed. It was as if she had made up her mind long ago how she felt about things. Although she was pretty and painted and all frills, she was strong too. She put a hand with very red nails on top of

Mr Roberts' bald head. 'Musn't talk with food in our mouths, must we?' she said.

Mr Roberts shook her hand off. 'These two rescued Ashton Vaughan from a watery grave,' he said. 'Did you know that, Mrs Hampson?'

'I thought you were a musician,' Mrs Roberts cried, pointing to Gladstone.

'You can still be a musician and rescue people from drowning,' Gladstone replied.

'But – I thought you were a student, or something...'

'Marian,' said Mr Roberts sharply, 'why don't you get new glasses, woman? This is Gladstone Williams. Martha Davies' son. Lives on Lower Hill.' It sounded like a police record.

'Lower Hill,' Mrs Roberts gasped.

I was very angry. 'I live on Lower Hill, too,' I said.

'Yes,' Mrs Roberts said, her face a deep red, 'but you're with our Gwynfor. In the County School.'

Eirlys Hampson laughed so much she had to reach for her handkerchief.

'Sense of humour, haven't we?' Mr Roberts said.

'Thank God,' Eirlys said.

'Right, then,' said Mr Roberts, speaking only to Gladstone, 'what about this friend of yours, then? This famous – or should I say norotrious – Ashton Vaughan?'

'Notorious,' Eirlys said softly.

Gladstone didn't say anything.

'I'm talking to you,' Mr Roberts shouted.

'Dada! Please!'

He pointed his knife at Gladstone. 'I'm talking to you, boy.'

'You're not in the shop now,' Gladstone said quietly. 'I'm not asking for tick, and I'm not one of your kicking boys.'

Mr Roberts sat there, mouth open, showing his teeth and food. I thought for a moment that he was going to choke, but he managed a swallow big enough for a horse, and sat bolt upright on his chair.

'Take care, boy,' he thundered. 'You're playing with fire.' He glanced at Eirlys. 'Everybody who mixes with the Vaughans plays with fire. Know that?' Eirlys winked at us again. 'Those two men are evil. I'm old enough to know when a man's evil or not. And I'm warning you, boy – it'll be a bad end for you, keeping company with a drunken reporbate like that...'

'Reprobate,' Eirlys said.

'What?' Mr Roberts was the colour of a summer thundercloud. 'What did you say, you cheeky bitch?'

Gladstone stood up, sending his cup spinning, 'Language, if you please, Mr Roberts. Remember your son is at the table.'

Mrs Roberts nodded earnestly. 'Yes, that's right. Gwynfor's here.'

This time Mr Roberts did choke.

Gladstone bowed to her. 'Thank you for the tea. Very nice of you to ask us...'

'Must come again,' Mrs Roberts said, a little uncertainly.

Mr Roberts recovered. 'You bloody halfwit!' he roared at his wife. 'You silly bloody woman!'

Gladstone led the way to the door. He opened it for me and stood there giving them all a long, cool look.

'Get out of my house!' Mr Roberts cried. 'Get out – you guttersnipe!'

In the hush that followed, Eirlys reached for the milk jug from the table. She raised it up, then very slowly poured its contents over Mr Roberts' bald head. 'Nice and cooling, milk,' she said. 'Be in the shop, if you want me, Marian.' Then she joined us at the door and ushered us out.

'Quick,' she said, 'before he recovers. You'd like a ride down, wouldn't you?'

XI

Eirlys brought the car to a screeching halt outside her shop. She switched off the engine and sat there tapping her hands lightly on the wheel. She seemed to be saying something under her breath.

'Nine, ten,' she said aloud. 'No – it's no good. I'll have to have a fag.'

She pulled the packet out of her handbag and lit one. Her hands were trembling, I noticed. 'There's nothing like a fag for bringing you round,' she said, and held out the packet, offering us one. We both refused. 'Nothing like a fag when you've just lost a good customer and made an enemy. But, boys bach, I couldn't resist it. There was the milk jug, and there was that nasty little man's head. I couldn't resist it...'

'No more than he deserved,' Gladstone said from the back seat. 'Nothing but a pig, that man...'

'Pig is right, but his wife is – was – one of my best customers. Can't keep customers if you pour milk over their husbands, can you?' She looked quite serious for a moment, then slowly a smile grew. 'Worth it, though. Oh, hell – it was worth it and no mistake.'

'You'll have all the ministers in town calling on you,' Gladstone said.

'Don't forget the deacons,' she said.

'Queuing up at the door...'

'And the police as well. The entire force. I'll be put in jail, drummed out of Chapel, branded for life I shouldn't wonder. But – still worth it, though.'

She smelled nice, of scent and powder. There were tiny golden hairs along her round, smooth arms. She *was* like a doll, with her waves set and shining in her blonde hair, her frilly silk dress, her painted fingernails. I thought she was very beautiful, like the film stars were at the pictures, even if she wasn't very slim like them.

'You should have asked him if he took milk,' Gladstone said.

'Now, then,' she said, arching her brows and opening wide her eyes, 'perhaps he only took cream?'

The little car shook with our laughter. Eirlys laughed so hard she had a coughing spell. 'Bloody cigs,' she said, 'they'll be the death of me yet.' Then she turned to me. 'Lew Morgan,' she began, 'I can guess what this one feels, but what about you? You look a proper dark horse.'

I was shy. 'Feel all right,' was all I could say.

She turned in her seat with a rustle of silk and looked at us both very steadily. 'Ashton's friends, eh? The whole town's heard about you lot. You *are* his friends, aren't you?'

109

'That's right,' Gladstone replied, but stiffly.

She nodded and was silent for a moment, examining us each in turn. There was nothing shy about Eirlys. 'What's he like, then?' she asked. 'All right, is he?'

'Haven't you heard?' Gladstone said, stiffly still. 'It's all over the town.'

'That's a shirty answer,' Eirlys commented with a smile. 'I'm not asking the town, though. I'm asking you.'

'They're all waiting for the worst to happen,' Gladstone said heatedly. 'It's a disgrace, that's what...'

'It's the Porthmawr hobby,' she said. 'They call it waiting for the fall.' She flicked ash through the open window. 'Don't get me wrong, will you? I wasn't asking about Ashton in order to tell his brother...'

Gladstone looked very stubborn. I found myself wishing he was nicer to her, more polite. 'If his brother wants to know...' he began.

'He can find out for himself,' Eirlys finished it for him. 'I know, I know...'

'He can take him home and offer him some help...'

'That's right,' Eirlys said, 'but I've heard the world is littered with people who tried to help Ashton Vaughan. That's the trouble with Porthmawr – there's always *some* truth in what they say...'

'Look,' Gladstone said, 'never mind what they say. He's just a helpless, drunken man. He can't help the way he is...'

'I wonder,' she said softly. 'I wonder if anyone can...'

'But he can't,' Gladstone insisted. 'It's – well, he can't.'

I sat there, my hands clasped tightly between my knees, not daring to join in. All I could see was Ashton's face, and that mouth twisting....

'I'm not trying to warn you off him,' Eirlys went on. 'My God – it isn't up to me to warn anybody. And I'm no tale-carrier, either. You can bank on that. I was only wondering why he'd come back here all of a sudden.'

Gladstone shrugged. 'Why shouldn't he come back? He belongs in Porthmawr. Maybe there was nowhere left for him to go.' He drew breath in deeply then asked, 'Doesn't his brother mention him at all?'

'Who's being nosy now, then?' she said. Then she shook her head slowly. 'No – not so as you'd notice.' She flicked her cigarette through the window. 'Maybe that's why I was asking…. Anyway, let's get out. Bet you the news has reached town already. No police about, are there?'

We got out of the car and stood with her by the shop window. 'We'll swear he made it up,' Gladstone said with a grin. 'Tell them you never poured milk…'

'Hush,' she said, 'walls have ears.' She opened the shop door. 'Pop in and say hello when you're passing,' she said. 'We'll buy a gallon or so of milk and make a christening list. All right?'

'All right,' we said.

'And if you run into any trouble, like – or if you want to tell me anything about our mutual interests – know what I mean? – well, pop in, like. All right?'

We said all right and went down the street smiling.

'She's a case,' I said.

'Fine,' he agreed. 'Tell you what – Marius can't be so bad if she goes with him.' Then he stopped in the middle of Market Street and roared with laughter. 'His shop,' he said. 'Roberts' High-class Grocers. Did you see the milk run down his face?'

We laughed so loud that one of the assistants came out of the shop and told us to move along.

'Tell you what,' Gladstone said, 'we won't be asked up there to tea again.'

That night we gathered, the four of us, around the fire in Gladstone's house. The children were in bed, but not yet asleep. Now and then there was a scream and a cry of 'Glaadstoone', but he didn't go up to them.

'Honestly,' he said, 'they've been the limit. I got home this evening and do you know what they were doing? They had poor old Walter standing there with his little thing in his hand, and they were making him wee into jam jars. Honestly, he was *pale* with it. Shouldn't wonder if he doesn't wet his bed for the next ten years.'

'Doctors and nurses?' Maxie inquired.

'Playing public houses, they said. It's that Dora. She starts them off. Look at this, will you?' He handed me a crumpled page from an exercise book. 'I find them all over the house.'

I looked at the letter:

My DEAR GLADSTON. AM leevin HOME sooN, Love from DORA xxxxx.

'I used to do that,' Dewi said, looking over my shoulder. 'I used to write letters all the time. Just remembered that now. I used to want to leave home, too. Still do...'

'Wants to join the Navy,' Maxie explained. 'Dewi wants to be a bloody captain...'

'Do I bloody hell,' Dewi said.

'Language,' Gladstone warned, taking the note from me.

'I've found dozens of these, but when I ask her what's the matter, all she says is Catherine...'

'Who's Catherine?'

'Her friend,' Gladstone said with a smile. 'The one who isn't there. She talks to Catherine all the time. Even in the lav. She says Catherine wants to go. Catherine's an Asiatic Princess, I think. Dora's the Lady in Waiting...'

'Like the May Queen,' Maxie put in.

'Yes,' Gladstone sighed, 'like the May Queen. I wish I *could* take them all away. Somewhere nice. Somewhere we could be by ourselves.' He looked around the kitchen. 'Somewhere nice. The way I see it this place is a little house on a beach, where the sun is shining all the time, like it does in the South Seas, and where everything's clean.' He clasped his bony knees and stared into the fire. 'One day we'll go. Just wait...'

We didn't make any comment. This was private, what Gladstone was saying.

'Anyway,' he went on suddenly, 'I asked you over because we've got to plan a visit...'

Dewi sat up, interested as a terrier promised a walk. 'A job?'

'A kind of a job.'

'No more boats,' Maxie said. 'My dad will kill me.'

'No boats,' Gladstone said.

'There's plenty of lead piping in that house on Bridge Street,' Dewi said. 'Mind you, it's not so clever with the light nights and that, but if we don't move in quick someone else will...'

113

'No lead piping,' Gladstone said.

'But we're going to pay a visit somewhere?'

He nodded.

'I'll buy,' I said. 'Where then?'

'The Point...'

'Oh, good God!' I said.

'Never, man,' Dewi joined in. 'Them dogs...'

'We're going to take a look at Marius Vaughan's house,' Gladstone declared flatly.

Oh, no, I thought. It's the wrong thing to do, I felt it instinctively. But Dewi was suddenly converted to the idea, wanted to go there and then. Maxie was still saying his father would kill him.

'They were telling me,' he added in his slow fashion, 'about some boys that went to have a look at the Point one night. He caught them – and you know what he did? Took them in the house and made them bend over and gave them the cane across the ass. Never got the police or nothing. Just did that...'

'Jack Bach's brother,' Dewi said. 'Said it hurt like hell...'

'And there's dogs,' Maxie went on.

Gladstone shook his head. 'There *was* a dog. It died last winter. Postman told me...'

'What are we going for?' I asked him, trying to catch his eye.

He ruffled my hair. 'Just a visit. A tour of inspection, you might call it...'

'But why?'

He was looking directly at me now, speaking to me as if in a private language. 'I'm curious. I'd go alone – only

114

having you with me might be handy. Lookouts and that. But I want to see. I – I can't explain, Lew, but I want to see what it's like...'

'Bloody great big house, our Tada says,' Dewi broke in. 'Great big rooms and that...'

'So I've heard,' Gladstone said. 'Saw it from a boat when we were out after mackerel.' He stretched his arms high above his head. 'I want to see how the other brother's going on,' he added.

'Ashton asked you?'

'No – nothing like that. He did say tonight that he bet his brother was having something nice for supper – not chips from the shop. That's what set me thinking. No, Lew, this is for myself...'

'To spy around?'

'Have a look, that's all,' Gladstone said. 'Are you game?'

I hesitated. It wouldn't work out, I knew – couldn't possibly work out. But I said all right.

'Dewi?'

'Draw one of your plans,' Dewi said.

'Maxie? Coming?'

Maxie was occupied with another worry. 'You know,' he said slowly, 'when you rub yourself and that – is it right that you'll go blind?'

Dewi laughed. 'Only three hundred times you've got and that's a fact. You're getting near it, so watch out.'

'Never mind about that,' Gladstone broke in. 'Are you coming or not?'

Maxie nodded. 'My dad will kill me, though,' he said.

Gladstone got up and stretched himself. 'All right, then. We'll try it tomorrow night.' He looked hard at me, his face

115

very pale and serious. 'I've got to *know*, Lew, haven't I?'

Know what? I thought. There didn't seem to be any reason that I could see for taking a chance with Marius Vaughan, but I said yes just the same.

We didn't go the next night, however. There was a thunderstorm in the afternoon and rain heavy enough to wash all of Porthmawr into the ocean. Lower Hill was flooded, as usual, and I helped Meira bail out. Even the lav in our yard rose like a fountain.

We didn't go on the following night, either – although it was a fine, warm one, after a fine, warm day. That night Ashton Vaughan went missing, and we had to comb the town for him. Up to us, Gladstone said: we couldn't go to the police. But we didn't find him until the following afternoon. He was sleeping it off in one of the railway carriages on the sidings. There was an empty bottle of gin next to him on the seat.

Gladstone went to work on him straight away, but it was a long time before he opened his eyes. At first I thought he was dead; he was so still there on the seat, the skin falling away from his nose leaving a line of white bone. But it was all lines, that face, as if it had been pinched and pressed and twisted, God knew by what. 'Best bloody advert I ever saw for Temperance,' Dewi remarked. 'Want to prop him up next to the pulpit – the pubs will be out of business in no time.'

It was a relief to hear Dewi say that. Now and then he came out with something that surprised you, made you look twice at him. I laughed, but Gladstone showed a grim and angry face.

116

Ashton Vaughan came round. We helped him with his boots and got him looking fairly presentable, then we took him along the back streets to his room.

'Better have an aspirin,' Gladstone suggested.

'Jesus Christ!' Ashton groaned. 'Not enough in the wide world for a head like mine,' he said. 'Look at my hands.' They were shaking badly. 'I'm a sick man – that's what I am. I'm a very sick man.'

Dewi said what I wanted to say. 'Why not pack in the drink, then?'

There was a silence you could have touched after that, then Gladstone started giving Dewi what for. 'No right to be saying that,' he said. 'You ought to be ashamed...'

'I still think he wants to give up the drink,' Dewi went on. 'It's no use crying when you're killing yourself, is it?'

'There's reasons for everything...'

'No!' Ashton cried, in a voice so loud that I jumped. 'No! He's right! He's dead right. The drink's killing me. I'm telling you, the drink's killing me!' I forced myself to look at him. His eyes were bloodshot and full of tears. 'I know what I'm doing to myself.... Boys, I know!' His shaking hands punched the air. 'Last night I had them. I had the visions, I tell you. All the crawling, slimy, filthy things you ever saw – all spewed up from the swamps of hell itself. And they were coming for me – coming for my throat!' He raised his hands as if to ward them off. 'Crawling out of the dark, coming for me... you see them and you don't see them... come and go, like that... but you can hear them all the time, purring like cats, see... and you try to get your hands on them, but they slide away, twist out of your fingers.... Oh, lads bach, they were after me!'

117

'Who were?' Maxie croaked. He was wide-eyed and all set to make for the door.

'Be quiet,' Gladstone ordered, giving Dewi a sharp, reproving look. 'It's all right, Mr Vaughan. There's no need to worry any more. Daylight now, and we're with you.'

Ashton lay back on his bed. 'They were there, though, kid. Saw them. Had to fight them off all night...'

'It's all right,' Gladstone said. 'You were ill...'

Ashton heaved himself on his feet again and raised one arm and pointed it at the window. 'By the Lord Jesus Christ I swear – not another drop!' he cried. 'It's a disease, I've got. The doctors said it was a disease. I need help, help. I'm desperate!' He was using a preacher's sing-song voice now. 'A desperate man, I am. I need help. Help. But where will it come from, tell me that...? I've got to stop the drink! I've got to stop the drink!' He still stood there, still pointing, long after he had stopped speaking – and that made it an act, nothing but a piece of acting.

Gladstone touched his arm gently and made him sit down again, but he went on babbling and crying for help, and saying he had no one, no one in the world, and vowing all the time never to touch another drop. Then, suddenly, he was on his feet again. 'Find his picture for me,' he cried. 'Find me Jupiter's picture.'

Gladstone knelt and searched under the bed and handed him the photograph.

'My brother Jupiter,' Ashton cried, 'oh, my brother Jupiter, will you never die?' He clutched the picture to his chest. 'Why does the beautiful have to die?' he asked in a hollow voice. 'Tell me that. Tell me that, for Christ's sake.' He lay back on the bed, Gladstone helping him to swing

118

his legs up. 'Jupiter, Jupiter, why did you have to die? Can anybody answer me that?' He closed his eyes.

'Come on,' Gladstone whispered to us. 'Let's be going. He wants to be by himself.' From the door I watched him cover Ashton with a blanket. Ashton never said a word, just lay there, eyes tightly shut, clasping the photo.

Outside, in the street, Gladstone started on Dewi straight away. 'What were you thinking of – talking like that to him...'

'He's in a hell of a state,' Dewi said calmly. 'He wants to give up drinking – quick...'

'What do you know about it?' Gladstone began. 'You don't know anything about it. You don't know what it's like...'

'Listen,' Dewi said.

'Oh, no.' Gladstone was really worked up. 'I'm just about fed up with these people who know the answers to everything.... Give up drinking? Easy as that? What do you know about it?'

'Don't keep on asking me that,' Dewi said, less calm now. 'There's something about that man – I don't know.'

'That's right,' Gladstone said sharply, 'you don't know...'

Something snapped in me. 'I do, though,' I said. 'I know what's the matter with him.' We stopped walking and made a circle on the pavement, 'He's a fraud,' I said, trying to keep my voice steady. 'He's just one big fraud.'

I saw Dewi's face light up in a big grin. 'Too bloody true,' he said. I didn't look at Gladstone, who seemed at that moment to be towering above me, ready with a deluge of protest.

But when he spoke his voice was very soft and slow. 'You mean he never saw any of those things? You mean he was acting?'

'That's what I think,' I said, keeping my head lowered. 'He's a fraud.'

We moved to the doorway of an empty shop. 'It was all one big act in there,' Gladstone went on. 'That's what you think?'

'Nearly as bad as Capel Mawr drama,' Dewi said.

'And he's a hopeless case? And cunning – thinks we're just muck from the harbour?'

I looked at him for the first time. 'It's true,' I said. 'You feel it too, don't you?'

It seemed a long time before Gladstone nodded his head. 'Yes – it's true. He's just a hopeless case...'

'Wouldn't trust him farther than I could kick him,' Dewi broke in. 'All of them things creeping up on him – it was acting, that...'

'All acting,' Gladstone agreed, 'except for one thing. About Jupiter – that wasn't acting...'

I wanted to destroy everything now. 'How do you know? It could be...'

'No, Lew. Jupiter died that day,' Gladstone said quietly, 'and nothing's been right ever since. That's what's been eating him up...'

'I don't know,' Dewi said with a sigh. 'You could be wrong...'

'Oh no.' Gladstone drew us nearer to him. 'They're different, the Vaughans. They're not like the town crowd at all. I don't know how to say it, but I *feel* they're different – as if they don't belong here, as if they should

120

be living at another time and in another place... at a time when nobody frowned on you because you were reckless, or because you didn't follow suit. Lew,' he gripped my shoulder tightly as if to force me to understand, 'they've got *style*, don't you see?'

Dewi grinned suddenly. 'Close up the pubs, then, shall we?' And we were all relaxed again, the quarrel broken up and gone.

'Tell you what,' Gladstone pleaded, 'what do you say we find out how the other one's taking it? What do you say we drop in on Marius Vaughan? He's Jupiter's brother too.'

XII

Although Gladstone had tried his best to make me keen on paying Marius Vaughan a visit, all I could do was worry and ask myself questions. What were we supposed to do when we got the Point, anyway? Would we knock on his door, or what? And if we knocked on his door what would we say, what *could* we say? This wasn't one of the grocers up on the Hill. This was Marius Vaughan.... And if we ever got around to knocking anywhere, or talking to anyone, what would we get for an answer? What *would* we get as an answer to: 'Mr Vaughan, excuse us calling, like, but we thought we'd drop around, like, and ask you how you're getting on, like, after all that terrible trouble you had when you accidentally shot your youngest brother dead, like, all these sixteen years ago...' Oh, good God, Gladstone must have been carried away again – as carried away as he had been when he tried to get us to play in that bloody percussion band in front of the whole Sunday school, or the time he had us turn out for the May Day procession, dressed in hearth rugs, as the Mabinogion. This visit to Marius Vaughan, I felt certain, was going to be just as embarrassing. I tossed and turned all night.

Owen hadn't helped any by staying up with me by the dying fire to talk about the Vaughans, although Meira kept on calling for him to go up. He had to tell me how he'd gone to the war on the same day as Marius Vaughan. (Owen had spent the war in the barracks in Wrexham.) And how a friend of his, who was in the know, had told him, in confidence of course, that Marius Vaughan had just about gone through all the money.... And how a pal of his, who been a waiter in the Red Dragon at the time, had told him about this big dance for the swells and how Marius Vaughan had fallen flat on his face when he was dancing, and how he'd stood there at the bar of the Dragon and *cried*. Not crying because he was drunk or anything, but crying because his leg had let him down in public, because he wasn't the tough boy he wanted to be.... Marius was only a small chap, but he made himself tough.... Thankfully I had heard Meira stamp out on the landing and shriek 'Owen!' and he had gone, double sharp, and I was glad. Mention of Marius Vaughan was touching an open nerve.... But Owen's gossip was something else to toss and turn over, even after sleep came reluctantly with the first light.

And it was all Marius next day, too, as we waited for the evening and darkness. Marius using his gun on a disobedient dog, Marius ramming another boat which had fouled him in the regatta, Marius bouncing the Rev A. H.

Jones down the steps of his house, Marius taking on some of the locals because they had laughed at his limp, Marius turning the hosepipe on the man from the Council.... Oh, God, he was likely to do anything, a law unto himself. When we crossed the town that night I was wound up tight as a mainspring, and so sensitive that it hurt.

Halfway along the road to the Point there was a gate plastered with Trespassers will be Prosecuted and Private Road and Keep Out. This far we had been before. When we came to it that night it was thick darkness everywhere and not a sign to be seen, but I knew they were there. It was very warm and still, too, with the sound of thunder behind us on the mountains.

'Once over this,' Dewi said, his voice high with excitement, 'and we're not in Porthmawr any more. We're in the Vaughan country.' And, because he too was wound up, he had a pee against the Keep Out on the gate.

We climbed over, Dewi running on ahead to act as scout, Maxie bringing up the rear. Maxie's nerves were on edge too: he never said a word, just followed along in the darkness, farting like a horse.

The road skirted the side of the harbour. I could see the white fence between us and the water now that my eyes were used to the dark. On the other side, Graig Lwyd towered above us. No escape anywhere, I thought.

'Sure about the dog, then?' I said to Gladstone.

'Dead. I told you. Postman said they haven't got another.'

We walked on, keeping to the grass verges most of the time in case there was anyone out and listening for us. Now and then Dewi up ahead gave his owl hoot, which wasn't really necessary, but none of us knew how to tell him about it.

He was back with us suddenly. 'Trees ahead,' he announced. 'Then it turns – the road – and we're there. Plenty of them rhododendrons. Been up to the front of the house – well, nearly. Like a big yard there, and a bit of a garden near the house. There's lights on.'

Something went deep in my stomach as he said that, and although I asked myself what did I expect, it didn't help at all.

'Listen to that machine for making the electric,' Dewi said.

We stood, tightly grouped, and listened to the hum of the generator. Something else that made Marius Vaughan different, I thought – no penny in the slot for him.

Gladstone came to life. 'All right. Let's go on. Keep together. Everybody look out.'

We came to the rhododendrons. Once around them we could see the light falling in a huge, broken square on the rockery and the yard. There was a car on the yard, a small one. Eirlys Hampson's car.

'What do we do now?' Dewi asked in a whisper. 'Knock on the door and ask for the rent?'

'Break a window,' Maxie suggested.

Gladstone, I felt, wasn't sure what to do either. He stood looking at the square of light as if it dazzled him. I could sense his indecision.

'Go back, shall we?' I said.

'Not now,' Dewi replied fiercely. 'Now we've come so far we've got to do something...'

'Follow me,' Gladstone said suddenly. 'Make for the

flower beds by the window.' And he was off at a run towards the house.

We followed, Dewi and Maxie racing past me. There was a small wall around the flower beds, but I never saw it. The first thing I knew I was falling flat on my face on warm, moist earth, and lying there, my heart loud as a drum.

'Lew! Here!' Gladstone hissed.

I looked up slowly. No doors had been opened. No one was shouting what for... Gladstone was kneeling by the window. I crawled over to, him. 'Take a look,' he said.

The curtains weren't drawn across the big bay window. I took a quick look then bobbed back again. All I saw was a large room and two people – a grey-haired man and Eirlys, both standing up, talking.... No, not talking, I thought. More like arguing.... I looked again, longer this time. Eirlys walking to the door, then turning to say something to him, finger pointing.... I bobbed back. She was coming out! I gripped Gladstone's arm, but before I could say anything there was a crash of splintering glass farther up the yard where Maxie and Dewi had vanished. Then came a wild, uncontrollable shriek of laughter from Dewi.

Gladstone and I ran across the square of light from the window, leaping over rose bushes on to the yard. By the time we reached the other two a light had been switched on and the yard was bright as day. We didn't realise it was on, however – not with the shock of seeing Maxie standing knee-deep in a flower frame, held there by broken glass, unable to move. Dewi was near by, bent double with laughing.

'Jumped straight in the bloody thing,' he cried. 'Trust old Maxie to bugger a job up!'

'Glass,' Maxie said. 'If I tear my trousers my dad will kill me!'

I looked up. 'The light's on!'

'It is indeed,' a voice said behind us. 'Stay where you are! Don't move!' Then he must have seen Maxie. 'Boy!' he roared. 'Get out of that bloody frame!'

Maxie just stood there shaking his head.

'Do you hear, boy? Get out of it!'

'Easier said than done,' Eirlys said very quietly but clearly.

'P-please, sir. Fell in it, sir,' Maxie said.

'Then fall out again, damn you!' Marius Vaughan snapped. 'You others – help him out.'

We managed to remove Maxie from the frame without any cuts or tears. Dewi was still giggling about it.

'Come on out, Maxie,' he whispered, 'then we'll make a run for it. Old peg leg there will never smell us.'

'No,' Gladstone ordered. 'We stay. He's recognised us by now, anyway.'

'That's enough of that talking,' Marius Vaughan said. 'Over here, all of you! At the double!'

'Let's rush him,' Dewi whispered as we turned to face the doorway where Marius and Eirlys stood. 'Four to one – we'll mince him up.'

'Quiet!' Gladstone snapped. 'Follow me...' He set off across the yard straight for the door. For a moment I was all for running, but I couldn't leave Gladstone to face him alone.

'Come on,' I said to the other two. 'Crazy,' Dewi muttered, but he and Maxie joined me, and we marched behind Gladstone, a small army going to our doom.

'Well, well,' Marius said when we reached the foot of

the steps, 'Ashton's friends. Don't tell me he's lurking in the shrubberies somewhere?'

He had a very English voice – a fake English voice, every word spoken as if it were underlined.

'Well – answer me. Is he with you or not?'

Gladstone shook his head.

'Right,' Marius Vaughan said, 'inside. You've got some explaining to do. Inside – quick!'

We filed in past him, Eirlys leading the way. She looked over her shoulder and gave us a smile, and I felt a little bit better. We were in a large room now, a room with a lot of furniture, and pictures on every wall. Marius Vaughan followed us in. The door closed with a smack, and deep down in my stomach something went again.

He lined us up against a wall and walked slowly in front of us, like an officer inspecting his men. He wasn't a tall man but he had wide, powerful shoulders. His hair and his moustache were pure white, only his eyebrows were still black. He wasn't like Ashton at all – his face smooth, unmarked, except for a scar, his clothes very smart. He looked very clean, somehow, and full of menace.

'Gladstone Williams and his gang,' he said, speaking to Eirlys. 'My brother's keepers, in fact.' He took up a position directly facing us, standing very straight and stiff. He had a stick in his right hand, but he wasn't leaning on it at all. 'All right,' he said, 'now tell me what you are doing on my property at this hour of the night. I assure you I have a right to know.'

Where had I heard that tone of voice before? In school, surely? And from a dozen or more sarcastic teachers who always asked their questions in the same kind of English.

'Struck dumb, are we? I suppose you think it's very unfair of me to ask you what you are doing here? After all I put that frame out there so that you could break it, didn't I? And all those notices on my gate don't really mean what they say....' A thought struck him. 'You do speak English, I suppose? Siarad Saesneg?' He even said that with an English accent.

'You know we speak English, Mr Vaughan,' Gladstone said.

'Ah, yes,' Marius said, moving so that he stood directly in front of Gladstone. 'We have met, haven't we? Gladstone Williams, would you be so kind perhaps as to tell me what you were doing outside there, and how my frame came to be broken?'

'It was my idea, sir,' Gladstone said. 'You can let the others go...'

The black eyebrows went up. He looked over his shoulder at Eirlys. 'Can I, indeed,' he said. 'How very kind of you to tell me what I can do, Gladstone Williams.'

He went down the line, then, asked us our names in turn, where we lived, what school...

'County, sir,' I said.

'Ah – then you *must* be able to read a little. What does it say on my gate, tell me that?'

'Trespassers will be Prosecuted,' I said.

'Well done. And what does that mean?'

'The police,' I said.

'Very good. I can see you are worthy of your place in the County School.'

I saw Eirlys pull a face and look away. I felt my temper rise. We were caught, weren't we? There was no need for him to play the sarky teacher like this. 'It also says Keep Out four times,' I said.

For a moment I thought he was going to hit me. The scar on his cheek reddened a little and his mouth tightened. But he looked over his shoulder at Eirlys and I thought he smiled.

'Well done, little sharp Welshman,' he said. 'Now perhaps *you*'ll tell me why you chose to disregard those notices?'

Little sharp Welshman! What did he think *he* was? He was Porthmawr born, too – as Welsh as any of us. If Dewi had rushed him then, I would have been with him, and to hell with the consequences.

Gladstone tried to explain. 'Mr Vaughan, it was all my idea. I brought them here. We didn't mean to break your frame...'

'An *accident*,' Maxie put in quickly.

'Accident be damned,' said Marius Vaughan. 'The fact remains that you were trespassing on my land.'

Eirlys got up. 'Let them go, Marius,' she said. 'They're only boys. Probably taking a short cut somewhere...'

'Aye, that's right,' Dewi said eagerly, 'going after lobsters we were...'

The rocks beyond the Point were a good place for lobsters. I felt relieved: we had to have some excuse, after all.

'Lobsters at this time of night?' Marius said. 'I don't believe you.'

'They don't look as if they've come on a social visit, anyway,' Eirlys said. 'Send them home, Marius.'

'Oh, no,' he said, shaking his head. 'You never know –

they might be a deputation from the Free Church Council, or something. They could even be here to tell me about progress in the missionary field in Madras. Come to, that, they might be the Watch Committee.'

'Have your fun, then,' said Eirlys.

'Well, my dear, what can it be? I ask you? I've no apples to steal, no poultry going begging – nothing much of value anywhere. So it intrigues me. Suddenly I get a visit from the town, and my visitors don't seem to know why they're here. Very interesting isn't it? Could they have come from Ashton, do you think?'

Eirlys picked up her coat from the back of a chair. 'I'm going, Marius. Looks as if...'

'Wait a minute – this might interest you, too.' They stood there, staring at each other. Eirlys had a smile on her face, but it wasn't a warm smile, and it wasn't for him. 'One never knows – does one?'

'Ashton didn't send us,' Gladstone said.

'Now then?' Eirlys said. She was walking towards the door, and with each step she took my heart sank lower.

'Then why did you come?' said Marius, speaking to us but keeping his eyes on Eirlys.

'To have a look, that's all.' Gladstone sounded genuinely ashamed.

'You mean Ashton sent you to spy on me?' Marius went on, still watching Eirlys.

'No, Mr Vaughan. Your brother had nothing to do with it.'

Eirlys turned by the door. She took a bunch of keys from her pocket and jingled them. 'So now you know,' she said lightly. 'I'm going...'

'Are you?' he said.

131

There seemed to be a struggle going on between them – only the eyes now, but previously, I felt sure, there had been words as well.

'I've got some work to do – on the books,' she said. 'Very important, the books...'

He looked away from her. She opened the door. 'See you, then, Marius,' she said. 'Don't bother to come to the door with me. They might escape, or something.' She smiled and gave us a wink. 'That would *never* do, would it?'

The door closed behind her. Marius looked as if he was going after her, but he held himself back. We heard the front door slam shut, then the click of her heels outside on the yard, then the door of her car as it closed. When the engine started up, Marius went over to the window and looked out, one hand raised to shield his eyes. He stood there like that for a while after the sound of the engine had dwindled and died. The room seemed to have stiffened in the silence, meanwhile. I was afraid that, once someone moved or spoke, everything would shatter and crumble before our eyes.

Then Marius turned to us, and he was a different man. For one thing, he looked older suddenly. For another he had a smile on his face – a weary sort of smile, but a smile all the same. 'Well now,' he said, but gently, very gently, 'I don't want you holding up that wall all night. Suppose you try sitting on that couch there.' I heard Dewi gasp. Asked to sit in Marius Vaughan's house! 'I'm tired of standing in front of you,' he went on. 'I get tired standing these days. Come on – sit down.'

We shuffled slowly to the couch, wondering what the catch would be. It was a long couch, big enough to take the four of us. Marius settled himself in an armchair opposite and lit a cigarette and inhaled deeply. 'Old wounds get going more at night, you know. But you wouldn't know about that, would you?' His tone was very gentle still, almost kind. 'Too young, all of you – but we weren't much older when we went off to war. Only boys, really. I find myself thinking a great deal about the war these days. About my father, too. He was a fine man, my father. He made you want to be like him. Used to swim out there in the bay, winter and summer, when he was turned seventy....' And on he went, talking like that about his father and the house and when he was a boy. What was he doing it for? Was he just playing with us? Was it the old game the teachers played – talking to you nice and soft before suddenly, when you weren't expecting it, ripping you to shreds? I watched him warily, then out of the corner of my eye saw Gladstone: he was at the other end of the couch, sitting well forward, his eyes fixed on Marius, rapt, following every word. And Marius, I felt, was speaking more to him than to the rest of us.

'In this room. He beat me. Took one of his sticks from the hall and thrashed me with it. That's what he did,' he went on. 'But I admired him, worshipped him. He said to the world – this is the kind of man I am, take it or leave it. *He* didn't go sucking around like that crowd in the town.' Dewi giggled appreciatively and I felt myself relax. 'They haven't got a good word for the Vaughans in the town, have they? It doesn't bother *me*, you know. *I* don't care what they think. My father taught me that.'

'We like the Vaughans,' Gladstone broke in eagerly. I saw him blush after he'd said it.

Marius stroked his moustache. 'Is that why you came?'

'Look, Mr Vaughan, we're sorry about the frame and everything. We shouldn't have come...'

'That's why you came, though? Because you like the Vaughans?'

'Well,' Gladstone began, looking at us as if he expected some support. 'Well – yes and no. I mean, Mr Vaughan, your brother never sent us...'

'Drunk all the time,' Dewi broke in.

Gladstone gave him a dirty look. 'It isn't *that*, Mr Vaughan. Your brother – well, he's a sick man...'

'You don't have to apologise for my brother,' Marius broke in.

'Well, he never sent us. If you know what I mean, Mr Vaughan – I don't think he's capable of asking us to come here. I mean – he never talks about you...'

Marius nodded briefly. 'Ashton and I fell out. It's a terrible thing when families fall out. Difficult to heal the breach, what?'

'But – why don't you, Mr Vaughan?' Gladstone asked, passion in his voice. 'I mean – why don't you...?' He choked into silence.

Marius Vaughan didn't reply straight away. He just sat there, looking down at his feet, and I thought that's done it – he'll be telling Gladstone to mind his own business, and getting back to that broken frame.... But, when he looked up, his face was drawn and somehow helpless. 'What would you suggest I do that I haven't already done? I've spoken to him – written – but there you are. Ashton's a special case.'

We sat waiting for more, but all he did was shake his head. He was stroking his false leg all the time.

'Mr Vaughan,' Gladstone said, 'if you like we can talk to him...'

'No, no, no,' Marius said softly. 'I've got to have time to think...'

'But he might listen to us...'

'I've got to have time to think, dammit! I know it's time he took his place here. I know. He can't go on living in this room of his for ever. Dammit all.' He stood up, his stick in his hand. 'Time he came back here. I know. I know.' He pointed with his stick to a high-backed wooden chair which stood against the far wall. 'Know what we called that chair? The flogging box! The old man – my father – made us lie on it, and let us have it. Not Ashton, though. Me. Oh, yes, it was nearly always me. I used to take the blame for Ashton. "Which one of you has transgressed this time?" he'd ask. Liked big words, the old man.... And I'd own up. It might have been a window smashed in the conservatory, or an oar missing from the boat, or one of his best fishing rods broken, or money gone from a drawer.... Anything like that, and most of the time it was old Ashton. But I stepped forward and owned up. Ashton was weak, you see. Always weak. Besides I was the oldest.' Marius closed his eyes so tightly that a vein stood out on his forehead. '"Trousers off!" the old man would say. "On the chair, boy!" And he'd be off to the hall to fetch his cane.' A shiver passed through him. 'Then he'd beat me – beat me till the blood came.' He pressed finger and thumb hard against his closed eyes. 'I never cried once. Never made a sound. Not in a hundred beatings. I

135

used to clamp my teeth tight, and close my mind to it. The next one *couldn't* be as bad, nor the next, nor the next... the old man would be breathing heavily like a warhorse above me.... The next one, the next one, the next...' I heard the thwack of the cane and the heavy breathing and the stifled gasp clear across the room.... 'By Christ, the old man had an arm on him – and I swear he couldn't count. Swear it. He'd start off going to give me ten of the best and finish off with twenty.' Marius gave a strange, high-pitched laugh. 'Then – it was over. "Trousers up!" he'd say. The room would be going round but I'd get myself sorted out – pull my pants up and make myself tidy. Old Ashton would be there by the window – crying. Always weak, Ashton... Then the old man would put his hand on my shoulder and say, "Never a sound, my boy". He'd say it in Welsh, always, though he hated the lingo. "You never made a sound."' He took his hand away from his face, but he didn't look angry or hurt or full of hate, or anything at all. He stared across the room at the chair. 'Always felt responsible for Ashton, somehow,' he said. 'Always did.'

The silence that followed seemed endless. I wanted to move my leg which had developed pins and needles, but I didn't dare.

Then Marius spoke again, so quickly that I didn't hear him. None of us heard him. 'What's the matter,' he said sharply, 'gone deaf, all of you? I said clear off.'

No one moved.

He turned to face us. 'Well – go on! Hoppit! I'll forget about the frame this time. Off you go – and don't come round here any more. Understand?'

I don't know who was the first to move towards the

door. I came to as we were backing out, nodding like geese. Then, when we had reached the door, he spoke again. 'Here a minute – you, Gladstone Williams.'

Without hesitation Gladstone went over to him, waving us out behind his back. Dewi had the door open and we ran down the hallway to the front door, and out on to the yard. Dewi and Maxie were off straight away into the darkness, but I stayed by the window and watched. Marius was saying something. Gladstone was nodding and smiling. Then Gladstone did one of those things that always made me feel embarrassed for him – he *bowed* to Marius, then tried to do a soldier's about turn, but made a mess of it, then marched stiff and straight out of the room. Oh, God, I said to myself, and crouched by the window to wait for him. But he too, once he was outside, must have felt the urge to get away fast. He went bounding past me, never even noticed I was there.

That left me on my own to see the white-haired man suddenly shake himself and spring into action. Three times, before I went floundering after the others, I saw him raise his stick high in the air and bring it down, vicious and hard, on the back of the chair in front of him. He wouldn't stop at three, I told myself as I ran: only his arm hanging limp and useless at his side would stop him.

XIII

'I'll go and wet my feet, kid,' Ashton said as he rolled his trousers up to his bony knees. 'By God, I'm dry all over. Drier than the Sahara.'

It was a hot day. In fact, the four days that Ashton had been without a drink had all been hot and thirsty. We watched him as he made his way down to the sea, stepping gingerly on the pebbles, still wearing his jacket and his hat.

'Pathetic, isn't he?' Gladstone remarked. 'Poor old soak. I wonder how long he'll last.'

'If I was him I'd be off to the Harp or somewhere,' Dewi said. 'He looks worse without having a drink...'

'He's got the shakes all right,' Gladstone agreed. His attitude towards Ashton had changed since our visit to the Point. He criticised him now as freely as the rest of us, although he insisted that we had to be kind and help him all we could. 'You never know,' he said, 'if we can get him to go back it might sort him out...'

'Have you had a word with him?' I asked.

'A lot of words. Lew. It's going to be a slow job.' He sighed deeply. 'I was telling Marius yesterday – you can't rush him. He's made up his mind nobody wants him, that's all.'

Gladstone had gone up to the Point every day since our visit. He never told us why Marius wanted to see him, but it wasn't too difficult to guess. Our job, Gladstone said, was to persuade Ashton that it was time he went home. 'Get the poor old thing back where he belongs. Shouldn't be living where he is, anyway. He's a Vaughan. Wasn't brought up like that...'

We had nothing from Gladstone now except the Vaughans. They had become the most important people alive; the world revolved around them. It was the Vaughans against the town, and the town was wrong, had been wrong all the time. What if we had been caught up on the Hill, then? he asked. Where would we have finished up? In the police station, that's where, with Super Edwards flapping a charge sheet long as your arm in our faces.... Oh, no, Marius had proved himself a gentleman with us. Although we had burst in on him like that, broken his frame and all, he had let us go. And not only that: he had been nice to us as well, even told us about himself, spoken to us as if we *were* somebody.... The town was wrong, that's all there was to it. All the town was interested in was knocking people down. Set them up – knock them down. One of their habits was destroying. Nobody had to be different, that was the trouble. They couldn't bear that. And the Vaughans – well,

139

they *were* different, weren't they? And not just different, either – *nobler*, somehow. Why, there was even something noble about Ashton, poor old hopeless Ashton. They had *style*, both of them…. And whatever they did, whether it was wrong or what, they looked the town and the world squarely in the face. They didn't say one thing and do another. If they cheated, they did so openly, and without quoting texts at you. They were *straight*…. Mind you, there was more to Marius than old Ashton. You had to admit that. Wasn't it strange how two brothers could be so different, but then little Walter there was different from Dora, really, wasn't he? We'd seen them both now, hadn't we? Even seen Marius close to. And they had one thing in common – clear as daylight, that was. They were both scarred men. Scarred by Jupiter dying, living in the shadow of his death…. It was more obvious in Ashton, perhaps, but they were both old before their time, weren't they? Anybody could see that – anybody, that is, who *wanted* to see…. They were two broken men….

The rest of us said very little when he went off like this about the Vaughans. I thought there was a lot in what he said, but I also thought he'd been carried away, too. Obsession came easily to Gladstone: it was because of this that I felt embarrassed for him now and then.

'When Ashton comes back,' he was saying earnestly, 'you three say you're going for a swim, and take the children with you. You know, it would be nice if they got together. I'll have a real talk with him…'

Maxie sat up, pointing, 'By God,' he cried, 'look at them headlamps…'

A girl visitor was running down to the sea, her breasts

bobbing inside her bathing costume.

'Steady on,' Dewi said, 'you'll be off to the bushes to shake hands with it, the way you're looking...'

'The children!' Gladstone warned.

The girl shrieked as she ran into the sea. 'She's a virgin,' Dewi remarked positively.

Maxie was up on his knees, alert and interested. 'How d'you know, then? How d'you tell?'

Dewi had Maxie on a hook, and we were smiling the three of us. 'Always scream,' he said. 'Never hear that before? Soon's they're in cold water – always scream...'

I was glad of a break like that from the Vaughans, but in a way I was sorry for Gladstone, too: start being serious about something and you find yourself talking to a world of comics.

It was after tea that Dewi came running with the news. 'He's going back!' he said. 'Gladstone says round to his house by six. Ashton's decided to go back!'

For a moment I thought it was another of Dewi's jokes, but he was dead serious. I hadn't seen him look so impressed since the night the man did the high-wire act when the circus came to Porthmawr. 'It's a fact, Lew,' he went on. 'You got to hand it to old Gladstone. Wants us at his house six o'clock – washed, he said. We're taking Ashton up there...'

'All he said was he wouldn't go without us,' Gladstone said. 'He wants us with him because he feels a bit strange about it, like....'

Tea at Gladstone's house that day had got mixed up with going to bed, so it was decided that the children should take their tea up with them. 'All right, play nurses with Walter if you like,' he cried, 'so long as you *don't go too far*.'

Martha had been called out on important business to do with a bet on a horse, Gladstone explained, so we gave him a hand with the children. But even so it took half an hour, which included Hamlet's Mistake, or the Murder in Harlech Castle, before they were up the stairs to stay. 'Right,' he said, looking at the jam on his hands, 'I'll be with you in ten minutes.' And he was, wearing a pair of white flannels that were a few inches short in the leg, and a blue shirt. On his head he put his boater which, although I felt it wasn't quite right, made the occasion one of the highest importance. 'We'll have to hurry,' he said. 'We've kept the poor man waiting long enough.'

By the time we reached the door below Ashton's room even I had a sense of mission. Gladstone went up to see if he was ready while the three of us stayed down in the street, pulling faces at old Maggie Thomas who was peering out at us through the windows of the house next door.

Gladstone came down in a hurry, and alone. 'He's packed everything,' he said, 'but he isn't there.'

The old woman was screaming something at us. Maxie pressed his nose flat against the glass, which made her jump back into the shadows of her room but not before we heard the words that echoed our own thoughts. 'Try the Fishers. Try the Fishers.'

Gladstone, without a word, ran up the stairs to Ashton's room. When he came down he was carrying Ashton's big suitcase and another bundle. We took them from him and followed as he set off rapidly towards the Fishers. It was turned seven, and that meant the pubs had been open for two hours.

142

We halted outside the Fishers. Gladstone went to the foot of the steps and stood there, fingering the brim of his boater. It was a big thing to enter a pub in Porthmawr in broad daylight.

'Try the back,' he announced suddenly. 'Better for getting him out, anyway.'

We followed him down a narrow alleyway to the yard of the Fishers. Most of the local customers used this entrance to the pub, and the door through which Gladstone, his confidence renewed, marched head held high was labelled 'Public Bar'. It was very quiet for a moment after the door had closed behind Gladstone, then there was a great, shattering roar of laughter. The three of us stood there in the beer-and-urine-smelling yard and didn't look at each other and didn't say anything.

Gladstone wasn't in the bar more than a minute, but it seemed longer. When he came out there were two red flushes on his cheeks. 'Been and gone,' he said breathlessly. 'Had a bottle in his pocket, too.'

'Bloody hell,' Dewi said as he picked up the suitcase, we'll have to go round them all.'

We went out to the sunlit street and began our tour of Porthmawr's pubs. There were eleven of them, but we didn't have to search them all. The windows of the Harp were open against the heat of evening, and through them we saw Ashton, half sprawled across a table. Gladstone's mother was there, too, already drunk as a monkey and telling everybody to be quiet because she was going to sing.

Gladstone mopped his forehead. 'There he is,' he said. He didn't say anything about his mother.

'I've got to sing, damn you all,' she was screaming.

'What is Wales without a song? The land of song. Nothing lovely as a song.' She was trying to climb up on a table and showing all her legs.

'I'll get the police for sure, Martha Davies,' Joe Pritchard, who kept the Harp, was shouting. 'There's no licence for singing...'

'Joe Pritchard, this the land of song, or isn't it?' She put her hand on Ashton's shoulder. 'My friend here – got a special request – "Aberystwyth". Nothing wrong in that, is there? My gentleman friend...'

'Back a bit,' Gladstone said. 'Come on.' He drew us away from the window. Ashton, we could see, was nodding his head and smiling foolishly. 'Listen – she's well away, Martha. Must have met Ashton. Going to be sick as a dog before the night's out – but never mind that now. The fact is it makes it difficult for me – her being there, like. If I go in, old Pritchard will think I've come for *her*.' He turned to me, appealing, 'Lew – will you go?'

I wanted to refuse. I would sooner have jumped in the harbour than gone in there in front of that crowd.

'All you have to do is ask to see Mr Pritchard. Tell him Ashton's wanted outside, urgent.' He measured me with a look. 'All right, then, Lew?'

I couldn't refuse. 'All right,' I said, and tried to stop the trembling in my knees.

Then Dewi gripped my arm. 'I'll come with you,' he said. 'Just up our street, this is.'

I was too grateful even to thank him. We hurried across the yard to the open back door of the Harp. The narrow passageway was lined with men, each one a glass in his hand. They weren't looking at us, however: Martha

144

had everyone's attention. They didn't notice us until we had reached the bar. Then the comments began. 'By God, this is a night – look what's blown in now... Old Joe will go out of his mind.... Hey, boys bach, what'll it be, then?' My face burned.

We pushed through to the door of the saloon, where Martha was still telling everyone she was going to sing. There was a crowd around the door. Dewi looked at me, and I looked at Dewi. I was all for giving it up as a bad job, but Dewi had other ideas.

'Paging Mr Vaughan!' he roared, in exactly the way they did at the pictures, American accent and all.

Everybody shut up as soon as he'd said it. A pin dropping in that place would have been thunder. Then the crowd around the door parted, and Joe Pritchard came through, wide and square and shirtsleeved, fingering his waxed moustache.

'Great God!' he cried when he saw us. 'What else is going to happen tonight?' He fixed his glare upon us. 'What are you young buggers doing in my pub, then?'

I knew it was my turn to speak. 'We've come for Mr Ashton Vaughan,' I said in my best County School voice. 'He's wanted...'

Joe Pritchard raised his great arms in the air. 'Get off these premises!' he roared. 'Clear out! By God, if the police should drop in this minute...'

'It's Ashton's little friends,' someone sneered.

'So they are, now...'

'I don't give a bugger who they are,' cried Joe. 'Get out of my pub! Now!'

He raised his arms again to shoo us out. I began to

145

back away, but Dewi stood firm. 'We're going,' he said, raising his voice because the row in the saloon had started again. 'Going now, Mr Pritchard – but tell Ashton Vaughan he's wanted outside urgent – will you?'

Joe Pritchard pulled hard at his nose. 'Tell him? Oh, hell, aye – I'll announce it ever so polite. But he won't be able to bloody well walk out, lad. Understand?' He swished his cloth at us. 'Now – out!'

'Tell him, though – will you, Mr Pritchard?'

'Out!' Joe roared. 'Out this minute!' He came for us. 'Out – or you'll have my boot up your backside!'

That was enough, even for Dewi. We charged through the grinning men out to the yard.

'No good?' Gladstone asked. Dewi shook his head. 'Don't go in, though. Joe Pritchard's ready to kill.'

We crouched near Ashton's luggage and felt depressed. It was such an anticlimax, somehow. 'Won't have to wait till closing time, will we?' Maxie asked. We told him to shut up, and sat there listening to Martha singing 'Aberystwyth'. She sang it well, too – drunk or sober, Martha had a voice smooth as syrup – but I couldn't help feeling sorry for Gladstone having to listen to it.

Then, suddenly, she broke off in mid-note and started to scream abuse at someone. Not long after there was a commotion at the back door, and two men appeared, humping Ashton between them. They were obviously under orders, because they ran quickly back into the pub and slammed the door shut, leaving him slumped on the doorstep. He wasn't out for the count, though, but one look told us he'd never manage the walk to the Point.

Someone in the pub was calling Martha a common

woman, but we were too deep in our own troubles to pay much attention. How did we move Ashton off that step, and having done that where did we move him to? His room, or the Point?

'The Point,' Gladstone said firmly.

'Taxi, then?' Dewi asked.

Gladstone shook his head. 'We're not going through his pockets, either. Too much of that done to drunken men.' He was searching the yard as he spoke, not bothering at all about the row going on in the pub.

'Going to be a big job carrying him,' Maxie said. 'That case and all...'

'Over there,' Gladstone broke in, pointing. 'That wheelbarrow. They won't notice if we take it...'

Dewi brought the barrow over. It was the kind used for shifting beer casks, without any sides to it, but with a big iron plate sticking up at the front. 'Not a *dignified* carriage,' Gladstone remarked. It was heavy, too – heavier still once we had propped Ashton Vaughan on it. We made him sit up, his back against the iron plate, and we put his suitcase on his lap to keep him down. 'The point of balance,' Gladstone kept saying, but we can't have found it before we were clear of the yard because Ashton fell off twice.

No one noticed us – no one said anything, anyway – and once on the road the going was easier. 'Two of you on either side to see he doesn't come off,' Gladstone ordered. 'We'll be there in no time.'

It was downhill all the way to the Square. Ashton only fell off once – at the feet of Llywelyn Philips who had been a missionary in Africa. 'What's the matter with that man?' he cried, nearly climbing out of his celluloid collar.

'Leprosy,' Dewi replied, as we propped Ashton back again. Now and then, before we reached the station corner, I looked back, and Llywelyn Philips was still standing in the middle of the road watching us.

When we stopped for a breather by the station, I was all for cutting down one of the back streets to the harbour, but Gladstone insisted that it was shorter through the town, and he didn't care who saw us. 'We'll have his coat over his face, though, for *decency's* sake,' he said, and we covered Ashton Vaughan's sagging head with his old mac.

Station Road was crowded, as I knew it would be. It looked as if all Porthmawr was out to take the evening air, or watch the antics of the visitors, or see us pass through. Then I heard the first roar of laughter which always preceded the coming of the Rev A. H. Jones, and there he was, arm in arm with his wife, on our side of the road too. He was pointing things out to his wife, and laughing because it was such a funny world – and we might have passed him unnoticed had not the wheelbarrow hit a stone and tipped Ashton off again.

'My goodness!' Mrs Jones screeched. 'It's a man!'

'Steady! Steady! Steady!' the Rev A. H. Jones cried, not to us but to his wife. Then he flung his arms around her and stood on tiptoe looking down at the inert figure on the pavement. 'Good gracious,' he said, 'is he dead? Wherever are you boys taking him?'

'To the bonfire,' Dewi said, as we hoisted Ashton back on the barrow.

The Rev A. H. Jones let go of his wife, fixed his glasses on his nose, and ventured closer. He was over his shock now, and curious as a puppy.

148

'Gladstone Williams!' he cried. 'Again! What are you up to, boy?'

'Not *up* to anything,' Gladstone replied as he draped the mac over Ashton's head. 'It's poor Mr Vaughan. He was on his way home, poor man, and was taken ill. We're putting Christian principles into practice, you might say.'

'He's drunk!' the Minister cried out. All the people watching must have heard him quite clearly.

Gladstone gripped the handles firmly. 'Drunk or sober, still in need of Christian charity,' he said. 'Would you like to help, then?'

The Minister leapt back. 'Certainly not!' he gasped. He reached for his wife's hand. 'Myfanwy,' he said, 'Myfanwy...'

'Whatever is Porthmawr coming to?' she said. 'Is *that* Ashton Vaughan?'

'Steady! Steady!' said the Rev A. H. Jones.

'And is *that* Gladstone Williams?'

A quick nod.

'Goodness,' she said, 'oh, goodness... hold me, A. H.'

'Plenty of room on the barrow,' Gladstone said as we set off once again towards the Square.

It was all very embarrassing, I thought, especially as Ashton had come to and was now singing under the mac. But I stuck close to Gladstone and tried not to look at anybody. Perhaps that was why I never saw Super Edwards until he was upon us, blocking our way, his hand up, as if we were a bus or something. 'Stop!' he cried. We were in the middle of the Square. 'Stop where you are!' Constable Matthews was at his side in an instant. We could tell what Ashton was singing now. It was 'Rock of Ages'.

149

'It's a drunk,' the constable said.

'Take the mac off him,' the Super ordered. The constable did so. 'By God,' said the Super, 'it's Ashton Vaughan!'

'He's all right,' Gladstone said.

'I can see that,' said the Super. 'Where d'you think you're taking him, then?'

'To his brother's,' Gladstone said.

'Good God!' The Super looked thunderstruck. He knelt by Ashton's side and sniffed.

'It's all arranged.'

The Super got to his feet again. 'Does Marius know? By God, won't he be glad to see him!'

We didn't bother to comment. Gladstone gripped the handles firmly. We took our places ready to move off.

'Shall I make a charge, sir?' Constable Matthews asked, stepping in front of us.

The Super shook his head. 'No. No charge. You *sure* you're taking him to the Point?'

'Quite sure,' Gladstone said.

'Where did you get the barrow, then?' the constable asked.

'On loan,' Gladstone said wearily. 'From the Harp.'

'And Marius knows he's coming?' the Super persisted.

'All arranged,' Gladstone said. 'The breach is healed. All's well with the Vaughans.'

'Good God,' the Super said, 'when is the day of judgement then?'

'Can we go?'

'Aye. Get him out of here fast as you can. Smells worse than a public bar. Get going...' The Super was grinning all over his face. 'That man had better be very careful,' Gladstone said as we carried on across the Square. 'He's likely to find himself on the mat before the Chief Constable.'

Once clear of the town and on the road to the Point the excitement died in us, and tiredness even overtook Gladstone. The stops became more frequent, the longest of all by Marius Vaughan's gate. We all had a pull on a fag there and listened to Ashton's muffled snores rise on the still, evening air.

Then Marius Vaughan's car came from the direction of the house. We opened the gate for him and stood there waiting. The car came to a halt. Marius wound down the window. He didn't really look at us at all – only at the wheelbarrow.

'What's that?' he asked, pointing.

'Your brother come home,' Gladstone replied grandly. We all felt rather proud at that moment. We had accomplished something. But Marius Vaughan, where I was concerned, soon altered that.

'Good God,' he said, more like a military Englishman than ever, 'is that the only way you could bring him? Like a pig from the market?'

We were tired and hot, and this wasn't the kind of talk we wanted to hear. Dewi at my side cleared his throat, all set for argument, but Gladstone took no offence.

'Well – you know how it is, Mr Vaughan. Told you he needs looking after...'

'You wheeled him across the town in *that*?' Marius went on. 'Had he no money for a taxi?'

'Never asked him,' Dewi said sharply.

'Then you should have done. Making a bloody carnival of it! I suppose he does know where he is?'

'He told us he'd come,' Gladstone replied, still very gently. 'He was all packed and everything, but he got in with a crowd at the Harp...'

'Well, good God,' Marius kept on saying. 'On a bloody wheelbarrow! Good God!' Then he tossed two half-crowns through the window. They fell on the dusty road with a chink that was somehow insulting. 'The taxi would have cost you that,' he said. 'You may as well have it...'

Gladstone picked up the money. 'You don't have to do that, Mr Vaughan.'

'Oh yes, he does,' Dewi said grimly.

'Didn't do it for the money...'

'Don't be silly, Gladstone. Don't give it him back.'

'Take it!' Marius snapped as he revved up the car. 'Carry on to the house. Hand him over to the housekeeper. She's got a room ready for him...'

The car began to move off, Marius still looking intently at the bundle on the barrow. 'Please, Mr Vaughan,' Gladstone said. 'It's all right. We don't want this...' But the car gathered speed and left us standing in a cloud of fine dust.

Gladstone turned to us, holding the two coins as if they were dirty. 'He needn't have done that,' he said. 'We didn't do it for money...'

'You mean we didn't do it for five bloody shillings,' Dewi broke in angrily. 'He could have said thank you very much as well, the bastard! Five bloody shillings!' He looked at Ashton on the barrow. 'All the trouble we've had with that bugger. We should have dumped him in the bloody harbour...'

152

Tempers broke suddenly. Dewi and Gladstone had a real set to. Gladstone threw the money on the ground. Dewi picked it up. Gladstone knocked it out of his hands, and Maxie scrambled after it, crying out that one half-crown was lost…. It was a poor end to the day.

Gladstone and I carried on to the house, leaving the other two scrabbling on hands and knees in the dust. Neither of us spoke. There was only the occasional squeak from the barrow and Ashton's irregular snoring to break a silence that was as heavy as doom.

XIV

During the week that followed I saw nothing of Gladstone. It was a very wet week, unfit for any visits to the beach, but that wasn't the only reason. The truth was that I'd had enough of the Vaughans – more than enough; the holidays had been given over to them, had gone quickly in their shadow, and I knew that Gladstone, were I to go down Lower Hill to his house, would still want to talk about them. So, apart from odd afternoons with Rowland Williams in his workshop, I stayed in and read Zane Grey and Edgar Wallace and talked to Meira and played draughts with Owen. I was like Dewi – I'd had a bellyful of the Vaughans.

We had spent the five shillings Marius had thrown at us on fish, chips and peas – a big feed in the cafe behind Johnson's Chips. Gladstone had talked of the Vaughans non-stop while Dewi and Maxie and I had pulled sly faces at one another. Gladstone was jubilant. 'I *never* thought Ashton would agree. Never. But we managed it, didn't we? We brought them together again. We succeeded where others have failed – old Super Edwards can put *that* in his pipe and smoke it.' I wanted to say that Ashton hadn't really gone of his own free will, had in fact been carted there dead drunk. And afterwards Dewi had called our journey across town a bloody farce. But we said nothing. If Gladstone wanted to see it as a triumphal procession, then fair enough. We let him talk. 'Two scarred men, Lew, all their passions dying now, and both with the same sickness. But they're together now, as they should be....' He carried on like that all the way home, and that's how I left him – eyes shining, face drawn and pale with excitement. I decided there and then that I would have a rest. I would wait until Gladstone had got over the Vaughans.

A wet week, and the visitors dwindling. Give it a few more days, Owen said, and there would be only the seagulls after a boat, and he would be back on the dole.

'Nice when they're gone, though,' Meira said. 'We can have the place to ourselves...'

'Lovely, that is,' Owen said.

'Poor things – going back to them big, dirty towns...'

Owen made a move on the draughtsboard. 'Very nice for us living in lovely old Porthmawr with no work, too. The gentlemen of Porthmawr – and all the work they do is sign on the dotted line. Know who said that, Lew?'

I shook my head.

'The Rev A. H. Jones, that's who. From the pulpit. It was a bit of fair social comment, coming from a man who's working the ass-end off his breeches...'

'Owen!' Meira said, very sharp.

'Only quoting, cariad,' he went on. 'Quoting my betters.' He gave me a wink. 'Not so long left of the holidays now, Lew?'

'Results on Wednesday,' I said. I had tried my Senior, and everybody knew how important *that* was – that and the Central Welsh Board.

'Think you've passed, Lew?'

'Don't know,' I said.

'Pass or fail – it's back to school for you,' Meira put in. 'Been paying in that club of Mrs Davies – enough for a new rig-out for you, boy.'

Owen and Meira, I decided, were the only two people I felt really secure with. I didn't belong to them, of course, but most of the time their kindness made me forget that. I didn't want to go back to school at all, but I would do if that was what they wanted. And that night I prayed that I had passed the Senior because I knew it would please them. And on Wednesday the news was good.

'Matriculated as well!' Owen cried. 'Meira, he's got the bloody matric!'

'Don't swear,' Meira said through her tears. 'Oh – pity his mam...'

'Been living with a bloody genius,' Owen went on. 'By God – it'll be college and all sorts for you now, boy.'

Straight off this niggling contempt I had for them came back. I was ashamed of it, had tried all I knew to scrub it out, but it was there – especially when they were like this – all emotion and kindness and love.

'Have him a teacher, shall we, Meira?' All Porthmawr hated the teaching profession, but they thought of nothing

156

else for their sons and daughters. 'Safe job – all them holidays...'

I turned away in disgust. A foreign correspondent was what I wanted to be – a foreign correspondent who was also a poet.

'Teacher, Lew?'

I shook my head.

'What then? Civil Service?'

'Never mind now what he's going to be,' Meira said. 'For a start, he's going back to the County, going to try for his Higher. Might make a Minister out of him...'

'Oh, no,' Owen protested, 'he's not joining the black battalion. For sure he's not...'

'No need to get excited,' Meira said. 'Only a suggestion.'

'Wales and Spain,' Owen went on fiercely, 'too many bloody priests, that's what...'

I left them arguing and went up Lower Hill to Rowland Willams' workshop. Rowland was standing at his bench, a half-finished coffin in front of him, a book propped against it. He looked up as I entered, then slipped a piece of paper to mark his place in the book, closed it and placed it carefully on one side. 'You've come to talk,' he said, 'so I'd better get some work done. You can't read and talk, but you can work. In fact, you have to.' He pointed a chisel at the coffin. 'There's someone waiting for this...'

'I passed,' I said.

'Matric?'

I nodded.

Rowland scratched his nose and looked me over carefully. 'Any book you like,' he said. 'Take it and keep it for ever.' Piles of dusty books stood up like gravestones on the workshop floor. Rowland, although a carpenter, had never got around to making shelves for them. 'Look around you,' he went on, 'take your time and pick one...'

'For passing? I'd rather you chose one.'

It was the right thing to say. Rowland grinned then turned to spit in the fire. 'Diplomat you're going to be, Lew? Knew I'd like to pick one, didn't you? All right. Let's say that one, shall we? Anton Chekhov – *The Cherry Orchard and Other Plays*.' He picked up the book and passed it to me after wiping the dust off its covers. 'You read it some time, Lew. When you're about twenty – read it then....'

I sat back on a stool and leafed through the pages while Rowland talked. It was a great honour to receive a book from Rowland, especially a book that had belonged to him. He had taken up his work again, was planing slowly, sending small curls of wood into the air, talking all the time. 'Drudgery, that's what this is. If you're creating something it's all right. Making something – like the great sculptors, like Michelangelo. People like that. Seeing something, feeling for it, shaping it. That's all right. But this – this stuff's no good at all. *Mending*, not making. Mending and coffins, coffins, coffins. By God, there's not much art about an old coffin, is there?'

He was launched now on a subject, a small, dark man, full of secrets – a dirty man, Meira said, but I didn't think so – talking quietly as the rain swished on the workshop window and made the fire spit. Soon he would get emotional, and then tell me that the trouble with the Welsh was an excess of emotion. I hugged my knees and listened only occasionally. The exams were passed and I was warm with success.

'...Lost an eye in the last one,' Rowland was saying. 'What will it be in the next, I wonder?'

I was all attention, suddenly. 'Is there going to be a war, Mr Williams?'

He rubbed his thumb across the bristles on his chin. 'Sure as tomorrow...'

'Serious, though? I saw the news in the pictures. War like the last one?'

'Worse.' His voice hardened. 'They all want one, you see. Building up for the big bang, all of them...'

Ever since I had started going to the pictures I had seen films about the war – all the guns and the grey men running in the mud, and the poison gas.... War scared me worse than Frankenstein. All I could think of when someone said war was Warner Baxter in a steel helmet swallowing aspirin and waiting to go over the top.

'All over Europe,' Rowland went on, 'men limping or carrying an empty sleeve in a pocket. Men with trenches across their hearts.... All of them crosses, Lew. All that one minute silence. Mockery, Lew! Mocking the dead! Scars everywhere, and men lying awake.... All those names, Lew. Jesus Christ!' Rowland threw a chisel on the bench in disgust. 'It's coming again. No doubt about it...'

I had a pain deep in my stomach as he spoke. Whatever you might say about Rowland – that he was small and bandy-legged and didn't wash much and had hairs growing out of his nostrils, stuff like that – yet you knew he spoke the truth, that he was a genuine man.

'Thirty-eight when they took me last time. Too old, Lew. A man's *very* sensitive, time he gets to thirty-eight...'

'Will it change everything, though, Mr Williams?'

159

Rowland took up a plane and squinted along the blade. 'The last one did,' he said softly. 'Can't see any reason why the next one shouldn't do the same.'

'Honestly?'

'Bound to,' he said flatly. 'Nothing else for it.'

I wanted to run away from the workshop then. It was all so inevitable. Nothing anyone could do about it. But outside the rain swept down and I stayed, feeling the way I felt at the pictures with all those guns thundering against the roof of the Palace.

'Marius Vaughan was in the war,' I said, just for something to say. 'Lost his leg.'

Rowland nodded. 'Captain in my unit. He'd have a word with me sometimes – us coming from the same place, him a boy, me already an old man, like. He was hard, Lew – much too hard, as if he feared men. I knew a boy come from over Llandrindod way – and he was all for shooting Marius Vaughan.'

'Great God,' I said.

'Never did, though,' Rowland went on. 'Was blown to bits first... Oh, hell, aye – there's scars everywhere, even on Marius Vaughan, I shouldn't wonder...'

'That's what Gladstone says,' I broke in.

Rowland's bushy eyebrows went up. 'He's a character, that Gladstone, and no mistake. Reckons Marius has a scar, does he? Thinks about people, Gladstone, doesn't he? Concerned about people.' He picked up the chisel and held it so that it was pointing towards his good eye. 'How would I feel, d'you think, if I jabbed this in my eye, Lew? Be a bit stupid, wouldn't it? Not much sense in doing it?' He turned and pointed the chisel at me. 'Know what – I was not so far from Marius Vaughan when that shell copped him. Saw him carried off...' Rowland looked at the smears of rain on the window, considering things carefully. 'Know what, Lew? I reckoned Marius Vaughan wanted that wound – was after a scar all the time. And not like the rest of us. Not to get out of that hell. No – I reckon he wanted hurt. Really wanted hurt.' It was very silent in the workshop, but somewhere in the distance a dog was howling. I was being told something, and I couldn't quite grasp it – like it is in a dream.

Rowland shook himself, then picked up a long piece of elm and carried it over to the sawing bench. 'Give a hand, Lew,' he called. I went over and watched him measure off. I wanted to ask him to explain, but somehow the moment had passed. He began to saw through the wood.

'No art in this job,' he grumbled. 'No art at all for the man with one basic qualification for an artist. Know what that is, Lew?'

He wasn't going to explain about Marius Vaughan. I shook my head.

'Not the matriculation, I can tell you that. No – that's only good for getting you in the Civil Service, God help you.' He stopped sawing. 'Lew – the one basic qualification for an artist is intolerance. After talent – intolerance. Now, I've no talent, Lew bach, but I'm sodden with intolerance.... Hold the wood, boy.'

He finished sawing, then carried the wood back to his bench and fixed it in a vice. 'A patcher-up, that's what I am. A creator of man's last resting place – and by God the dead are *uninteresting*, aren't they? Ashes to ashes and dust to dust, if it's a box you're after, Rol Williams' a

161

must. Doesn't scan, Lew, but not bad, eh?'

I went back the next afternoon, hoping he would start on Marius Vaughan again, but that day we had the Spanish Civil War, Herr Hitler, and the League of Nations.

Even during this week away from Gladstone, the Vaughans still managed to come through. I was thinking about Marius Vaughan being carried away on a stretcher, and Rowland Williams watching, and the rain coming down, and the mud everywhere, when Eirlys Hampson came running out of her shop and called after me.

'Head in the clouds you've got,' she said, laughing. She always seemed to say everything through a smile. 'What were you pondering on, then? And what's the idea of passing without even a wink?'

I was in the shop now, very embarrassed because there were knickers everywhere, but liking it all the same because Eirlys was making a fuss, flirting with me all the time.

'Just thinking,' I said.

'Aye – and take your eyes off those private clothes, old brainbox,' she said, shielding my eyes. 'For shame on you.' She smelled nice – of powder and scent. She was wearing a silk blouse and I could see her shoulders and her arms through it. 'Now, tell me Lew Morgan,' she said, ruffling my hair, 'how's the Vaughan Society going on, then?'

'Don't know what you mean,' I said.

'You got him to go back, didn't you?'

I nodded. There was a woman in the shop doorway looking in. I felt myself blushing because I was going to be seen in there, alone with Eirlys.

'Miracle worker, your friend Gladstone.' The woman

came in. 'Oh, damn,' Eirlys said, lowering her voice and not smiling. 'Thought we might have a chat about how our mutual friends are getting on at the Point.' She gave the woman a look that would have turned away a dog. 'Anyway, call again, love – will you?'

'All right, Mrs Hampson,' I said.

'That's a good boy.' She came to the door with me, her arm around my shoulders, holding my head against her breast. 'This old bitch,' she whispered, 'be here for hours, ask to see everything, then finish up buying a penny elastic....'

My face was burning when I got out to the rain, but I thought she was nice all the same. It didn't strike me for a long time that *she* should have known how things were at the Point without calling me in.

The Vaughans kept coming through. It was annoying, but it was inescapable. They were different from anyone I knew in Porthmawr, and because they were different, even without sight or sound of them, they intruded on me all the time. It was a relief when, at the end of that week, Gladstone's inimitable knock came on our front door.

'Lew – come round, can you?' he said, not facing me directly at all.

'They're at the pictures,' I said. 'I'll leave a note.'

It wasn't until I reached his house that I saw why he had shown me only one side of his face. The other bore a bruise below the eye, a bruise which seemed to grow and darken even as I looked at it.

XV

What happened to you, then?' I asked. 'Have a fight?'

Gladstone shook his head and knelt by the fire and made a great business of tidying up. I crouched beside, him. 'Harry Knock-Knees, was it? That crowd?'

He smiled then, but went on shaking his head. 'Big fool – that's what I am! Big fool!' He stirred the fire with the poker. 'Do you ever do things, Lew, that make you crumple up inside afterwards? Just thinking about them makes you feel all withered up? Do you?'

'All the time,' I said.

He stood up and walked the length of the room and back again. 'Lew – I went up there. Tonight – just before it got dark.'

'To the Point?' I got to my feet as well. 'You didn't cop that there, did you?'

He nodded, then turned away hastily. I knew I was

saying all the wrong things, but I couldn't help it.

'You never had a *fight* with the Vaughans, did you?'

'Not a fight. I was thrown out.' He came back to me and seized my arm. 'Lew – this doesn't matter.' He jabbed his thumb hard in the centre of the bruise. I winced for him. 'This doesn't matter at all...'

'Marius Vaughan hit you?'

'It doesn't matter, Lew. He didn't hit me. Just sort of pushed me out and I fell. Knocked against the door as I fell.'

'Pushed you?' was all I could say.

Gladstone brushed the hair back clear of his forehead and tried to smile. 'Well – I made a mistake, didn't I? I went up there. Nosing around – that's what I was doing. Lew – I shouldn't have gone...'

'Well you did,' I said. 'You did – and that was no reason for throwing you out.'

Gladstone clapped his hands impatiently. 'I wasn't thrown out, Lew. Nobody did that to me.'

'Pushed then,' I said.

'He just asked me to leave, that's all. And we sort of collided – had a collision – and big fool me fell against the door.'

He looked at me, waiting for me to comment, but there was nothing I could say.

'I shouldn't have gone up there,' he went on. 'Sit down, somewhere, Lew. Don't stand looking as if you're going to take on the whole town.'

'Not the whole town,' I said. 'Just the Vaughans.'

His hands came up in despair. 'No, no, Lew. Don't be childish, now. It wasn't the Vaughans. It was me. I should

165

never have gone up there. Never in a month of Sundays, I shouldn't... I should've minded my own business and let them be.'

I moved to the old rocking chair by the fire and he went over to the couch which was his bed. He sat down heavily, then clasped his head in his hands. The silence seemed to go on forever, and how to break it was beyond me.

Then he stirred and smiled. 'Heard some good news about you, haven't I? Congratulations, Lew. Always said you were going to be an intellectual.'

'Oh – hell,' I said.

'Never you mind hell – you're going to be an intellectual. I know it. And an intellectual man, Lew, is the finest there is.' His eyes, suddenly, were no longer dulled. 'That's what I think – an intellectual is *different*, Lew. He's got *style*. I like people who have style – know what I mean?' He was sitting forward eagerly now, not talking to me or to anyone – just letting words and ideas wipe out, for a time at least, what had happened to him up at the Point. 'I wish I had real learning inside my head. I wish I was an intellectual man with style – with a style of his own... and I'll tell you something else, Lew – I wish I was a cosmopolitan as well – not a stuck-in-the-mud native of Porthmawr. A real cosmopolitan, able to move freely about the world, mixing with high and low, able to talk about the *big* things, *important* things, like art and music and books. That's what I wish.' He sighed deeply, then leaned forward to stir the fire into life. 'Ashes,' he said, 'that's all you've got here. Ashes and mud. The trouble with us, Lew, is we're sunk in the mud of Porthmawr respectability. This is the primeval swamp of respectability. They invented the word here. The

166

clean front and cuffs – and the dirty shirt underneath.'

He put the poker down. 'They ought to have maps in school – like those average rainfall ones, only these would show the distribution of Hypocrites per square mile.' He grinned, and I knew he was feeling better. 'Be black all over, this place would... brighten up the old Geography lesson too, wouldn't it?'

'Fair enough,' I agreed.

'And let's have textbooks as well. Guides to the young – how to tell a hypocrite, how to detect a fraud.' The idea delighted him. His eyes were shining now. 'We'll line them up for inspection – the people with two voices, Lew, one for posh English, one for poor Welsh. The ones who come back from England and *can't remember* any Welsh, poor things. The ones who pronounce Porthmawr 'Pommower' to suit the English. The ones who tell us to love Wales – in *English*!' He sucked in his cheeks and did an imitation for me. 'Then there's the other crowd – the ones who want to shut everything out that isn't Welsh. We'll have them in as well. The ones who say no to everything... all frauds, Lew bach – and we've got them here in this little half and half town. I tell you Owen Glyndwr would spit right in their eye. He had *style*, Lew. He wasn't a respectable fraud forever changing to suit the company....'

The excitement left him suddenly. 'What's the use?' he said, and for a moment he was silent again.

'Lew – honest to God, some days I feel I'm choking here,' he went on. 'Don't know what stops me getting the little ones together, packing a bag and away to go...'

'Go on, then,' I said, keeping my voice light, but worried all the same because he was so serious with it.

'You'd never go. Told me yourself...'

'Not *for ever*, maybe. But – there must be somewhere to go to, Lew, somewhere nice.' He picked up an old school atlas – it had Porthmawr Council School stamped on its cover – and opened it at the middle page. 'Plenty of places here – the Mediterranean Sea, Athens, Rome, Alexandria.... Oh, hell, spoilt for choice, once you've worked out the getting there.' He closed the atlas and threw it down behind him. 'It's either go away, or stay. And if you stay you have to be like the Vaughans.'

'Never,' I said, looking at the bruise on his cheek. 'What did you want to go there for? You shouldn't have gone.'

He stood up quickly. 'I know. I know I shouldn't. You've *no* idea how *ashamed* I feel about it. I was interfering, breaking in on them – acting like all the people in Porthmawr would. *Spying*, Lew...'

'What made you go, then?'

He paced up and down the kitchen, his hands tightly clasped in front of him. 'I wanted to see for myself, I suppose. I couldn't wait. Wanted to find out if it was working out – if they managed to bury Jupiter at last.' Standing there directly under the light he was all skin and bone, somehow. His arms were limp at his side, the palms of his hands turned towards me, appealing. '*You* know what I mean, don't you?'

Why does he have to ask me? I thought. What makes him think that *I* understand? But I nodded, though: there was nothing else I could do.

Then the children upstairs began to cry, and before Gladstone had moved from his position under the light they had come tumbling downstairs and into the room, and were pressed against him, little old people in their nightshirts, faces puffed with sleep and tears.

'Now then,' he said as he crouched down to them. 'Now then, what's this?'

'Had nightmares,' Dora sobbed.

'Not *all* of you?' He was touching them and kissing them and smoothing back their hair. 'Not at the same time?'

'It was terrible,' Dora said.

Gladstone felt Walter's bottom. 'Not wet the bed, have you?'

'Never,' Walter said firmly.

'Tell me, then. What did you have nightmares about?'

'Chips,' Walter said.

'And cockroaches,' Mair added.

'That's a mixture, for sure.' Gladstone smiled, and Walter and Mair smiled with him. 'Recovered now?' They nodded. 'Then off to Lew by the fire, while I talk to Dora...'

They came running to me and occupied my knees. They smelled of old feather bed and sleep, and were nice and soft and warm.

'Only me had the real nightmare,' Dora sobbed.

'Grammar,' Gladstone cried.

'Only me *have* the real nightmare, then,' she said.

'Oh, God,' he said, picking her up, 'come over here by the fire and tell me...'

Dora buried her face in his shoulder. 'I'm going to have a baby,' she cried. 'That's what I was dreaming about – having a baby.'

Gladstone sat down with her and held her close. 'Some day you will – not now.'

'It was a baby with blue eyes, and it came out of my belly. Out of *here*...'

Mair giggled foolishly on my knee.

'Where did all this information come from?' Gladstone asked sternly. 'Who's been talking? That one next door?'

Dora pressed her face deeper against his chest, but there was a nod too. 'Said I had a big belly, and that was because there was a baby in there – and it would come out, and there would be blood and everything...'

Gladstone smiled and kissed her ear. 'Such ignorance,' he said softly. 'Such crazy old talk...'

Dora's face emerged, puffed and tear-stained. 'Not true, then?'

'Not true,' he agreed. 'A baby comes from heaven...'

'From my belly, she said.'

'From heaven, and there's no blood. Pink and shiny and hungry, that's how it comes. All ready for you to love.'

'From my *belly*, though,' Dora protested.

'Well – it's a nice belly...'

Dora's head came up. Her chin began to tremble. 'It's true, then? What she said is true?'

Gladstone gave an elaborate sigh. 'Answer me a question, that's all. How old are you?'

'Eight,' Dora said.

'Then it can't happen for another ten years – at least. Answer me another – are you married?'

She giggled. 'No. Of *course* not.'

'Can't have a baby without a husband,' Gladstone said quickly. 'Impossible. Ask anybody...'

'Annie next door did. Mam said she did...'

Gladstone did his sigh again. 'Well – he was a kind of a husband she had. Not a proper one. Believe me, or believe me not – no husband, no baby. And in any case you're not old enough yet...'

'But when I'm old enough – from my belly? *Not* from my *belly*.' She shook her head. 'No – not from there, eh?'

'Where d'you suggest then? From your arm? Your head? Your big toe?'

'Silly,' she said.

'Well – it's got to come from somewhere, poor pink and hungry thing. Never thought of that, did you?'

She shook her head slowly, but the idea struck her as being right. She smiled. 'From my belly,' she said.

'When you're married, too,' Gladstone went on. 'Don't forget *that*.'

Dora came off his knee. 'It's very disappointing,' she said, 'but if you say so, then it must be right.' Another thought occurred to her: 'How did it get in my belly, then?'

'One thing at a time,' Gladstone said smoothly. 'That's the secret of a long and happy life. Best you understand what I've told you before we go on to lesson two. Not going to cry any more, are you?'

'Not at the moment,' Dora said. 'Anyway – it's very disappointing.'

'I know,' Gladstone said, 'I know.' He wasn't acting it up because I was there. 'The trouble is it gets more disappointing as you go on...'

'Like ice cream?'

'And toffee apples.'

Dora giggled. 'What's that on your face, then?' She touched the bruise very gently.

171

'The price of one question too many,' he replied, looking at me.

We had *Oliver Williams-Hughes-Jones* by Charles Dickens after that – the revised version, Gladstone said. He hurried it a bit, though, because it was late, and didn't make much of Fagin Price in case the children had another nightmare. No sooner had he got them back up the stairs than Dewi and Maxie burst in.

'This time of night,' Gladstone said. 'Who threw you out and from where?'

'Not tonight,' Dewi said. 'Three times last week, though. From the Palace.'

'Just thought we'd call round,' Maxie said, 'as we hadn't been...'

'What happened to your face?' Dewi asked.

Gladstone said something about falling out of bed, and I felt special because he wasn't telling them a truth. I realised then, too, that I wasn't the only one who had decided on a holiday from the Vaughans.

'Oh,' Dewi said, 'well – thought we'd come as we hadn't seen you for a bit, like.'

'Don't apologise,' Gladstone said, 'just get the Woodbines out.' So we had the fags going, and Gladstone made some tea, and Dewi swore like the Royal Welch, and Maxie told us how the pictures last week needed something to brighten them up – preferably a human mole. It was an occasion and a party all of a sudden.

The clock was striking eleven when Martha came in like someone in a drama, her face white, tears like rivers on her powdered cheeks, lipstick smeared.

'Gladstone, Gladstone,' she cried. 'Oh, my God, my God.' She threw herself down on the sofa.

Martha often came in like that, often threw herself on the sofa and moaned away and showed all her legs. It was 'moods' Gladstone always said – women over forty had moods all the time, and it was best to leave them alone. We carried on with our game of Pontoon for matches, and smiled and winked at one another. It could have been 'moods', it could have been gin – no matter which where Martha was concerned. None of us, not even Gladstone, looked on her like we did other women. Martha was a special case, a comic and a dead loss. We liked her, but we knew she was hopeless, so we let her be.

'Oh, God, God, God,' she cried. 'Oh poor little Jesus Christ, our Lord, Amen.... Gladstone, Gladstone!'

'Pay pontoons only,' said Gladstone.

'Speak to me, damn you,' Martha cried.

'And five-card tricks,' said Gladstone.

Martha sat up on the sofa and clasped her ears tight and began to scream. Gladstone was over to her at once, his hand on her mouth.

'Quiet, woman,' he said, 'you'll wake the children.'

Martha stopped screaming immediately. 'Let them hear,' she said sulkily. 'Everybody should hear...'

'Have yourself a cup of tea and calm down,' Gladstone told her. 'Wipe your face, too. It's a proper mess.'

He came back and crouched with us at the hearth. 'All got cards, then?'

'Your face would be a mess too if you'd heard what I've heard,' Martha said. 'Murder in Porthmawr...'

Gladstone put his cards down. 'Murder? Tonight?'

Martha had a mirror up in front of her face now. 'Don't ask me. Don't ask me because I won't tell you. I've been insulted enough. Coming home upset like I did, and getting the cold shoulder. Just don't ask me, that's all. I'm not telling anything.'

'I heard about it,' Dewi put in. 'Know all about it, as a matter of fact...'

'You never do, then. How long've you been here? Been here an hour or more, haven't you?'

'At the pictures it was,' Dewi said. 'James Cagney shot the other one – bang, bang, like that. Everybody's heard...'

'Which one?' Gladstone's question was a whipcrack across the room.

Martha lowered the mirror. 'I'm not telling you any more...' her voice trailed away, and she began to sob again. 'Ashton,' she said, 'brother killing brother. Ashton killed his brother dead!'

We were on our feet, Gladstone running to the door. I had followed him without thinking, was running now at his side down Lower Hill. Behind us Dewi and Maxie followed, Dewi saying murder, murder, murder, over and over again. There were no lights anywhere. Porthmawr was a dead town, murdered, dead.

At the edge of the Square, Dewi cried out in pain and fell to his knees. We all stopped and crowded around him.

'Dewi's shot!' Maxie cried. 'Bullet came from over there!'

'Bullet my ass,' Dewi groaned, 'got a stitch, that's all!'

'Oh – come on,' Gladstone said sharply, and turned away.

'Where to?' Maxie asked. 'Where we going?'

I heard Gladstone gasp in the darkness. He came back to

us. 'Don't know,' he said in a voice so changed that I thought it was one of the others who had spoken. 'Don't know.'

'Police station, that's where,' Dewi said as he struggled to his feet. 'Where else would we go?'

'That's right,' Gladstone said, and set off across the Square in the direction of Market Street. Maxie and I followed with Dewi, who was limping badly and cursing.

The light outside the police station must have been the only one in Porthmawr that night, and there was a small crowd, all caps and shawls, standing under it, talking softly. At the top of the police station steps stood Constable Matthews, thumbs hooked in top pockets, stiff with importance.

Gladstone pushed his way to the front. 'Is it true, then?' he was saying. 'Is it true?'

Ned Evans turned with beer on his breath and said, 'Hell aye, boy. Shot him dead, see.' Ned was a South Walian and spoke very quickly. 'Housekeeper comes home, see – and there's Ashton sitting in a chair, the gun on his knees, and the other one on the floor.... Bloody pantomime for you, that is...'

'Shouldn't talk like that,' Gladstone said.

Ned Evans bunched up a big collier's fist. 'Not telling me the way to talk, are you, boy?'

'You haven't the slightest idea what's behind it,' Gladstone said, sticking his ground.

Ned Evans laughed. 'By God, now – is that right?' He turned to the crowd. 'Hey lads, here's Martha's boy – knows all about the *motive* and all, see.'

'Go and sober your mam up,' someone said to Gladstone.

'Oh – be careful now. He's a *great* friend of the

175

Vaughans, that one...' there was a lot of laughter... 'oh, hell, aye – a very great friend.'

Constable Matthews came down the steps, stiff-legged, but quick. 'What's going on, then? All this laughing.'

'Constable,' a beery voice broke out, 'someone here that knows all about it. Knows the *motive*, see.'

There was more laughter.

'Any more of this,' said Constable Matthews, 'and I'll clear the lot of you.... The Super...'

'Missing a bit of *evidence*, you are,' someone said.

'Come on,' I whispered. 'Gladstone, come on.'

I pulled at his arm. He held firm for a while, then gradually backed away with me.

'He's *escaping*,' a voice cried. The laughter rippled across the crowd.

'Now then,' Constable Matthews was saying, 'warned you, haven't I? Clear the lot of you, that's what I'll do.'

I pulled Gladstone back. 'Never mind them,' I said. 'Come on home.' He allowed me to do it, too, but once away from the crowd he shook himself clear of me and walked off into the darkness. I saw his face briefly before he vanished: it was all broken up, like old china.

Meira and Owen were on the doorstep, waiting for me.

'No right to be out with murders going on,' Meira said, and I felt a terrible contempt for her. What did *she* know about it, anyway? And there was Owen launching straight into *his* version, as if he'd been there, as if he understood.... But I stayed up with them a long time just the same, and listened to it all.... Marius on the floor, half his face blown off by the shotgun; Ashton *sleeping* in the chair when the police burst in; a mirror shattered on the wall....

'Bad luck, breaking mirrors,' Meira said. 'Where was that blondie, then? Eirlys Hampson. Was she there?'

I would have stamped off to bed there and then, only I was afraid that the Vaughans would be there, waiting for me as soon as I closed my eyes.

XVI

Porthmawr next day came to a dead stop with the wonder of it. Wherever you looked people stood talking and tut-tutting and glancing up at the sky and doing the shiver that meant someone was walking over their graves. Voices were pitched at low, faces had a funeral set; and there was a tension in the air that was full of what had happened, and what would happen, and fear.

But not for Polly.

She had sent me out for the papers, had examined each report carefully through her magnifying glass, like a lawyer studying a brief. She was Portia, suddenly, precise and careful of speech, and brimming with jurisprudence.

'Hang him, will they?' I asked.

'See that,' she replied, tapping the *Mail*, 'Porthmawr spelt wrong, such ignorance. Never make a mistake with Addis Ababa, do they?'

178

'Hang him, though?'

She placed the glass down carefully and stood, then smoothed down her black dress, then stroked her high, white forehead with the tips of thumb and forefinger. 'We know the procedure, don't we?' she said. 'Monday morning, Magistrates' Court. That's the official appearance for the remand. Then they'll take him away until they have the case ready. Prison, of course. Now – there should be a coroner's inquest, I think.' She looked at the *Family Lawyer* next to the Bible on the sideboard. 'I'll have to look that up....'

'The court will be here – in Porthmawr?'

'Scene of the crime, cariad,' she said, 'won't it be marvellous?'

Oh, poor old boozy Ashton Vaughan, I thought.

'We know what *that* verdict will be, of course. Then will come the Assizes. Judge *and* jury. The black cap.' She mimed it for me. 'The judge passing the sentence. "You shall be taken to the place whence you came..."'

Be quiet, be quiet, I wanted to say, this isn't one of the great murderers, for God's sake. Be quiet.

But Polly's prophecies never materialised. Fate, as Owen said, stepped in. Ashton never got as far as the Assizes, never as far as the Magistrates'. He appeared in court, though, on that Monday morning, and the charge was read out. Super Edwards kept the public out, but of course everyone knew what had gone on.

'How do you plead...?'

I was standing outside the police station with Dewi at the time.

'Guilty, that's what he'll say,' Dewi said. 'I plead guilty but insane....'

179

'Not that,' I protested, 'can't say that.'

'Course he can,' Dewi insisted. 'His brain's pickled in alcohol...'

'But he can't say that.'

'All his nerves have rotted away,' Dewi went on. 'That's the last stage – when it pickles the nerves. Then you're insane.'

Dewi was wrong, too. Ashton Vaughan had appeared before the magistrates that morning, and had been asked the question.

'Got to go to the lavatory,' he'd replied.

The question was asked again, and Ashton had told them his bowels were giving him hell. Then Super Edwards had said, 'Mr Vaughan, we have to know how you plead – guilty or not guilty?' And Ashton, loud and clear, had answered, 'Guilty, you silly bugger. No lawyers by request.'

That was the story we heard that day, and everyone said it had come from Super Edwards himself. Ashton had been remanded in custody – we all had procedure and phraseology right to a T – and he'd been taken, not to a cell to await his escort, but to the lavatory. Ten minutes later they broke the door down when he didn't answer, and they found him sitting there, dead.

'Poison!' Porthmawr cried hopefully, and they were wrong again. Ashton Vaughan had had a heart attack.

Monday was a day to remember. We were surfing along on the waves of tragedy, not sorrowing perhaps, but living at a new pitch of excitement.

'By God, it's like the pictures,' Dewi said.

180

'Like Capel Mawr drama, only better,' Maxie put in.

We walked the town all day, hoping something else would happen. None of us mentioned Gladstone. None of us suggested that we go and see him, either.

On Tuesday the town was still tight-lipped and tragic. Two brothers dead, they whispered, one by his own brother's hand, the other by the hand of fate. The ravens of the hunting Vaughans had come home to roost... that's the kind of thing they were saying. In a prayer meeting at Capel Mawr that day, the Rev A. H. Jones added his voice: 'The mills of God grind slowly,' he said, 'but they grind exceeding small.' It was a quotation that caught on, was repeated by all the Bible-punchers in town, eyes half-closed and all.

By Wednesday, however, the wave of tragedy had hit shore. The jokers were out. 'He died with his pants down,' was a favourite. 'The killer never pulled the chain,' was another. Dewi had them all off pat. 'Know why Ashton bumped off Marius, then? Wouldn't let him have any toilet paper, get it?'

I thought of Gladstone and Eirlys Hampson. 'Shouldn't say things like that,' I said.

'Come to Jesus,' Dewi jeered, so we had a fight.

'Heard this one,' Meira said at dinnertime. 'Old Evans Cymric Dairy – know how *dry* he is, don't you – said it would never have happened, the shooting I mean, if Ashton had taken his working medicine regular. "Should have had his Andrews, missus fech, like the rest of us," he says.'

'Not right,' I said.

'Oh, I don't know,' Meira said. 'Didn't really like the Vaughans, did you?' She giggled. 'Can't help laughing, neither.'

181

And that was true. It was wrong, but you had to laugh. Like the town, I was tickled too – it was no use pretending I wasn't.

'Heard this one down the dole,' Owen said. 'Poem. See if I can remember: "Ashton Vaughan did live on gin, It rotted away his brain: Shot his brother – oh, what a sin, And forgot to pull the chain." Like it, then?'

Meira liked it so much she had the hiccups.

'So there we are,' Rowland Williams said, 'both dead at one fell swoop, and the town wetting its pants laughing. The interesting thing about us is this craving we have for the comic. Anything, we have discovered, at the right time, can produce the belly laugh – and that's their real love, Lew. They'll never admit it, mind; none of us will. We like to think – in the small hours, times like that – of our tragic existence; we like to think of the *nobility* of man. But the frame is so grotesque, so comic, Lew.... What we see in the mirror is so ripe for the big belly laugh, so we let fly with a typhoon of laughter, and the world is doubled up, eyes streaming. He was watching himself in the window of the workshop as he spoke, gauging there his gestures with the chisel. 'In the twentieth century there is no place for *Hamlet*, Lew – follow me, do you?'

'Well, Mr Williams,' I began.

He threw the chisel down. 'What I am saying, boy,' he went on sharply, 'is that we are unwilling, probably by now incapable, of recognising and appreciating the dignity of man. Are you with me?'

I nodded, but he wasn't looking at me.

182

'This laughter is a killer,' he went on, and he was angry now. 'A killer – tell Gladstone Williams that, will you? Tell him to shape his mouth in a grin straight away, tell him quick, Lew, before the howls and screeches drown him.... Oh, by God, he's taking a chance, that boy – never a smile, never a giggle.... You tell him I said this laughing's a killer. Tell him I said that.'

Then, suddenly, and for the first time to my knowledge, Rowland lost his temper. He picked up a mallet from the bench and flung it into the far corner of the workshop. It made a clatter and raised a cloud of dust, and left a silence deep as eternity. Rowland never turned to give me a grin of apology, either – just stood there looking at his reflection in the workshop window. I left him like that.

'Cheated the gallows,' Polly said sorrowfully. 'Have they fixed the inquest, then?'

'Friday – after the funeral.'

'You've got to try and get in – understand? I want a full report – who said what – everything. And you can watch the funeral for me, too. Can't leave Tada, more's the pity.'

Poor old boozy Ashton Vaughan, I thought. Were all the great murderers like him?

Dewi and Maxie and I joined the crowd across the road from the police station on the morning they buried the Vaughans. We were moved along twice by Constable Matthews, but we shuffled back and waited in the sunshine with the rest.

The clock on St Mary's church struck ten, and the first of the coffins came out. Hats came off. All talking stopped.

The coffin went into the first hearse – Marius or Ashton? I wondered. Then came the second coffin, and at that moment I saw Gladstone. He was on the other side of the road, wearing a black suit that looked new to me, a white shirt and a black tie. He was carrying two bunches of flowers. He looked fine – taller, somehow, and distinguished.

I gave Dewi the nudge. 'Gladstone.'

'Going with them by God,' Dewi said, and the crowd murmured as if echoing his words.

As the second coffin was pushed into the other hearse, the Rev A. H. Jones came down the steps with the Vaughans' housekeeper. He helped her into his car and took his place behind the wheel. In the car behind his were a couple of Capel Mawr deacons, and after them Super Edwards and a sergeant in the police car. There was no sign of Eirlys Hampson.

Car doors were closing, engines starting up, but nobody, I felt, looked at anything or anyone but Gladstone. He stepped off the pavement and walked very slowly past the cars to the second hearse. The driver of the hearse came out, then opened the back of the hearse and let Gladstone place one bunch of flowers on the coffin. They walked together to the first hearse. Super Edwards got out of his car and stood by it on the pavement, watching. Gladstone put his other bunch of flowers on the coffin then said something to the driver. They walked back to the second hearse, and Gladstone opened the cab door and squeezed himself in next to one of the bearers. Super Edwards got back in his car, the funeral moved off, and all around me the mouths hung open, but no one was saying a word.

Dewi, Maxie and I, after the last car had gone past, stepped out in the road and watched them until they disappeared around the corner of St Mary's Crescent.

'Let's follow,' Dewi said.

We walked to the corner, then fell into a trot down the hill towards the cemetery. We gave them plenty of time to clear from the entrance before we went in, and even then we kept our distance.

From where we were standing by the trees we could only hear a murmur of what the Rev A. H. Jones was saying; he didn't take long anyway. I was watching Gladstone, so stiff and straight by the open graves, his arms tightly clasped across his chest, his head lowered. It was a clear, sunny morning. Beyond the cemetery wall you could see the mountains, very cool and clean looking.

'Two graves,' Maxie whispered. 'Should have buried them together.'

Dewi turned on him fiercely. 'One of them murdered the other, old fool,' he said.

Then it was all over, and the Rev A. H. Jones was leading them all away, the housekeeper crying on his arm. I saw Super Edwards turn to Gladstone and say something, then Gladstone left the graveside and walked towards the gate. The Super and the sergeant smiled at each other, and whispered: having a joke about Gladstone, I thought.

'I'll give him a whistle,' Dewi said, but Gladstone never turned. He walked on to the gate and we saw him climb into the front of the hearse. He was a stranger to us that day, but even so I wanted to go after him and tell him I'd seen the smile on the Super's face. But I didn't. I stayed there by the trees and watched the two gravediggers get on with their job.

The inquest was at two. I ran over to the police station straight after dinner, knowing full well there was little chance of getting in, but even so I hardly expected the doors to be closed and already a crowd outside.

Dewi and Maxie joined me. 'Been shut for half an hour, them doors,' Dewi said. 'Full house – like Saturday night pictures.'

'Seen Gladstone?'

They shook their heads, and we took up position at the edge of the crowd. The coroner and the police doctor, wearing black bowlers, marched up the steps looking important.

'See them two going in now,' Maxie said, 'police special detectives. Scotland Yard.'

'Gerraway!' Dewi said.

I had no idea how long an inquest took. I wasn't even sure why there should be an inquest at all now that both of them were down the road there in the cemetery. By three o'clock my legs ached with standing, and all the crowd around me had begun to look like birds of prey. Then, shortly after quarter past three by the church clock, the door opened. Constable Matthews came out first, then Gladstone, then Super Edwards.

'Gladstone,' Dewi said. 'Trouble!'

Super Edwards looked angry. He held Gladstone's arm with one hand and pointed down the steps with the other. You didn't need to hear to know that Gladstone was being ordered out.

'Thrown out,' Dewi whispered. 'Like us at the pictures!'

Gladstone came slowly down the steps, shaking his head. Super Edwards and the constable went back inside. The door closed behind them.

'Come on,' Dewi said. 'See what's happened, then.'

We ran across to the police station gate, but the birds of prey were there before us, crowding around Gladstone, yelling their questions. We tried to charge our way through to him, but they were scrum-tight. A loud cheer arose. We backed away to get a better view over their heads, and there was Gladstone pulling himself on to the wall, hanging on to the railings. Oh, God, I almost cried aloud, let him get down.

'Quiet then,' someone shouted, 'quiet for the main man.'

Gladstone nearly slipped off the wall, but managed to hang on. 'I will,' he cried, 'I will tell you what I told them in there.' He made himself more secure on the wall so that he was facing them directly. He looked better now, fine in fact, but I still wanted him to get down.

'Threw you out, did they?' someone cried.

'What's it about then? A bit of quiet, boys, so's he'll tell us....'

Men at the back of the crowd were standing tiptoe and whispering that it was Martha's boy, pal of the Vaughans, bit of a bloody young fool, queer and that.

'I tried to tell them what was behind this tragic business,' Gladstone said, 'but they wouldn't let me speak....'

'Talks nice....'

'Quiet, man. Let him tell us....'

'I tried to tell them why Ashton Vaughan shot his own brother dead. There were mitigating circumstances.'

Someone laughed loud and coarse.

'What's them? Catching, are they?'

'It's about Jupiter,' Gladstone said. 'You don't kill your

187

own brother for no reason. Jupiter – that's what's behind it all.' I cringed inside for him – not because I thought he was wrong, but because I knew they wouldn't understand... and any minute that police station door was going to open.

'Sixteen years ago,' Gladstone went on, 'Jupiter Vaughan was shot dead by his brother Marius Vaughan. It was an accident, though – might have happened to anybody. But Jupiter Vaughan was special. He was young and beautiful.' The same coarse laugh broke across the crowd – not just one laugh, though, but many. 'And this boy's death is what caused Ashton to kill his own brother. They couldn't live with that death, either of them... that's what's behind it....' Gladstone's confidence ebbed, his voice trailed off.

'Sherlock Holmes has spoken,' a voice cried.

'Give him a chance, man,' a deeper voice said.

Gladstone almost slipped off the wall. The sleeve of his jacket was caught in one of the railing spikes and he was trying to free himself. 'Look,' he said, anger coming through, 'these two men, from the day he died – the day Jupiter died – were broken by his death. Not like ordinary men at all...'

'Damn right you are there, boy.'

'They were scarred. They were broken men.' Gladstone cried out above the din.

'Bloody rough, they were, for sure.'

'Aye – and better than us, don't forget.'

'You don't understand – you don't understand. They weren't *bad* men.'

'Not so bloody much.'

'Lording it over us...'

Gladstone was speaking again, but I couldn't hear him now for the noise.

'The Vaughans never loved anybody except themselves,' a voice broke through.

'It was remembering all their lives this terrible thing that had happened to their brother,' Gladstone said in the hush that followed. 'They were broken men, both of them. Ashton didn't mean to kill his brother. It was Jupiter's death lay between them...'

'Get off the wall, nancy boy,' the same voice cried, and I knew then that it was Harry Knock-Knees. 'Talking cock you are.'

I saw Gladstone's mouth open and close, but the noise of the crowd drowned everything. They were urging Harry Knock-Knees to pull Gladstone down, they were telling Gladstone to come down and see Harry off. It was a riot, suddenly. I was watching Gladstone so closely that I never saw the police station door open, never saw Super Edwards and the two constables rush out. The crowd backed away so quickly that we had to turn and run to avoid being trampled. By the time I looked again, Gladstone had been pulled down off the wall, was being marched up the police station steps between the two constables. His tie was off, and there was a rent right to the shoulder in one sleeve of his jacket.

Super Edwards remained at the gate, pointing and waving. 'Everybody move on!' he ordered. 'Causing a public disturbance. Have you no shame?'

'Bloody Hitlers!' someone shouted, and for a moment it looked as if the Super might take them on by himself, but all he did was lower his eyebrows and glare. The crowd knew that glare, knew his memory for faces, too. Slowly they retreated towards us, but I wasn't really watching them. All I could see was the half-closed door of the police station through which Gladstone had been bundled.

'Gone to the cell!' Dewi whispered.

'Have to bail him out now, for sure,' Maxie added. 'Disturbing the peace is worse than bigamy.'

'Shut up,' I yelled at him. 'Close your silly mouth!'

Maxie jumped back as if I'd hit him, but I didn't care about Maxie or his feelings. Inside I was curling up for Gladstone, sick for him almost. Why had he bothered to tell them what he thought, how he felt? Didn't he know, for God's sake, that you had to keep things like that private?

XVII

Super Edwards kept Gladstone in the cell until eight o'clock that night. Gladstone had a talking-to, and a warning, and was told to go home to await farther questioning. By then, of course, all Porthmawr knew about it, and the jokers were out again.

Next day it was worse still. There was Gladstone, hanging on to the police station railings, on the *front* page of all the papers. Even Polly was amused when she wasn't telling me how disappointed she was because I'd failed to get in to the inquest.

'Demonstration at inquest,' she read out. 'Police warn crowd. Disgraceful!' She drummed her fingers on Gladstone's picture. 'Mind you, Lew – they're hushing it up. Any fool can tell that. The powers that be are hushing it up. Where was *she*, for instance? No word about *her*, is there?'

Polly was a dribbling witch, suddenly, crying for blood

like the old crones around the guillotine did in all those pictures I'd seen about the French Revolution. I was wasting my time talking to her.

'Was she there?'

'Never saw her,' I said.

'Well – what *did* you see, then? Only your friend like a monkey on the wall?'

'Gladstone's all right,' I said.

She pulled at her long nose. Was it the light, or something? Had I never seen the spying fox behind her eyes before? 'Wants watching, if you ask me,' she said. 'What did he mean – about Jupiter?'

'It's a theory, that's all.'

'Not right in the head, that boy. With your brains you shouldn't make a friend of someone like that.'

Forcing me to answer, urging me to defend Gladstone and so tell her things. Had she always got me to talk, to tell the tale, in the same way? 'Matter of opinion,' I said. 'He's a brilliant person.'

'Fancy! He'll need to be brilliant, too – all the trouble that's waiting for him.'

'What trouble?'

'Wait and see. You don't think they're going to let him make a laughing stock of himself – getting his name in the paper, and a picture – without...'

'What can they do?' Old curtain shifter, I thought. Old prophet of doom. 'It's none of their business.'

'He's only a boy, and he's got too many crazy notions, don't forget. What did he say, then? Tell me again what you think he was trying to say.'

I looked at the Captain asleep like an enormous child

in his chair. 'Why don't you ask Tada?' I said, and was sorry straight away because it was a blow, and must have been very unexpected, and must have hurt, too.

'I see,' Polly said in a voice out of the North Pole, 'I see. Perhaps we'd better go. We are obviously not in a good mood.' She turned her back on me, picked up the magnifying glass and began to examine the paper again. As I was leaving, she called after me, 'Won't bang the door, will we? *Tada* might wake up and tell me.'

I was four inches tall as I went out, and very angry. I'd seen through Polly, I kept telling myself, but I wasn't really pleased about it.

'Can any man afford to be naked?' Rowland asked. 'That is the question we would have to debate, if we were detached enough to want to debate anything. Can any man, we would ask ourselves, afford to unclothe – no, no, that's a doubtful metaphor – to *unmask* is better. Can any man afford to unmask – to show his face to the world, his real face?'

'You were there, Mr Williams? Never saw you.'

Rowland took another pull at the bottle. 'Among the vulgar and the uninformed, boy. Oh, Gladstone Williams, what an error you made.'

'Shouldn't have done it, should he?' Rowland drunk at this time of year! It was incredible. Only on Armistice Day was he ever on the bottle, and then only on ruby wine, I'd heard. But today the liquid looked lighter, more like whisky.

'You'll excuse me, Lew Morgan, passed matriculation and all set to be a Civil Servant? I *never* offer a drink. It's against my Methodist principles.' He was in his Sunday best, even wore a collar and tie. 'Made an error of judgement, our friend did – possibly an error of taste as well. He has backed, if you will excuse me, a *dying* cause,' Rowland giggled. 'I was near the photographer, you know – that representative of the great British Press – and I jogged his bloody arm, I did! But to no avail, apparently. No – our friend, our mutual friend, has made the faulty assumption that because men have attachments of gristle and skin on either side of their heads, therefore they can hear. And understand. *Fatal* mistake, Lew! The world, let me tell you, is deaf, stone deaf. But, as I said, were we in debate, we would have to ask ourselves only one question – a fundamental question – did I tell you I was a fundamentalist, Lew? A dusty fundamentalist with wood chips in his hair and resin clotting his nostrils – that's what I am... and we would have to ask this question – can any man afford to show himself to the world?' He waved his arms and grinned foolishly, then had to sit down. 'Oh, Gladstone, Gladstone, you haven't a chance – and that's from the man who has debated like hell, but never made the gesture himself. You haven't a chance, boy. That you may be right is not the point at issue – who the hell said right is might? What you must understand is that you are in error, Gladstone. You have shown yourself. And that's the error only the mad make – and you know what they do with the mad, don't you, Gladstone?'

'I'm Lew,' I said.

He looked at me and blinked rapidly. 'So y'are. By God, so y'are.' He had a spell of soundless laughing, then got to his feet and did a jig in the restricted space between his bench and the pile of timber on which he had been sitting. He picked up a mallet and began to beat time to the tune he hummed. 'That's what's wrong with us, Lew – we've no *dance* music.' He nearly fell over as he tried to turn around. 'Today, no work, boy. Know that? It's not November the eleventh, is it? They're not out at the war memorials, are they? I'm not drowning the Somme... but I'll not touch tool or wood just the same. Today shall be for rational debate, nothing more.' He saw himself mirrored in the window and came to a stop. The smile left his face. Then he began to swear. 'Rowland Williams,' he cried, 'you...' and it was all the swearing I knew and many, many more I'd never heard but knew to be swearing by their hardness and viciousness and the spittle forming on his lower lip. God was there and the body, and private parts and the faeces, and sex... obscenity on obscenity, until I thought the timbers of the old workshop oozed filth, and I jumped up and made for the door, afraid.

'Stop, Lew!' he cried. 'Oh, stop, stop...'

'Going to see Gladstone, Mr Williams.'

'But stop! Don't go! Stay, Lew – stay for me to tell you I'm sorry.' He came up to me and placed his rough, horny hands around my ears and rocked me. 'You never heard,' I could hear him saying, 'what can I say to you? Never heard me, did you, Lew? I'm sorry, boy – *sorry*. Oh, God, what can I do?' Then he brought his face close to mine and kissed me on the forehead. I flung myself away from him, so violently that I banged my head against the door. I was dazed for a moment and went down to my knees. I saw Rowland back away from me. 'Oh, Jesus Christ,' he was saying, 'oh, Jesus Christ.' He choked on the words.

I stood up and tried to speak, but my mouth was dry and no words would come out. I wanted to tell him it was all right, that I understood, that I knew he hadn't meant anything wrong, that he was sorry about the swearing... but I couldn't say it. He stood there by the bench, his shoulders shaking, and I couldn't say anything.

Then he seemed to grip himself, to mould himself right again. 'Lew,' he said softly, in his old Sunday-school voice, 'the moral seems to be, don't get drunk, except on Armistice Day.'

'That's right, Mr Williams,' I said, laughing too loud.

He made his face smile. 'Rowland Williams the wit,' he said. 'Old snake-tongued Williams.' He raised the bottle and drank. 'Off to see Gladstone, you said?'

'Think I'll be going, then.'

'Aye – I'm sorry, Lew.'

'It's all right,' I said, too warmly, 'it's all right.'

'Aye – well. Going to see Gladstone, then?'

I opened the door, tried to be slow about it in case he thought I was running away. 'Be going now,' I said.

'Come and tell me what he says, though – everything?' he pleaded.

'All right,' I said, and closed the door behind me before he could start apologising again. It was raining, and I was glad of the freshness of it on my face.

'This morning,' said Gladstone, 'I had Super Edwards for an hour. Said join the Army, boy. A fine life is the Army.'

The four of us had the fire stoked up with driftwood, and we had chips out of paper. Upstairs, the last scream of the evening had been drowned by sleep. Martha, of course, was out.

'Why don't you join the Army, lad?' Gladstone went

196

on, imitating the Super's voice. 'Why, I said, is there going to be a war, Super? Never again, he says – read the papers. Never again. You could join as a boy, he says. It's a good life. Plenty of good discipline. He kept on talking about discipline all the time. Discipline and fresh air. Besides, he says, you want to get away from here. Looking after children isn't for a boy of your age. Not manly...' Gladstone grinned as he lit a Woodbine. 'Martha was here. Ever since she saw my picture in the paper she's been treating me like a film star – until the Super came, that is. Then all she said was that's right, Super – you tell him – lowering the family name like that. The *family name*, think of that! And all he kept saying was discipline is a necessary thing.'

'My Uncle Ted joined the Army,' Dewi said. 'Always talking about spit and bloody polish, he was.'

'I told him I wasn't in agreement with the war machine,' Gladstone went on. 'Told him I was basically a pacifist.' He rubbed his long, thin nose thoughtfully. 'He seemed to go blue when I said that. Then he said he could charge me – disturbing the peace, inciting a mob to violence, interrupting an inquest on dead men... I ought to be ashamed of myself. Had I been carried away, or what? Well, I said, the coroner asked if there was anyone who could throw light on the case, so I got up. He meant the police, the Super said.... But you never mentioned Jupiter, I said.... The Super lost his temper then. Jupiter's been dead and buried these sixteen years, he said. Life isn't a fairy tale – that's what you're making of it. A fairy tale... They'd been to France, I said, they'd seen all that dying, but it was the boy's death that broke them.... They were rough men, he said. And we had a really interesting argument, except that Martha kept interrupting. You can't just say he shot his brother dead, I told him. What do you know about it? he says. What do you know about the law?' Gladstone rolled his chip paper into a ball and threw it in the fire. 'It isn't a question of law, I said. It's just that you ought to account for things. The discussion went to pieces after that. He said join the Army, make a man of you... I said I didn't think the uniform matched my eyes... stuff like that. Very common it was. Write to Wrexham, he said. Gave me the address, too.'

I was horrified. 'Not going to, are you?'

'Not until they come and fetch me...'

'All over town they're talking about you,' I said.

'Let them talk. The Vaughans are in the earth now. Someone's got to speak for them.' He touched the fading bruise on his face. 'I should never have gone up there – only I thought I could help them. *Saint* Gladstone, that's me. I should have known that nobody says thank you for help.'

'What about *her*?' I said.

'Eirlys? I bet they're dissecting her too, aren't they? Poor woman. I expect she was too overcome with grief to show her face.'

It was a rough night outside, the rain sweeping up Lower Hill, but we heard the knocking on the door through it all. Gladstone leapt up and went to the window and moved the blind aside. 'Oh, my God,' he said, 'the Rev A. H. Jones and somebody else...'

Maxie, Dewi and I were at the back door almost before he had finished speaking. Once in the backyard we could scale the wall and be clear and away.

'Lew!' Gladstone called. 'Come back!'

Maxie and Dewi charged past me, one of them knocking over the cinder bucket.

'Can't,' I protested. 'Not my place...'

Gladstone gripped my arm. 'Moral support,' he begged. 'There's *two* of them.'

I let him lead me back to the fireplace, then he went to open the front door. When I next looked up it was into the shining, smiling face of the Rev A. H. Jones. Behind him towered Mrs Meirion-Pughe, long beak twitching as she took in the room.

The Minister bounced straight for me. 'Edward – isn't it?' he cried.

'Lew,' I said.

He slapped his forehead with the palm of his hand, but gently so that he wouldn't upset the line of his wig. 'Of course! Of course! Lew Davies.'

'Morgan,' I said.

'Morgan,' he agreed smoothly, 'of course.' He pinched my arm and said success, bravo, well done, matriculated, many a great man has come from a poor home, many many many a great man, onwards now Llywelyn...

You old comic, I thought, why do you have to talk like that? He bounded past me to the fire and held his hands out to it. 'Thank our dear Lord for a fire on such a dreadful night,' he cried.

Alderman Mrs Meirion-Pughe, with the gesture of the soldiers in the costume films, swung off her cloak and handed it to Gladstone. 'Hang it up, boy,' she ordered. 'A terrible night to be out.'

I looked at her thick, bright-green frock, the rows of

199

yellow beads at her throat, the rubber overshoes on her feet, her noble chin with the immense beak above it... and I was saying comic, comic, comic to myself – and so was Gladstone, for his eyes were shining.

'Do I smell cigarettes?' Mrs Meirion-Pughe cried. 'Not been smoking, have you?'

'It's the children,' Gladstone said. 'They always go through a packet before bed...'

'Boy!' she said in a voice of thunder.

'Softly,' said Gladstone. 'Don't want to wake them up, do we?' He brought a chair for her to sit, but she waved him aside. 'Going to be difficult, A. H.,' she said. 'Told you so, didn't I?'

'Ha, ha,' said the Minister, still holding his hands to the fire.

'A. H., a prayer if you please.'

'Of course,' said the Minister, 'a lovely idea.'

He turned to face us, smiling still, then he clasped his hands and closed his eyes. Mrs Meirion-Pughe immediately fell to her knees. Capel Mawr knew her as a great prayer at all the meetings. She always took a long time at it, and always became very emotional, and wept.

'Our Father,' said the Minister. I looked across at Gladstone. He winked at me then lowered his head. His eyes weren't closed, though. He was watching the broad-shouldered, kneeling woman, and his face looked very sad. 'Guide us in all our ways about the world,' said the Minister. 'Let us always do that which is right in your eyes....' He didn't say anything after that for what seemed a long time, then he said 'Amen'.

Mrs Meirion-Pughe came floundering up to her full

height. Only Gladstone was taller than she, but since he was so thin she seemed to dwarf him, too. 'Very short, A. H.,' she said, 'But down to business, eh?'

'Ha, ha,' said the Minister. 'Yes, of course.' And he sat on the chair nearest the fire. He held his hands out to the blaze again and said what a night, what a dreadful herald of a long winter.

Mrs Meirion-Pughe sniffed very loudly, then fixed her eyes on me. 'You,' she said, 'are in the way.' She was well known for her directness. 'Don't live here, do you?' Close to, like this, I could see the thin, black moustache running across her upper lip. It fascinated me.

'Matriculated,' the Minister said to the fire. 'A brilliant brain.'

'Why don't you run along and see if your mother wants you?' Mrs Meirion-Pughe suggested. 'We have important things to discuss.'

'Then Lew will have to stay,' Gladstone broke in. 'If anybody likes a discussion, it's Lew. He's got a flair for it – especially on theological themes.'

'Cut along, boy,' Mrs Meirion-Pughe commanded.

'You should hear him on the Prophet Jeremiah,' Gladstone went on. 'And I've always thought he has a real feeling for the Song of Songs, which is the "Song of Solomon".'

Mrs Meirion-Pughe swung round on him. 'You mind your tongue, boy,' she said very fiercely, but very quietly.

'Sorry,' Gladstone said, 'thought you'd come over for a little discussion on such matters.'

'We'll tell you why we've come – soon enough. As soon as this little boy has gone home to his mother.'

201

'Matriculated,' the Minister said to the fire, 'done *very* well.'

'And he's not going home,' Gladstone said flatly. 'Lew stays. Anything you have to say to me can be said in front of him. He's the soul of discretion. In fact, he was christened Lew Discretion Morgan – though he rarely uses his middle name, for reasons that will no doubt be obvi...'

'Enough!' Mrs Meirion-Pughe roared. 'Quite enough of your cheek!' Her nose twitched angrily. 'So – you do realise, Gladstone Williams, that it is time someone spoke to you?'

'I only assumed you'd come to talk,' Gladstone said. 'I could be wrong. After all – neither of you has been farther than the doorstep before...'

Mrs Meirion-Pughe reared up, almost the way swans do, except that swans are more graceful. '*Watch your tongue*, boy,' she warned in a hollow voice. 'That tongue of yours will get you into serious trouble...'

'Impossible to see everybody,' the Minister protested. 'Many sheep in my flock...'

'How true,' Gladstone said, and I feared for him. These two weren't like Gwynfor Roberts' mother and father up there on the Hill.

'Beautifully put, A. H.,' said Mrs Meirion-Pughe, but there was a bit of irony creeping up on her, too, when she added, 'Perhaps you'd like me to begin?'

'Well – perhaps – yes.' The Minister gave her a little wave.

'I know,' Gladstone said, 'you've come to give me a row because I got up at the inquest, because I spoke to the crowd from off the police station wall, and because I got my picture in the paper. Is that right?'

'Not a row,' the Minister broke in. 'No, no – we are not the police force, are we, Mrs Meirion-Pughe?'

'The police force came this morning,' Gladstone said. 'They suggested the British Army as a way to salvation. What do you recommend?'

Oh, careful, careful, I thought.

'Gladstone,' said the Minister reprovingly.

'Gladstone Williams!' barked Mrs Meirion-Pughe.

Ever since that night at the Band of Hope when Gladstone had done his sermon on the Parable of the Sower – using real grass seed which he cast over the children – Mrs Meirion-Pughe had watched him very carefully.

'Blasphemer!' she cried. 'Sacrilegious fool! Son of darkness! Wicked, wicked boy!'

'Mrs Meirion-Pughe,' the Minister protested, 'steady!' Then he spoke to Gladstone, but his eyes were fearfully on the woman all the time. 'We've come for a chat – just a little chat, that's all...'

'Come to tell him in the sight of God to mend his ways,' she broke in harshly. 'Come to tell him to have no farther association with men of evil character, men who can pervert the mind, twist the soul...'

'Dead men,' Gladstone said.

Mrs Meirion-Pughe had started to froth a little at the mouth. 'One of them,' she cried in a strange, high voice, 'dead by his own brother's hand. The other one a murderer. Does that mean nothing to you?'

'A dead murderer,' Gladstone said.

Mrs Meirion-Pughe leaned forward, her face very close to Gladstone's. 'Death excuses everything, is that right? You silly boy! You've spent the summer in the company of murderers! You've made yourself a party to their evil ways. You've been their servant, their tool – the tool of sinful men. They've *used* you! And now you've brought shame on your Chapel by making an *exhibition* of yourself – walking at their funeral, interrupting the processes of the law, *posing* for that picture...'

'That,' Gladstone said flatly, 'I didn't do...'

'Posed for it,' she insisted. 'Trying to be smart. You always try to be so smart, don't you? Foolish, foolish boy!' Her voice dropped now to a curious, flat monotone, her eyes were closed, and the saliva ran from the corners of her mouth. 'Without shame,' she went on, 'corrupt, without fundamental decency. You have chosen the ways of darkness – scoffer, blasphemer, sinner that you are.... Your mind is warped....'

'Steady now, Mrs Meirion-Pughe,' the Minister said. 'Oh, steady, steady...'

I looked at Gladstone as she continued. Her long beak was barely six inches from his averted face. 'It's a stony road you're on,' she said, 'and all is black around you.' Gladstone's mouth was clenched tight. 'The night is dark and you are far from home – and there is nothing, nothing to guide you, except for one, small light up there on the hill.... Do you see it, foolish boy? Answer me – do you see it?' I knew by Gladstone's eyes, by the movement of muscle in his throat, that he was inwardly convulsed with laughter. 'The one solitary light that can save you....' Her hand came up in a dramatic wave, and Gladstone had to move his head to avoid it.... 'See it? See it now? That one small light on the hill? Do you know what it is? Do you, foolish boy? Answer me! Answer!'

Gladstone swallowed hard. 'I didn't pose for the picture,' he said, and had to clamp his mouth tight again to stop the laughter.

Mrs Meirion-Pughe stepped back from him. 'Well, you *stupid* boy! You silly, stupid boy,' she said. 'You must be blind!'

'Not blind,' Gladstone said. 'Simply in the kitchen of our house, with the electric burning up the meter.... And stop calling me stupid....'

Mrs Meirion-Pughe swung round on the Minister. 'Speak to him,' she commanded. 'Can't you see how far gone he is?'

The Rev A. H. Jones clasped and unclasped his hands, got up and sat down again. 'Well – yes. Yes. Ha, ha!'

Mrs Meirion-Pughe glared at him, then advanced towards Gladstone again. 'Since no one else will speak to you, Gladstone Williams, then I shall. Answer me a few simple questions, please. Now – do you know the difference between Right and Wrong? Do you?'

Gladstone looked bewildered. 'On a Sunday-school level, do you mean? I mean, are we talking about basic right and wrong, or what is right and wrong for the world around us?'

'Did you hear that?' Mrs Meirion-Pughe flung the question at the Minister. 'Boy,' she said, 'boy – answer me this. You do know that there is Good and Bad in the world, don't you?'

Gladstone nodded very emphatically.

'And you realise that in the words of our Lord Jesus Christ we are told to cast aside the Bad and clasp our arms tight around the Good?' She hugged herself to illustrate the point.

'Mrs Meirion-Pughe,' Gladstone said gently, 'they were both good men. I only spoke up at the inquest...'

'Good men?' she cried. 'A murderer! Is a murderer a good man, boy?'

Gladstone sighed. 'It's possible...'

Mrs Meirion-Pughe seemed to do a kind of dance of rage. 'What are you saying, boy? You've been baptised, haven't you? Been received in as a full member of the House of God? Been taught in Sunday school, if nowhere else, that we must live by the principles He laid down, He who died for us....'

'The pity of it,' Gladstone said. He was very serious now. 'That is the pity of it.... The poor man...'

Mrs Meirion-Pughe flailed her arms. She was as near to being out of control as she ever would be. 'What did you say?' she cried in a voice that wasn't far off a scream.

'Softly, if you please,' Gladstone said. 'You'll waken the children.'

'Blasphemy!' she cried out.

'No, no, no,' said Gladstone. 'It's just that you're approaching things wrongly...'

She leapt at him and seized him by the shoulders. 'Blasphemer!' she cried. Her mouth was wet with spit, and the spit came as she talked, too. Her eyes were wide and glaring, like the eyes in the Boris Karloff films at the Palace. I felt I ought to be afraid, but this wasn't the pictures: this was real.

'Where is your mother?' she cried.

'Stop it,' Gladstone said. 'Stop it!' She was a powerful woman, and was rocking him none too gently.

'Where is your mother?'

'Steady, steady,' the Rev A. H. Jones said.

'At the Harp, waiting on,' said Gladstone. 'Give over!'

'Waiting on!' Mrs Meirion-Pughe shrieked. 'Consorting with drunken, lustful men!'

'Quite so,' Gladstone said. 'She's a very sensitive person who needs love.... Now, give over!'

He shook her hands away. '*You* need beating,' she said. 'You need beating until you are senseless. The Evil needs beating out of you!' She charged back at him, then with a terrible swiftness struck him across the cheek. It wasn't a hard blow, but it was loud.

The Minister leapt up. 'Mrs Meirion-Pughe,' he called. He pulled her away from Gladstone. 'What are you doing, my dear woman? You mustn't strike the boy.'

She was beyond control. 'Must beat the Evil out of him,' she was saying. 'Beat him and pray for him... I'll pray for him. That's what I'll do. I'll pray. She fell to her knees, hands clasped, head lowered.

The Rev A. H. Jones looked down at her, and the distaste was obvious in his face. 'Mrs Meirion-Pughe,' he said softly, but very distinctly, 'get up, woman!'

Her head snapped back so sharply that her hat fell off. She unclasped her hands, then picked up her hat. With a terrible, menacing slowness she got to her feet, and with the stiffness of a soldier turned to face the Minister. Her chin stood out, hard, rock-like, and above it the long beak quivered, examining the air.

'Were you speaking to me, A. H.?' she asked in a frozen voice.

The Minister's hands fluttered. 'Now, now, Mrs Meirion-Pughe, please...' He was trying to take her arm –

he always liked holding on to people when he talked to them – but she was rigid and unyielding.

'I asked you a question,' she said. 'Were you speaking to me?'

The Rev A. H. Jones was hopping nervously from foot to foot. 'I did – ha, ha – well, I did speak to you, certainly...'

'In *that* tone of voice?' She was a good two feet taller than him, and she hung over him, somehow, as if preparing for the pounce. 'Whilst you have been *warming* your hands at the fire I have been doing your work.'

'I was going to...' the Minister mumbled.

'Exactly!' she cried. 'Going to. But *when*? Tell me *when*?'

'Now then, Mrs Meirion-Pughe, ha, ha,' was all he could say.

'I saw it as our duty,' she went on, 'to come here on this dreadful night to try and show this misguided youth – get me my cloak, Gladstone Williams – point out the path of righteousness'

'Quite so, Mrs Meirion-Pughe. I was going...'

'But what *did* you do?' she went on, and it wasn't really a question at all. 'You made yourself comfortable. We can be *too* comfortable, can't we?' She snatched her cloak from Gladstone's hands and swung it over her shoulders. 'You warmed yourself by the fire,' she said as she rapidly buttoned the cloak all the way down: it nearly reached the floor. 'Warmed yourself,' she said again as she stamped to the door. 'What does self-denial mean, I wonder?' Then, before she went on, she delivered the parting shot. 'I shall see you again, my boy.' This was to Gladstone, but she used exactly the same tone when she said to the Minister, 'I shall call a meeting of the deacons in the morning. I shall make a full report.'

As the door closed, the Minister sat down with a thump. He remained there for some time without speaking, his hands tightly clenched in his lap. Gladstone and I looked at each other: we were both sorry for him.

'Cup of tea?' Gladstone suggested, but the Minister was too stunned to hear.

Then, suddenly, he was on his feet. 'I must go,' he said as he clamped his hat on his head. He bounced across the room to the door. 'Think about it, Gladstone. Think about what the good lady said,' he cried. He kept his back to us. 'I must go.' He opened the door. 'A terrible night, terrible...' And he was off into the street.

Gladstone went to the door and closed it. When he came back to the fire he had a smile on his face which I took to mean that we were going to discuss his visitors.

'She's a religious maniac,' I said.

He stirred the fire thoughtfully. 'People like that,' he said.

'And *he* was scared.'

'Lew,' Gladstone said firmly, 'tell you what – let's not speak about what happened to anyone, eh? I mean – well, let's forget about it, keep it to ourselves, shall we?'

I nodded, but all the same I resented the way he'd said it. I felt much younger than him at that moment, and uncomfortable – as if it was my duty, as well, to go out and leave him alone.

XVIII

Sunday night, the last night of the holiday that old Evans Thomas had ushered in with a death.

All week I had seen nothing of Gladstone, but Meira had told me often enough that he was being visited by the deacons. 'No good, that boy. Don't you be seeing him any more, understand? Don't want those deacons and that come-to-Jesus woman all over my kitchen.' I hadn't carried the tale about the Rev A. H. Jones and Mrs Meirion-Pughe home, although I knew that the holy falling out would have been hot news. But since they were on about Gladstone all the time, and how a County School boy with a matriculation certificate to his credit and everything shouldn't associate with a funny one like that, I kept it to myself. Besides, wasn't Mrs Meirion-Pughe just a demented old woman, and the Minister soft as sponge – and didn't I want to be like Gladstone and feel sorry for them?

On that Sunday night I recognised his knock and was out with him on Lower Hill before Meira and Owen could start their objections.

'Let us have a cold walk in what has become an icy town – or are you afraid of being seen in my company?'

'Don't be bloody silly,' I said.

'Some fresh air, then – it's been all *hot* air recently. Terribly fatiguing, you know.'

He looked tired, too. There were dark shadows under his eyes, and a rash of pimples had sprung up along his cheeks, and there was a desperate gaiety about him.

'Still bloody, and more or less unbowed as well,' he said, 'though I'm beginning to wonder what *part* of the Square they'll burn me on.'

Rapidly we walked the town. Porthmawr without the visitors had shrunk already to winter size, and was quieter than falling snow. Out towards the beach everything was grey, even the gulls.

'My little grey home in the west of Wales,' said Gladstone. 'How I do love thee – in spite of what you are. Lew – it's been a bloody procession. All the Big Noises from the Big Seat, all dead comic in a sad sort of way, and they've just discovered the existence of me. It's a Crusade, Lew. Did you ever think how the Heathen felt? Did anyone? All those people on their white chargers, with red crosses blazing on their shields, coming for you... and me on a black donkey – a black donkey with a limp, and only my sense of humour as a spear. And my sense of humour is rusting away, mate – getting blunt as hell.'

We walked over the dunes and on to the beach. There was a smell of coming winter everywhere; firm wet sand

211

and no footprints. The sea was the grey of dark ashes. We threw stones at it.

'Hypocrisy,' said Gladstone, 'fraud and deceit and humbug. They've got to be very special words for me. Hypocrisy – my cunning foe. Did I tell you they've bought Martha? A few bob and a loaf of bread and a packet of tea – and she's talking of starting Chapel again. Still gets out every night, though. Imagine the inner struggle in her breast, Lew. Gin or Genesis? Oh, it's a black and comic world, all right.'

We walked along at the sea's edge. We were the last men, I thought. Only us and the gulls were left. The bombardment had been and gone; the bombers out of the newsreels had circled and dropped their burden. Only us.

'I've had the good doctor, too,' Gladstone was saying. 'Dr Gwynn of the hairy hands. He says things like if there wasn't any Christ it would be necessary to invent one. Then he tells me he's adapted that from a famous Frenchman's famous saying. A twister, Lew... religion and Jesus Christ are a necessary safety valve – that's what he says. Good psychology, Lew... when you think of it, I've got quite a wide choice: I can be hysterical like Mrs Meirion-Pughe, or I can be psychological like Dr Gwynn. And no matter which I choose – they all lead to the right road.' He flung a stone viciously out to sea, and wrenched his shoulder – which made him smile. 'Tell you what, Lew, let's go and look at the old *Moonbeam*, shall we?'

We walked back across the beach and on to the mud where the old boat lay. She was much as we had left her, except that the cabin door had gone. 'How long is it, Lew, since he came aboard that day – breathing seven kinds of beer over us? Oh, by God, it's the Vaughans they always come back to... Old Abraham Evans even asked me how much money I'd got out of them. "You never did it for nothing," he says, and if he hadn't been so old I'd have thrown him out.' He sat on the edge of the bunk and tapped his heels on the floor. 'Came in through that door, a tall, wrecked man in tweeds, straight from every bar in the world and crying out for pity...'

I felt uneasy down there in the gloom of the cabin. 'Go on deck, shall we?' I said.

'I've got a better plan,' he said. 'Let's go and see Eirlys.'

'*Now*?' I said. 'Eirlys Hampson.' I felt my knees go weak. It was all wrong, what he was suggesting. One of those wrong things he came up with now and then – like talking to those men outside the police station, like wearing a Panama hat, like telling the Sunday school that the missionaries ought to stay at home – wrong like that, yet not wrong at all really, except that by the act you revealed yourself. 'I can't,' I said. 'I definitely can't.'

But ten minutes later, when it was dark, I was standing with him at the door of Eirlys' shop, and he had his finger on the bell.

She came to the door straight away, and although I hung back a bit I could smell her powder and scent, was caught instantly by her laugh. 'Two men!' she said. 'In you come quick, before anyone sees you and gives me a worse name than I've got already. Straight up you go!' Her giggles ushered us up the stairs. 'On Sunday night, too,' she said.

Above the shop there was a smart, bright room. Everything in it looked new – the couch and two chairs, the

213

big wireless purring out dance music, the ornaments along the mantelpiece, the polished table which held a vase full of shining roses: polished and rounded and smooth, everything. She had a bright-eyed budgie in a fancy cage, and he looked new, too. 'Sit you down,' she cried, 'don't stand about looking awkward.' She covered the budgie's cage with a cloth that had the same pattern as the curtains. 'Always cover him up when gentlemen come to call,' she said, laughing still. I sat down nervously. The cushion was of velvet and whistled under me.

'Hear the whistle?' she said. 'Special those. Full of air, see. You want to see some of the faces of the people who've sat on *them* for the first time.' She switched off the wireless and looked at herself in the oval mirror above the fireplace. 'Bet I look a sight, don't I? Caught me on the hop, you did. Just out of the bath! Good job I *was* out, though – else I'd have had to come down in a towel!' Her laughter filled the room. Gladstone made his face into a smile, and I did the same. Eirlys didn't look hollow-eyed, or ravaged by grief, or anything. She was wearing a dress with red flowers on it, and the smell of her powder and scent was everywhere. She had a red, permanent smile on her beautiful mouth, and already I felt we were tramps, and out of place, and was worried in case she was laughing at us.

'What's Lew Morgan looking at, then?' she demanded. 'Got a spot on my nose, have I?'

I blushed. She looked at me so directly, so wide-eyed. 'No,' I said.

'Right, then – just keep your eyes to yourself,' she said – said it with a big smile. 'Poor old me,' she went on, 'all alone with the *News of the World*, I was. All alone and in the doldrums.' She rolled her eyes at us. 'When I was a little girl, nobody seemed to move all day Sunday. Just ate and sat still as frogs... and I feel the same today – as if moving's all wrong.' She held out a packet of cigarettes. 'Have a fag, shall we? Go on – it's all right.'

We shook our heads.

'You have a puff, don't you?' she insisted. 'Go on – let me lead you down the primrose path.'

Gladstone took one, but I went on saying no. I was sure I'd make a mess of it, anyway – drop ash on the carpet, even be sick....

'Very charming room you have here,' Gladstone remarked in his high-class voice. I squirmed for him, especially when she replied, 'By jove, old thing, you're right,' in exactly the same voice.

She sat back on her chair and pulled her legs up under her and showed a lot of silk stocking. I tried, but I couldn't keep my eyes off her legs. She rested her head back and showed a wide, plump throat, the powder making lines on it. 'Three years,' she said to the ceiling. 'That's how long I've been back in this hole. Ever since old Auntie died. Sometimes I think I'll sell up and get back to Manchester.' A quick look at us. 'Ever been?'

'We've not been anywhere,' said Gladstone. 'Have we, Lew?'

'Plenty of life there,' she went on. 'Nobody watching you all the time, either.... Know anybody anxious for a ladies' clothes shop going cheap?'

Rounded and smooth and clean-looking, yet there was something blowsy about her too, something that Meira

215

would call common. Little things – the way she was sitting, the cast of her mouth sometimes, her hand holding the cigarette, this laughing all the time – added up and made her a painted doll; but she was still beautiful to me. I couldn't stop looking at her.

'Get clean away from this hole,' she was saying. 'It's a dead man's town, that's all.'

I saw Gladstone stiffen, the way you do when you've felt a sharp pain. I thought he was going to say something, but he only glanced at me and brought the cigarette up to his mouth.

'A dump. Ever noticed the way they open doors, here? Just enough to sneak in and sneak out again without letting in too much fresh air.' She laughed, then sat up and stubbed out her cigarette and smiled. 'You'll know all about *that*, won't you, Gladstone Williams?'

'I went to the funeral,' Gladstone said calmly. 'I said my piece...'

She giggled. 'I know, boy. Always knew you'd make a name for yourself. Picture in the paper and all...'

'Didn't do it for that...'

'I know – but there you were in the front page. Oh – I *did* laugh.' She hesitated. 'I was pleased – that's why I laughed. Anything to shake this lot up, eh? Had an old cow in the shop yesterday morning, and you know what she said to me? "Not in mourning, then?" – that's what! Oh, I had her out in the street before she could turn round, I can tell you. Told her to bugger off – excuse my French! Oh, yes – I know how narrow-minded they can be, too.'

'That's *awful*,' Gladstone said with real feeling. 'Dreadful...'

'You've not to bother,' she said with a laugh as she settled herself back again. 'And don't *you* bother, either. They'll have you dancing up and down like a puppet on a string, if you do.'

'Not me,' Gladstone said quietly. 'They won't have me dancing...'

She laughed. 'I should think not, but mind how you go all the same. Those Vaughans weren't worth it...'

She carried on talking after she'd said that, and I wasn't quite sure if I'd heard her right. Neither was Gladstone: he turned to me, making a silent appeal, but she was looking at me then, and all I could do was nod.

'You know, I'm glad you came,' she was saying. 'Really am. I wanted to have a chat with someone – not just anyone, mind – a girl's got to be careful in this little room... oh, God, yes. But – we were all associated with the Vaughans, weren't we?' She kept on smiling as she talked. 'You might say only us really knew much about them... and if I was to tell somebody all I know, they'd only start talking like that cow in the shop, start saying sour grapes... that kind of thing. You know how people are, don't you?'

'We didn't come to pry into your affairs,' said Gladstone.

She giggled. 'I know. I know. We've been in league, you and me, ever since I let old whatsisname have it with the milk jug – that right?'

I remembered the milk flowing along the bald head, and started to like her again.

'I don't mind if you tell everybody what I'm going to tell you,' she said. 'Don't care. Don't give a damn for them...'

'Is it about Jupiter?' Gladstone broke in.

'It's about a lot of things,' she said. 'You've been doing some talking about Jupiter, haven't you. Well – I'll have a word with you about that in a minute. First of all just you guess how much money Marius got out of me. Out of me, don't forget – and I'm not a simple young girl any more. Go on – just you guess.'

I kept my eyes on the budgie's cage. This wasn't at all what I expected, and I daren't look to see how Gladstone was taking it.

He laughed. 'Well, of course, Lew and I don't know anything about money. Never had any, have we, Lew?'

'Three hundred,' she said with a giggle. 'Close on three hundred pound.' She sat up quickly and clapped a hand over her knee. 'Oh, my God, a ladder,' she said, and lifted her skirt up and examined her stocking, dabbing at it. I looked away, embarrassed. 'They were terrible people,' she went on. 'You thought you were doing them a good turn by getting old Ashton to go back, weren't you? Ever ask yourself why Marius wanted him back all of a sudden?' She licked her finger and dabbed away at her stocking. 'He was broke, that's why. Ashton had his allowance still, and little Eirlys wasn't forking out any more. So – let's have Ashton back, let's have something coming in... that was the motto.' She covered her legs. 'Oh – beg pardon, gentlemen. I forgot you were watching.' She gave us a big smile and rolled her eyes at us. 'Marius Vaughan got me for three hundred,' she went on, 'and when he saw there wasn't any more – I'd seen the light, I can tell you – he got working on Ashton....'

'It's an interesting theory,' Gladstone said.

Eirlys looked at him steadily. 'The *truth*, that's what.

218

Listen, Gladstone Williams, you've been letting go with some theories, too, haven't you? Who told you all that stuff about Jupiter? Ashton, was it?'

There was a spring in my stomach that was steadily getting tighter. I looked at Gladstone: his face was pale as alabaster, and might crack, I thought – crack and crumble at any moment. Did she not see that?

'Did Ashton tell you when he was drunk?'

'No,' Gladstone said stiffly, 'I worked it out.... You could tell, anyway. Just being in their company you could tell...'

'Tell what?'

Gladstone shifted uneasily on his seat. 'That it was Jupiter's death made them the way they were. They weren't angels...'

'You can say *that* again,' she said with a laugh. 'My God, you can say that.' She lit another cigarette. 'Listen – you watch your step, young man. You've got some of this all wrong. Now – I don't mind you annoying the stuffed shirts of this town. Oh, no. But you've got some of it wrong...'

'Very likely. Can't know everything about them...'

'Listen.' She inhaled deeply before she went on. 'Ever asked yourself who killed Jupiter?'

'That's not the point...'

'Just you ask yourself, though.' She looked at me. 'Lew Morgan, here's a question for a bright lad. Who killed Jupiter Vaughan? Go on, tell me.'

I was cornered, and I hated her. 'I don't know,' I said.

'Course you know. Who do people say killed Jupiter, then?'

'Marius, I suppose,' I said. Did she have to keep on

219

smiling like that? Was she blind, or something? Couldn't she see Gladstone's face.

She clicked finger and thumb at me. 'Wrong,' she said. 'And this is the truth. Got it from the party concerned himself – and he loved talking about himself, I can tell you.' She paused deliberately and looked, wide-eyed, at each of us in turn. 'It was *Ashton*,' she said. 'Poor old Ashton, boozed up, went and shot his brother dead. But d'you know what Marius did? He took the blame...'

'Protecting his brother,' Gladstone broke in.

'What for? Why protect him? It was an accident – that's what everybody'd say. Why protect him? Why take the blame?'

'Doesn't alter anything, anyway,' Gladstone said quietly.

'Doesn't alter?' she cried, all exaggerated surprise. 'Listen – don't you see what Marius Vaughan really was? He was *mental*. Wanted to be everything. Old Ashton wasn't *worthy* enough to take the blame for shooting his brother. Oh, dear me no. He was a soak, a hopeless soak. And Marius wanted to be *everything*...' She went on like that, and she should have been screaming it out, her hair down over her face, and sweating... But she never even raised her voice, never stopped talking through a smile.

'He was protecting Ashton,' Gladstone said.

'*Killing* Ashton, you mean,' she replied. 'That's what he did.... Oh, I know what they tell you. Don't speak ill of the dead. All that kind of thing. But you really should know about those two. They were the roughest going, both of them.... Well, maybe Ashton, being a boozer, couldn't help it, but that other one – in a class by himself, he was....'

I was listening for Gladstone's heavy breathing,

watching the words bite into him.... On and on, she went:
I wasn't even clear about what she was saying any more.

'Straight from the horse's mouth... take it for fact.... Bet
you've never heard anything queerer than that, have you?
Wanting to take the blame.... He even wanted to be hurt....'

And smiling still, and quiet-voiced, and laughing – like
someone describing something comic at the pictures....
Can't you see him? I wanted to cry out. Don't you know
what you're doing to him?

'...Marius made Ashton a hopeless case. You can see
that, can't you.' She gave a little girlish laugh. 'Don't ask
me why. I'm only a woman. Don't ask *me* to fathom these
things out... but it was war between them since they were
small, and Jupiter was just something else to quarrel
over... I mean, imagine quarrelling over who shot him!
That's what I call mental, that is... I told the police, you
know. They came before the inquest, and I told them. And
you know what else I told them?' There was a knocking at
the back of the house as she spoke. She heard it too: she
glanced at the clock on the mantelpiece, pursed up her
mouth, then smiled. 'I told them that Ashton very likely
had said no about the money. I even told them I thought
Marius had probably *dared* Ashton to shoot him.' She
rolled her eyes and giggled. 'And he did!'

For the first time, at that moment, she saw Gladstone's
face. 'Hey, *love*,' she cried, 'whatever's the matter? You're
the colour of paper, honestly.' She leaned forward and put
her hand on his knee. 'Not going to be sick, are you?'

'I'm all right,' Gladstone said.

'Hey – I've not up*set* you, have I? Look – I was only
telling you the real truth in case you got yourself in big

221

trouble. If you made any more speeches and that, I mean.' She reached out to touch his face but he drew back. 'Don't take it to heart,' she said. 'They weren't worth it, either of them. Look – it cost me *three hundred* to find out.' She tried to laugh, but it wasn't a great success. She was uneasy now. 'Hey – you're all right, aren't you, love?'

There was a dead silence. We heard the knocking again.

My tongue was dry but I managed to say, 'Someone there.'

'It can wait,' she said. 'Look, Gladstone, I thought we were chums...'

He was forcing himself to recover, even managed a strained laugh before he said, 'We're friends still. It was only that I thought you loved him.' He said it in his high-class voice, too – and that only made her roll her eyes and giggle again. 'We had a *business* arrangement!' she said. She put her hands on her breasts and held them there. 'That's all we had, *honest*...' She even fluttered her eyelashes.

Gladstone got up. 'I think we'll go now...'

I was at the door in a flash. 'Listen...' she said. She was on her feet too, rubbing her hands up and down her thighs. 'Listen...'

'You've got a visitor,' Gladstone said.

'Oh, look – listen – come round again and have a chat about it, will you?'

Gladstone bowed to her. 'With pleasure. We'll come – some time.'

'I mean – I've en*joyed* talking to you.'

'Been a pleasure...'

'You're all right? Really?'

'Right as rain,' he said. Then he overdid it by bowing

again which made her clap her hands to her mouth.

'Honestly,' she said. 'I don't know...'

'Good night,' he said and came slowly to the door, but once through it he was down the stairs in leaps, and was fumbling at the shop door. I ran after him, Eirlys crying out behind me. A box tripped me up, and by the time I reached the street there was no sign of him.

A fine drizzle was falling. I searched around for him, and found him eventually under a gas lamp on Harbour View, letting the rain fall on his face. 'My dear old chap,' he said, 'old boy, dear old bean – I've just been sick.' Then he began to laugh, but it wasn't really laughing at all.

XIX

I went back to school, and they said you've done well, Morgan, well done my boy, but don't let it get to your head now, and no slacking off, the sixth form is a big jump, a great big jump, we must stick to it, mustn't we? And I said yessir, yesmiss, and thought all the time about Gladstone under that lamp, about Eirlys Hampson who had broken him with a giggle and a flood of talk.

Yet, once school was over, I came home to tea and did the keen schoolboy act for Meira. I didn't go to see how he was; so the first news came from Dewi and Maxie.

'Paralysed!' Maxie said, hopping up and down on the pavement in his excitement.

'Don't be bloody stupid,' Dewi told him. 'Just lies there,' he said to me. 'Lies there on the sofa as if he's fast asleep...'

'In a trance then,' Maxie said.

I stepped out on the pavement and closed our door behind me. 'All right last night...'

'It's like he's gone to sleep,' Dewi said. 'Like a mental collapse.'

That angered me. 'What are you, then? A bloody doctor?'

'That's my theory,' Dewi said evenly. 'His nerves have collapsed.'

'Bloody rubbish,' I said, and buttoned up my new blazer and marched off down Lower Hill towards Gladstone's. Paralysed! In a trance! Oh, God, I thought, is Dewi right?

We reached Gladstone's door as the Rev A. H. Jones and Abraham Evans and Dr Gwynn were leaving. I held back, but they were around me in no time. 'My dear boy,' said the Minister. 'Know him, don't you?' he said to the others. 'My dear boy – Lew Davies...'

'Morgan.'

'Of course. We were only talking about you. Really brilliant,' he explained to the other two. 'Lives on *this street*.'

Dr Gwynn took over. 'You are a friend of this – unfortunate boy?' Dr Gwynn was all jowls and rimless glasses. He had a strong South Wales accent, and I had heard that his name had once been Jones, but he'd changed it to Gwynn because Jones was so common sounding. 'You are a friend of Gladstone Williams, boy?'

'What's the matter with him?' I said.

Dr Gwynn put a hairy hand on my shoulder and looked up at the grey skies for an answer. 'Shock,' he said.

'Too many bothering him,' said Dewi behind me. 'Too many busybodies.'

225

'What did that boy say?' Dr Gwynn growled.

'Ask him to help,' said Abraham Evans through his white moustache. 'Close friends. Bring him round...'

'Boy,' said Dr Gwynn, 'we want you to go in there and talk to him.'

'Talk to him,' said Abraham Evans.

'Yes, talk to him,' said the Minister.

'A little prayer, too,' Abraham Evans suggested.

'Psychological factors,' boomed the doctor. 'You may be able to reach him, bring him round.'

'Shock him back, eh, Doctor?' said Abraham Evans.

'No shock,' commanded the doctor, 'on no account, remember... factors... deep rooted... I want to know what he says when he awakes, remember...'

I shook his hand off my shoulder. Three crows, I thought, grotesque old crows, black-suited, black-hatted. I wasn't going to tell them anything, ever. I tried to push past the doctor, but he had once played rugby and his natural instinct was to push back. I made myself taller and looked him straight in his glasses and said, 'Get out of the way...'

'Tell them to piss off,' Dewi whispered behind me.

Dr Gwynn held me for a moment to show how strong he was, then he stepped aside. Dewi opened the door of Gladstone's house and in we went. 'County School,' they said, 'manners, manners...' Dewi banged the door in their faces. We leaned against it, the three of us, and listened to their protests. Then Dr Gwynn boomed above the rest, 'Might do the trick, friends. Yes – might do the trick. And that boy will tell us...'

I looked at Dewi's scarred face. 'Never in this bloody life,' I said.

We went into the kitchen, Dewi and Maxie making a show of stepping aside to let me go first. I didn't know what to expect, and for a moment in my excitement saw nothing. But there were the children, crouched together on one side of the fireplace, wide-eyed and watching me; and there was Martha at the back door, a cigarette in her mouth and all messed up, but watching, too. They all looked towards the sofa. Gladstone was there under the blankets, and I thought then how he would have relished being in my shoes, faced with a comparable situation... and how he would have known exactly what to do, unlike me.

'Gladstone's sick,' Dora said.

'Go on, then, Lew,' Martha said. Then added tearfully, 'I can't manage. Can't really. Beyond me, it is.'

I went stiffly to Gladstone's side and looked down at his face on the pillow. He was very pale, his mouth firmly closed, his eyelids as if they had been scaled down. This is how he'll look when he's dead, I thought – and oh, God, what am I supposed to do? Why are they all so quiet, so hopeful of me? Ought I to touch his face or his hand? What should I say? I stood there and gulped and tried to hold on to one racing thought after another.

'Talk, then. Go on,' said Martha, in the same voice as she must have used when she asked me to say something in French. A voice that expected magic.

'When did it happen?' I managed to say.

She came into the room. 'This morning.' She sat down and acted it for me. 'Having a cup of tea. Like we always do. Then he *looks* at me all of a sudden. Oh – it was a look fit to send the shivers through you. Honestly! Then – he gets up and goes to the sofa and lies down. "Not so well?"

227

I asked him. "Feeling sick, cariad bach, are you?" Not a word did he answer. He lies down and pulls the blankets over him – and goes off to sleep.' Martha waved her hands helplessly. 'I never thought. I mean, he never *took* anything. I told Doctor he never took anything...' and by twelve o'clock she got worried and tried to wake him. 'Pinched him, even!' Then she'd sent for Dr Gwynn.

'Fatal mistake,' Dewi commented.

'Very nice, he was,' Martha protested. 'Been giving Gladstone talks and everything...'

'No wonder he's sleeping, then,' Dewi said.

'It isn't sleep, though,' Martha said with a break in her voice. 'Not real sleep at all...'

'Never moved?' I said.

Poor Martha broke down. 'He's got to have something to bring him round,' she sobbed. 'That's what Dr Gwynn said. He wanted me – his mother – to talk to him...'

Dewi made a disgusted face.

'Lew bach,' Martha said through her tears, 'say something to him. Dr Gwynn told me you're to say something to him...'

I was leading actor again, my face a beetroot red, the palms of my hands wet. I knelt by the sofa. 'Gladstone,' I said, not to Gladstone at all but to the rest of them.

'Any sign?' said Martha, coming closer.

'Gladstone – it's me. Lew.' I was too loud as well.

'Say some more,' she said. 'Saw his mouth move then.'

Dewi came to my support. 'I know what he was saying too,' he said firmly. 'He was saying to go away and leave me alone...'

I got quickly to my feet. 'That's the best thing,' I said.

'Did he really say that?' Martha asked.

'Course he did,' Dewi went on. 'How would you like to be woken up if you were enjoying a good sleep?'

'The doctor said...'

'Only having a good sleep,' Dewi went on. 'Leave him alone. He'll wake up.'

I felt better now. 'That's right,' I joined in. 'He'll be all right tomorrow...'

'They can give them injections,' Maxie said.

'Listen to the lunatic,' said Dewi.

I looked down at Gladstone while they had one of their arguments and I thought no, he'll not wake up, he'll never wake up, he'll be like that for ever, like the 'Lady of Shalott' by Tennyson.... Oh, God, if only there was blood or a wound, something obvious like that. You'd know then why he was sleeping.

'Percussion,' said Maxie.

'That's *bands*, old fool,' Dewi cried. 'Concussion you mean – and you're still wrong. Just let him sleep it out in peace. He'll be all right.'

Everybody wanted Gladstone to be all right, so everybody agreed with Dewi. And I was more than glad because it let me out.... We all cheered up then: Walter said something comic, and Maxie made another one of his mistakes. There were smiles all round until Dewi suggested that we go. 'No, stay,' said Martha. 'Stay, stay for a bit. He might come round tonight – you never know. Doctor said it might be a coma, like.' So we stayed for an hour and tried a half-hearted game with the children. Gladstone never moved, though – never changed his position on the couch, even.

When we got outside, Dewi stopped saying it was going to be all right. 'Gives you the creeps, Lew. Seeing him like that.'

'We've got to think of something,' I said. 'I don't know what – but something.'

'Might be all right tomorrow,' Maxie said, and we all agreed, but not very hopefully.

That was Monday night. Straight after school every day that week I went to see him, but he hadn't moved – just lay there as if some terrible drug was working on him. On Wednesday, Martha said that a specialist was going to be sent for. 'Who's going to pay for that?' she asked. 'It's not right, is it? He's always been queer.'

Her attitude towards Gladstone changed as the days went by. She had stopped crying, and every time she spoke of him it was grudgingly, as if she resented his long sleep. 'Just can't keep up,' she complained to me, and the dust everywhere, the ashes in the grate, the newspaper spread on the table, and the cigarette stumps proved how right she was. 'Not been to work for a week,' she said. 'What's going to happen to my babies, then?' But she managed to get out to the Harp every night just the same.

'You don't want to be going round there so often,' Meira said. 'Might catch something...'

'Sleep isn't contagious,' I said.

'Contagious! Well – listen to the County School.'

'My opinion,' said Owen, 'is that he isn't right – never was.'

'Tell me what right is,' I said.

'Well – like us.' Owen laughed. 'By damn, that's not

saying much, is it? Give me time and I'll work it out for you.' He made a move on the draughtsboard. 'Don't worry, Lew – it'll clear itself.'

Owen and Meira refused to fight with me, which was annoying in a way because by Thursday I was all set for an argument, and dreamed hopefully of catching one of the jokers of Porthmawr with Gladstone's name on his lips.

Polly said, 'There was a case in Liverpool some years ago – exactly the same – only it was a girl...'

'How could it be the same if it was a girl?' I asked smartly, and Polly became dry and withering, and talked in her best legal manner of people who changed, of certain parties who altered.

Then Rowland Williams caught me up on the street. 'You passed me,' he said. 'Never even looked...'

I said sorry, and that I had a lot on my mind. There was a week's growth of black beard on his chin, and his eyes were bloodshot, but there was no smell of drink on him.

'That's the trouble,' he said. 'The mind's the trouble.' He looked down at his boots and added, 'Thought you might not want to be seen talking to a comic character like me.'

I said that was soft for a start, then I told him about Gladstone.

'I know,' he broke in. 'I know.' And he was wringing his hands, almost breaking up in front of me, I thought. 'It's what happens,' he said. 'You show yourself and...' He had to lean against a wall for a moment. 'I'm all right,' he said. 'Been through worse and I'm all right.' He gripped my arm tight. 'Listen – know what the Nationalist Party's done, don't you? Burnt an aerodrome in Pwllheli to the ground! Know that, don't you?'

'Saw it in the paper, Mr Williams.'

'But it isn't enough,' he went on, tightening his grip on my arm. 'I'm with them, Lew – but they mustn't stop there. They're too late by a hundred years and more, but I'm with them.... It's a great fire we want that'll scorch away all the institutions of mediocrity – a great flame burning bright in the shabby dark, celebrating a dignity we have lost.... Oh, Lew bach, this bloody business between birth and death! We need a conflagration that will leave in its ashes a new birth, a fresh start...'

This was Rowland Williams, once so sharp, so lucid – and I wasn't following him at all. 'Didn't know you were a Nationalist, Mr Williams,' I said.

He came straight to attention. 'Not talking about Nationalism,' he snapped. '*Burning* is what I'm talking about. Can't you understand? I'm talking about humanity, about being alive, about the cancer that's eating away at head and heart...' He turned on his heel and shuffled off up Lower Hill, muttering angrily. Had he been six feet tall and clean and handsome perhaps my mouth wouldn't have shaped itself for a smile, perhaps I wouldn't have said 'Bloody hell!' again and again as a substitute for laughing aloud.

On Friday night I waited until I saw Martha go out before I went over to Gladstone. I was tired of her always expecting me to perform the miracle. Three times that day I had been in a fight because someone had asked after the 'sleeping beauty': I was in no mood to talk to anyone.

Nothing had changed at Gladstone's, except that the kitchen was dirtier still. The children were asleep, the silence in the house still holding traces of their cries. I removed a dirty blouse which Martha had thrown down on the rocking chair and sat down. Gladstone didn't seem to have moved at all. His face was the same, still mask-like, but paler if anything. The rash had cleared, but that was the only change. I sat there a long time, frustration gnawing at me, trying without success to will him awake.

Then, suddenly, the children awoke upstairs, shouting and protesting in a brief, sleepy quarrel. Automatically I looked up, and must have stayed liked that until the noise had died down. When I returned to my former position Gladstone's eyes were open and his face was turned towards me, and he was smiling.

I jumped up, as if stung, and went on wobbly legs to him. 'Well, good God,' I said. 'Good God.'

'What on earth were you looking at up there?' he asked, and raised himself up on the pillow.

'Lie down,' I said. 'Lie down – you're weak. I'll fetch the doctor.'

His familiar laugh echoed in the kitchen. 'A glass of water will do,' he said. 'I'm a bit parched. You look as if you've seen a ghost.'

'Don't talk,' I called over my shoulder as I went to the tap in the yard. 'Don't strain yourself.'

'I've had a good sleep,' he said. 'What day is today?'

'Here,' I said. 'Drink this. Don't talk.'

'But I'm ready for talk now,' he said, and he sat up on the sofa and drank all the water. 'What day?'

'Friday.'

He whistled softly. 'Monday to Friday! Still the same week, is it?'

'Seems much longer,' I said. 'Get the doctor, shall I?'

'Don't need any quack at all,' he replied. 'Refreshed and ready, that's me.' He cast his eyes over the kitchen. 'Things have got on top of me, haven't they?' he said in Martha's voice. 'Children all right, Lew?'

'All right except that they've been upset. Lie down, now. Get your bearings first.'

'Bearings?' he said with a laugh. 'Good God, Lew – that's why I went to sleep!' He flung back the blankets, swung his legs over the side of the sofa, and stood up: I moved nearer to him, certain he would fall, but there was no need. He stretched his arms upwards and sideways. 'A bit of exercise, Lew. To restore circulation.' He sat down again on the sofa and looked at his long, bony legs. 'Know what? I'll have to get a pair of pyjamas, Lew. Not right sleeping in your underclothes, is it? I'll have to get a pair – black, with a golden dragon on the pocket.' He winked at me. 'Two things I want to do,' he said in his actor's voice, 'two things ere my life is ended. The first is to play the piano in a nightclub, the second is to have a pair of black pyjamas with a golden dragon on the pocket. What say you?'

'Make a cup of tea, shall I?'

'Can't play the piano, though,' he went on. 'Put the kettle on – and go and wake the children.'

'Wake the children!' He was out of his mind, surely? 'They'll bring the house down.'

'Exactly,' he said. 'I think I'd like that. Very much. Go on, then. Kettle on first then up you go.'

I stood, open-mouthed, in front of him. I couldn't believe that he was serious, but he pointed upwards and said it was all right, and I found myself blundering up the stairs. It was dark on the landing, but although I was as noisy as an army there was no sound from the children's room. I opened the door, and the thought struck me: what if, by the time I had them awake and down the stairs, he had settled down on the sofa again and gone to sleep? The very idea threw me in a panic. I knocked the candle off its saucer and had to grope after it on hands and knees. Then, when it was finally alight, I was much too quick, much too rough. Walter first, then Mair, then Dora, were scratching and rubbing and crying like warm kittens newly disturbed. 'Come on,' I said, 'got a surprise for you in the kitchen.' I went down ahead of them, anxious now for Gladstone, but he was awake, trousers and shirt on as well. The children stumbled down the stairs behind me, complaining and crying, but when they saw Gladstone and realised he was awake, they were on to him in a rush. It was worth seeing. I felt as if I'd done something fine.

Ten minutes it took for the excitement to die down. Walter was really overcome and wet himself twice.

'Bladder trouble,' Dora told him, 'that's what you've got.'

They crowded around him, and went off into 'The Lord Is My Shepherd', very serious and tune-pure, followed by 'Dacw Mam yn Dwad', flat out but a bit ragged. And all the time Gladstone was touching and examining them, as if he expected to find a snail behind an ear. 'Look at their hair,' he tutted. 'Just look at that tidemark...'

Walter broke off in the middle of a note. 'Sleep well, did you?' he asked.

'Except when the linnets were singing,' Gladstone replied.

He was awake, a part of us once again. I kept on saying that to myself as item followed item in the concert. Back from the dead – my emotions were on free rein – old Gladstone back from the dead, the same as ever. But was he? Throughout Mars versus Wales by H. G. Wells I watched him carefully, and he *was* the same, surely? There seemed to be no change in voice or face as he recited 'The Mermaid of Porthmawr' and the terrible fate that befell her in the May Day procession 1933.... Yet, when he wasn't saying or doing anything, just looking at the children, there was a difference – all the lines of an old sadness were there.

At ten, Martha came in, three sheets to the wind and smelling like a brewery. At the sight of Gladstone she immediately fell to her knees and crawled the rest of the way to him. 'Oh my God, my God,' she cried in a strangled voice. 'He's back – never thought to see him no more in this life. Thought I was going to be left to struggle on alone with my babies....' She knelt at his feet, her chin on his knee, and went on like that, tears coursing down her cheeks. Gladstone and the children stroked her hair and said there, there, and giggled and winked at one another, too. It wasn't long before she was asleep, and in sleep looked strangely young and rather pretty. I helped Gladstone lift her up on the sofa. Dora removed her shoes, and they all settled her down for the night, as they would have done a baby.

There followed the pantomime of getting the children back to bed – everyone whispering and walking tiptoe and eyes shining, mouths smiling, because Mam was snoring and Gladstone was back in the land of the living.

When they were finally gone, Gladstone and I made tea

and toasted bread, and talked. But all the talking was about what had happened, and I did most of it. There was nothing about why he had gone off like that. He seemed to regard it as a normal thing to do, almost as if he had deliberately set himself the task of sleeping from Monday to Friday.

He came with me to the door. 'Let's walk the town,' I suggested in fun. He shook his head and breathed in deeply. 'Ever noticed the air of Lower Hill, Lew? One part salt, to one part mountain damp, to one part old lavatories.' We laughed together and looked out at the darkened houses. Then, piercing sharp, came the curlew's cry from the harbour somewhere. Gladstone shivered beside me. 'Smelly and beautiful,' he whispered. 'That's what it is all the time.'

For a while I stayed with him, then said I'd see him in the morning. 'All right,' he said, 'come over in the morning.' Before I reached our door I looked back: he was still there, his giant's shadow sprawled across the street.

XX

In the morning he was gone.

'Stolen my babies,' Martha wept. 'Taken my little ones away...'

The Super straddled a chair. 'Tell me again, Mrs Davies,' he ordered, 'from the beginning.' He glared at me from under bushy eyebrows. 'Stand there, you – and get your ideas sorted out.'

'He must've gone loony,' Martha cried. Her face was blotched and swollen with weeping. 'All that sleeping. He was always queer.' She came for me suddenly and caught me by the shoulders. 'You know all about it, Lew Morgan. Don't tell lies – you do.'

'Never told me anything,' I said. I was struggling to free myself: she was yelling in my face and her breath smelled worse than the harbour at low tide. 'I'm as shocked as you are.'

'Oh, no you're not. Nobody's as shocked as me.'

'We'll come to Master Morgan in a minute,' said the Super heavily. 'Just you calm yourself, Mrs Davies. Calm down now. Tell me what happened last night, when you got home.'

'He was awake,' she cried. 'The more I think of it, the more I can see he was pretending all the time.' She rounded on the Super as if he was responsible for it all. 'That boy never was sick, I bet you. I bet he woke up *every night* when I was out. Bet you anything he'd be prowling around here once I'd got to bed.' Her whole body shuddered at the thought. '*Noises* I used to hear...'

'Let's get back to last night,' said the Super. 'He was awake...'

'Wasn't he?' Martha yelled at me. 'Weren't you here? Wasn't he awake?'

'Half past eight or so,' I said, 'he woke up then.' It was still early and I was straight from bed, still bewildered. And Gladstone, she said, had run away with the children – without giving me any hint. 'He woke up and we had the children down...'

'That's a lie for a start,' Martha cried. 'They never were down, my babies. They were in bed – tucked up nice and snug in their little bed...'

'They were here when you came in,' I said. 'Then you went to sleep on the sofa...' I had to stop there because Martha went into a sobbing fit. The Super beckoned me over, pulled me closer to his chair.

'Lew Morgan – you're on oath...'

'Sir.'

'Going to tell me everything, aren't you?'

239

'Nothing to tell, sir. Don't know anything.'

The Super drew breath in, very sharp. 'Look at that poor woman there. You going to let that poor woman suffer?'

'No, sir, but I don't know anything.'

'Woke up this morning that poor woman did. Been to sleep on the sofa there. Woke up to an empty house. Your friend Gladstone woke up and gone. Her little children gone too. Think of that. Go on – think of it. Think how she feels.'

'Awful,' sobbed Martha. 'I feel awful.'

'And all she can remember is that he was awake last night – and you were here...'

'I was here,' I agreed, 'but he never told me anything. Never a word.'

'His best friend,' said the Super. 'Never told him anything – his *best* friend?'

'No, sir.'

'And you want *me* to believe *that*?'

'Yes, sir. Never told me he was going, sir.'

The Super got to his feet very slowly. Everything about him said menacing. 'Lew Morgan,' he began...

'What's all the fuss, then?' I said hurriedly. 'He's probably only gone for a walk. Taken them for a walk.'

'Clever,' said the Super, allowing himself a brief laugh. 'Gone for a walk, is that it? Gone for a walk and took with him all the children's clothes.'

Oh, my God, I thought. 'To the laundry?' I managed to whisper.

'All their personal effects – in a suitcase...'

'The only one we've got,' Martha sobbed.

'And,' the Super concluded, drawing himself to his full

height, 'there's money gone as well.' He glowered down at me. 'Gone for a walk, you say? Tell you what – let's you and me go for a walk. To the police station.'

'No breakfast,' I protested weakly.

'You'll remember better on an empty stomach,' said the Super.

I was there all morning. Shortly after ten, Dewi and Maxie joined me. The questions went on. 'There's a general alarm out,' said the Super. 'Kidnapping, that's what they call it in the States...'

Maxie rose to that one. 'Fry them on the electric chair,' he said.

'Shut up,' said the Super.

'Seen them on the pictures...'

'If you don't shut up,' said the Super, 'I'll be doing some frying myself.'

'He was only making a comment,' Dewi joined in.

'And you shut up as well.' Super Edwards by now was breathing heavily. 'Lew Morgan, I'm going to ask you once more...'

'Maybe he decided to go underground,' Maxie put in.

'What d'you mean,' the Super said, 'underground?'

'Well – there was this human mole, see. He went under the ground all the time. Burrowed down. Like a mole, see. That's why they called him the human mole.... He'd come up when he was ready. Catch everybody bending...'

The Super let Maxie go through it all, even sent a couple of constables to have a look at the old quarry workings.

'You know something, don't you?' he said in the nearest he could get to a whisper. 'You're in this, all of

241

you – *accessories before the fact....*' He was all things that morning: now pleading, now threatening, now reasonable. But we had nothing to tell. Perhaps he had begun to realise this when, at one, he sent us home for dinner. 'Report back at two sharp,' he roared. 'I'm going to get to the bottom of this.'

The interrogation continued over dinner, Meira all sentimental and sorry for Martha, but worried for me as well; Owen in one of his amused and cynical moods, yet anxious to know if I was hiding something. 'Where would *you* go, then – if you was running away with three little children?' That was the biggest question of all, I thought – until Meira asked 'Why did he take the children, then?'

I kept quiet and put on an innocent face. By the middle of the afternoon, once the Super had chased us out, I was beginning to enjoy my new status. I was in the know, hiding something.... Bet he knows, they would be saying in the town, he's a dark one, bet he's been in on this from the start.... As I walked the town among the squat, raw farming people who had come in for the shops and the pictures, I turned up the collar of my coat and hunched my shoulders, and affected a small smile that was, I thought, both knowing and mysterious.... But once darkness had fallen my anxiety for Gladstone came to the fore: miles away, cold, maybe hungry, he'd be, the children fretting and whining. Dewi was in the same mood. 'Should never have taken them children,' he said. Maxie came up with a succession of daft ideas. 'Perhaps he's still in Porthmawr,' was the only one we acted on. We went down to the *Moonbeam*, but there was no one – nothing to see, either, except the mud around her deeply

242

printed by size ten policeman's boots. That night I slept fitfully, in and out of a black dream.

Meira in the morning was strict and very serious. I was sent off to chapel 'to think about things properly', and there they must have spotted me because every second word was truthfulness, and the sermon was about the evil of deceit.... At two, in spite of all protests, I was ordered to the Sunday school. 'Mr Williams won't be there for a start,' I said, 'and you can't have a class without the teacher.' But he was – clean suited, clean shaven and clear of eye. Quietly, gently, he took us through a few verses from the Acts of the Apostles, but he soon gave that up and began to talk about Wales. 'A conquered people, an ancient, conquered people,' he said. 'We are frustrated by the facts of history, bogged down by the very thing that gives us brilliance and colour – our emotions....' Oh, it was the same old Rowland, and I was glad to find him so again. Dewi and Maxie helped me out in giving him all the details about Gladstone. He was very interested but showed no excitement. 'It doesn't matter *where* he's gone,' he said at the end. 'To go is to protest.'

He looked all set for a long speech, but at that moment we were collared by Abraham Evans and Dr Gwynn. They took us to the small vestry where Mrs Meirion-Pughe and the Rev A. H. Jones were waiting. They lined us up against the wall, as if for a firing squad, and they closed the door. Dr Gwynn leaned back against it, for all the world one of Edward G. Robinson's henchmen at the pictures. The Minister looked very nervous and very uncomfortable.

'Well, Mr Jones?' Mrs Meirion-Pughe said.

The Minister shuffled a bit, then stepped forward and looked at each of us in turn. 'Does any one of you know anything about the disappearance of Gladstone Williams and these little children? Dewi Price?'

'No, sir.'

'Ah – Max – ah – *you*.' He pointed at Maxie.

'So help me God, no.'

'Lew Morgan?'

'No,' I said.

The Minister crunched his false teeth. 'Honestly, now?'

We all nodded.

'Right,' he said, and stepped aside, letting us go.

Mrs Meirion-Pughe charged forward. 'Just a minute, Mr Jones,' she snapped. 'What about the Bible?'

The Minister kept his back to her and closed his eyes. 'There will be no swearing on the Bible,' he said slowly but firmly. 'There will be no swearing on anything. I believe these boys. Open the door. Let them go.'

We went out in a silence that could only be measured in kilowatts.

That night – in reality, the early hours of Monday morning – Rowland Williams' workshop on Lower Hill, Porthmawr, Wales, became an enormous bonfire, a great flame, as he had said, burning in the shabby dark. Rowland set it off himself; timber exposed to long, damp years does not burn with such intense brightness without a can or two of petrol.... And, in any case, Rowland was inside the workshop, at the centre of the great glow and the blazing heat. He came running out, so the morning stories had it, like a human torch, bursting out of the fire in an explosion of sparks. They exaggerated. Rowland came out of the fire slowly, almost reluctantly. He was wearing his long greatcoat, singed it is true, but not on fire; and he came with sleepwalker's arms straight for me where I stood at the front of the crowd. His hands were blackened stumps and stinking. I cowered back, but he wasn't making for me or anyone else. The crowd parted for him. Only the hiss and crackle of the burning workshop could be heard. Rowland went floundering through to the darkness of Lower Hill, and we left the fire and followed him, all of us, until he fell. He looked very small lying there on the worn sett-stones. I kept back and wept for him.

XXI

The new teacher to replace old Evans Thomas had arrived.
He was all pallor and pimples, and it was obvious by the
row he gave me for being late, by the way he escorted me
personally to the Head for giving cheek that he was new to
the game.... Mr Penry told him off in front of me for
leaving Sixth Form Arts to their own devices, then ordered
him back, gave me a smile as if in apology and asked me to
sit down. In no time at all we were having one of his
inquiries – one trap question after another, interrupted only
by good advice about my choice of friends.... My friends,
one in hospital with charred hands, the other God knew
where, were all right, and I told him they were all right.

'You have revealed considerable promise,' he said. By
now it was an insult. I wanted to say don't you know a
good memory when you see one, wanted to swear at him
too, and hated myself because I hadn't got the courage.

He gave up after break. I went back to the class: we had the new teacher again, and the carve-up was in full swing. I kept out of it until Goronwy Jones, always the boy for trouble, put his face close to mine and began to sing the one about my wandering boy. That did it. We fought on the desks, on the floor, out in the corridor. It took Mr Penry himself to part us. We had the cane and a lecture and were suspended for the rest of the day. So I arrived home at ten to twelve in time to catch Meira on her return from the station. She called me wicked, said it was all the bad company I'd been keeping, then added, 'Making a spectacle of himself – *bowing* to all that crowd watching him come off the train with them little children – policeman guarding them and everything...'

'He's back?' I cried. 'Gladstone's back?' And the tears came just as freely as they had done for Rowland Williams.

'Went to Chester,' Walter told me.

'My poor babies!' Martha wailed at the door as she took another pound of sugar from someone full of questions and sympathy.

'It's a Roman town,' Dora told me. 'They had to build it to conquer Wales. Have a little bridge going over the street and everything.'

'Like they were returned to me from the dead, Mrs bach,' Martha was saying.

'Had a lovely time,' Mair said. 'Real comic it was...'

Martha came back from the door and showered them all with kisses. 'My little babies! All right now you're with your mami, eh?'

'All right before,' Walter said.

'When's Gladstone coming back?' Dora inquired.

Martha refused to look at me. 'Oh – he'll be back...'

'Going to be a case?' I said.

She shook her head, still avoiding my eyes. 'It's the police, see. Told them I didn't want a case, though what he did was *cruel* – taking my babies. And he's seventeen and everything...'

'What's he doing at the police station?' I said.

'Well,' she said, reaching for a cigarette, 'wants warning, doesn't he? Wants teaching a lesson. Not right what he did...'

'Keeping him there a long time,' I said.

'Super said to leave him cool his heels in a cell...'

She was all guilty about something, and I was determined to find out what it was. 'He'll be home tonight, then, will he?'

Martha jogged little Walter up and down on her knee. 'Well – they got to decide, haven't they?'

'Decide what?'

'What to do with him. It's been all wrong, him at home with children and getting funny ideas. Reading and that all the time. Mrs Meirion-Pughe said it was all wrong.'

'Did she?' I said. 'So what will they decide? Off to a school somewhere?'

Martha gave a loud, false laugh. 'I told you – no case. I'm not bringing a case against my own. I just signed this paper...'

'Paper? To say what?'

She held a finger to her lips and pointed at the children. 'Well – so they can *decide*, that's all. I mean – he might take them from me again. Might try...'

I wanted to say 'while you're boozing at the Harp', but I couldn't be cruel to Martha. She was too soft, too hopeless, too easy a target. 'I'm going to see him,' I said.

Martha opened her mouth wide. 'S – E – A,' she spelt out. Then she waved a finger up and down. 'You know – waves...'

Horror chilled me. Gladstone going to sea – being shipped out! Oh, good God no, it wasn't possible. Only in the olden days did they send you to sea....

'Good place fixed for him,' Martha went on. 'I had to sign this paper because of his age, see. Super and everybody says it'll do him good, make a man of him.'

I marched past her to the door, Walter and Mair tagging on and whooping after me. But they were soon back to the kitchen when Dora, high-pitched and incredulous, cried out, 'Mami, you don't mean Gladstone has to go to *sea*, do you?' I didn't wait to hear how Martha tackled that one.

Super Edwards himself came to the long counter in the police station. 'Another one,' he said as he buttoned up his jacket. 'Just chased your pals away.'

I tried to keep my voice steady. 'Can I have a word with Gladstone, please?'

The Super had only recently finished his tea. He brushed his moustache and sucked at his teeth while he pondered my request. 'Been a *lot* of trouble, you lads,' he sighed. 'All summer. Got away with a lot. Know that, don't you?' I nodded. 'That one in there's got off *very lucky*. Should have had the stick across his backside. Know *that*, don't you?' I had to nod in case he wouldn't let me in to

249

see Gladstone. 'He's daft, that one. Keeps on asking me what *books* I've read!' The Super pawed his face. 'But daft or not – what's got my goat is he's not even *sorry* for all the trouble he's caused. He's *enjoying* himself in there! What's a bright boy like you want to talk to *him* for?'

He went on like that for ten minutes, and I nodded and said yessir. Then, quite unexpectedly, he raised the hinged part of the counter. 'Five minutes is all you've got,' he said, and he led me through his office to a large, bare room that smelled of disinfectant. 'Sit on that side of the table,' he ordered. 'Remember this is a *special* privilege I'm giving.' Then he went out leaving the door open.

When he returned with Gladstone, I stood up. 'Down!' barked the Super. 'Here's your friend.' He motioned Gladstone to the chair across the table from me. 'I'll be in my office, listening to every word,' he added. 'No *monkey business*, don't forget.' Then he turned and looked at Gladstone and laughed.

'Very nice of you to come, Lew,' Gladstone said in a very affected accent. 'Why don't you sit down yourself, Super – and have a good *discussion* with us?'

The Super went out saying, 'Had enough of you and your bloody discussions.'

'Did you get my note, Lew?' Gladstone said, winking at me. The Super turned quickly and came back and leaned against the doorpost. 'I tied it to the pigeon's leg and told the bird to fly straight to Lew Morgan's palatial residence on Lower Hill....'

Give over clowning, I was going to say, but the Super broke in with, 'What pigeon? What note's that?'

'Well, of course,' Gladstone went on, still keeping up his

250

affected accent, 'is it not a well-known fact that in each cell there has to be a bird? I said *pigeon*, but perhaps it was a starling, or a robin – it doesn't really matter – a bird to carry a message to a friend. Why – even in the Old Testament...'

'Oh, God!' said the Super.

'All I wanted was the pills,' Gladstone went on. 'Did you bring them, Lew?'

'What pills?' the Super roared at me. 'You've not brought this daft bugger any pills, have you?'

I shook my head. Why did Gladstone have to be like this? Why couldn't he be serious?

'I'm not having you doing away with yourself in my cells,' the Super said. 'Now you watch out, boy – I've had enough of your funny business.' The Super went out, banging the door shut behind him, then remembered and pushed it open again.

'No time for clowning,' I said.

Gladstone swept the long hair clear of his forehead. 'A debatable point, Lew. But when you are a failure, and you're about to be deported – what else can you do?'

'Change your voice,' I said. 'You're only talking to me...'

His face split into a broad grin. 'But I've been to England, Lew – for the first time in my life, and by courtesy of the London, Midland and Scottish railway in one of their most luxurious cattle trucks. You know how you're supposed to talk when you've been to England, don't you? Well – I've been.'

I was annoyed with him now. 'Give over,' I said sharply. 'What did you want to go for, anyway?'

'To see foreign parts, Lew,' he said in his normal voice. 'To taste strange air. To give the little ones a treat...'

251

'In a cattle truck,' I said.

He was surprised at my tone. 'Well – truthfully it wasn't a cattle truck. It was a guard's van with no guard. I only said cattle truck because it sounded more adventurous. It was a guard's van on a long goods train, and the damn thing went non-stop all the way to Chester. Something mysterious there, Lew.' He pointed a finger at me. 'Why should a goods train leave Wales at five on a Saturday morning and go non-stop to Chester? Intrigue somewhere, Lew bach. Who knows how many political prisoners were being shipped out from their native land in those cattle trucks?'

Impatiently I pushed my chair back. 'Be serious,' I said, 'we've all been worried about you...'

For a brief moment his face became grave, then the smile was back again. 'Been serious all summer, me,' he said, back again with that ridiculous accent. 'I'm a failure, old chap. I've even become an Anglicised Welshman after two days! Can't fail more than that, can you?'

'Give up,' I said. 'Talk properly...'

'Been in England so long I've forgotten all my Welsh.'

'Jesus!' I said angrily. 'Twll tîn bob Sais...'

'Exactly, old chap! That's just it.' His eyes sparkled even in that dim light. 'That's the whole trouble. You say to yourself where can I escape to, assuming that I want to escape? And the only answer is England! The other side of the dyke!' He clapped his hands loudly above the table. The Super appeared in the doorway and glared at us, then retired again. 'I'm a failure,' Gladstone went on, lowering his voice a little, 'because I picked the wrong train and the wrong time of year. Now, if it had been spring I might have made something of it – but not in the wet and the cold.

252

And there's these trains – why isn't there a train leaving Porthmawr station and going non-stop to Paris, say? Or, better still, a non-stopper to the Mediterranean, or the Nile, or Samarkand... ? Is that a place, Lew – Samarkand?'

I kicked the table leg. 'You're mocking me, that's what...'

'No, Lew!' he said earnestly. 'That's not true. I'm just telling you that if you want to escape you *have* to go to England, and that's the snag. When I realised what I'd done to those little children, I practically *gave* us up to the police.' Then, all too briefly for my liking, he was very serious, 'I could have gone on, but I hadn't anywhere in mind – except here.'

'But you're *letting* them send you to sea,' I cried out angrily.

'Tomorrow,' he admitted, the smile back on his face. 'The Super's coming with me. He wanted to beat me this afternoon, but the Rev A. H. Jones wouldn't let him. Oh, they had a long chat about my future – public enemy number one, that's me – and they were on the phone and all sorts. Now it's all fixed. I'm off on the South America run with Captain Jenkins – he's a Bible puncher too – and Martha has signed the paper to let me go...'

'But you don't want to go,' I protested.

He shrugged. 'I wouldn't say that...'

'You're giving in to them, letting them do what they want!' I was angry with him again, angrier still because he was smiling. 'You won't, will you? You'll clear off in Liverpool?' He shook his head decisively. 'But why?' I said. 'Why?'

He placed his hands very carefully on the table, fingers pointed as if he was going to play the piano. 'Lew,' he said

253

slowly, 'if I skip out, *they'll* be the winners.' I was baffled, and he could see it, too. 'Besides,' he added gently, 'I'm ready for something new. Buenos Aires – might be all right, Lew. Yes – let's say I'm ready for something new...'

The heavy silence that followed was broken by the scrape of the Super's chair. I opened my mouth to speak, but Gladstone pulled a book out of his pocket and waved me silent with it. 'I want you to have this, Lew,' he said. 'Found it in a railway carriage in Chester. Never knew such books existed... I've been wasting my time, really have.'

I took the book and read out the title. '*Salammbo* by Gustave Flaubert...'

The Super came in, but Gladstone went on talking. 'Some of the pages are missing – but you'll be shaken, Lew. I've never read anything like it.... I'll have to get on to these Frenchmen, and no mistake. Pity I can't read the language – you lose things in translation – but that might come, don't you think so, Super?'

'You've had long enough,' the Super said to me.

'Let him stay,' said Gladstone. 'The Super's got a nice place here, Lew. First time I've ever had a room of my very own.'

'Out,' the Super said to me. 'Come on.' He looked down at Gladstone. 'Oh – you're going to be sorted out, boy bach! You'd better get all the rest you can – get all your talking done, too. Captain Jenkins won't give you any time for talk...'

'How terribly Victorian,' Gladstone said in his affected voice. The veins bunched up on the Super's brow.

'Out!' he said again, then added with a laugh, 'say *goodbye* to your friend.'

My throat was dry. I couldn't get a word out.

'*Au revoir*, Super,' Gladstone said. 'Lew – kiss the little ones for me. Kiss old Martha too – if you like. Tell them I'll be home by Christmas, all bronzed and smelling of foreign parts. It'll be a Friday night, Lew. On the last stopper – the 8.23. You be there.' He held out his hand. I felt very shy as I took it. 'And, Lew,' he added, 'many thanks for the file and the cold chisel...'

'Out!' the Super roared, and I marched past his pointing arm. In the office I heard Gladstone start up again. 'Super,' he was saying, 'how do you stand under the *Habeas Corpus* Act in my case?'

I went out and walked the town in the wet, but it didn't help much.

Gladstone went away on the first train in the morning. None of us saw him go. That night I went to the Palace with Dewi and Maxie to see Laurel and Hardy. We fell off the seats laughing. Even Maxie thought it was terrible that we could be like that. 'Go and piss on it, shall we?' he said, looking back at the cinema. But they decided to go window-smashing instead. I didn't go with them. After that night we didn't meet as often, didn't have as much to do with one another.

Winter, black and damp and suffocating, fell on Porthmawr. As the months dragged on to Christmas there was less and less talk of Gladstone and the Vaughans, hardly a mention of the fire in Rowland's workshop. The town was taking a look at its future, and in public meetings and private committee they debated (for the tenth time since 1918) whether or not to build a promenade with boarding houses, whether or not to become a *proper* holiday resort like Rhyl, or Colwyn Bay, or Llandudno. The side issues were brought out and aired once again – the Welsh way of life, for instance, and the Sabbath, and the future of the language, and the unemployment question, and the drift into England... an ocean of talk into which the whole town plunged. Even Polly – we were friends again now – came out with some strong opinions when she wasn't discussing Royalty and divorce, morganatic marriages and another Prince of Wales in trouble.

Meira, however, took no part in all this. She had become withdrawn and secretive, and each day more beautiful, a new lustre in her hair, a new sheen in her eyes. I noticed how she sat for hours in a daydream, noticed how she was filling out, too. Then, on a sleet-lashed December night, I was running for the doctor; and next morning there was blood on the bedclothes soaking in the old tub in the kitchen, and Meira was shrivelled and bitter upstairs, and Owen silent and resentful by the fire.

Before Christmas, the Rev A. H. Jones had gone to a new chapel in the south, and Eirlys Hampson had sold up and returned to Manchester. There was a lot of spiteful chatter, of course – especially about Eirlys, and particularly when *Mr* Meirion-Pughe, only three weeks after his wife had died of a swift and terrible cancer, was off to Manchester too. 'But how do you know?' I asked Polly. 'Been *seen* there,' she replied grimly, 'more often than that.'

Then there was Martha and the children. In the first week of December, the week of Meira's trouble, they left suddenly and without goodbyes, furniture van and all, for Birmingham and an uncle newly a widower. The news that

256

they had gone shattered me. There was no reason for Gladstone to return to Porthmawr now.

But I kept hoping. The day after they left, another letter arrived. It was headed 'On the way Home', and was posted in the Canary Islands. His other letters, all very long, had been high farce and in his worst manner – as if he was deliberately hiding from me – and this was no better. Consider the non-existence of canaries in the Canary Islands, he began. Was this another instance of the general fraud, the worldwide conspiracy that said something was, when it was not? Pages of that, pages about a master plan to move the Azores ('why *do* they have such vulgar names?'), pages about Walt Whitman ('newly discovered, a *marvellous* poet'), but not a word about how he felt. Except a postscript in pencil hurriedly scrawled, an arrow that found its target: 'It is astonishing,' he wrote, 'how *alone* I feel.'

Not much hope, then. Yet, on many a Friday night, before and after Christmas, I went down to the station and waited in the white steam and the hissing gaslight for the 8.23. Rowland Williams was always there, his hands hidden in a kind of muff. We spoke occasionally, but only about trivialities. There was never anyone else. And nobody came.

Foreword by Philip Pullman

Born in Norwich in 1946, Philip Pullman is a world-renowned writer. He was educated in England, Zimbabwe and Australia before his family settled in north Wales where he attended Ysgol Ardudwy, Harlech. His novels have won every major award for children's fiction, and are now also established as adult bestsellers. The *His Dark Materials* trilogy came third in the BBC's 2003 Big Read competition to find the nation's favourite book. In 2005 he was awarded the Astrid Lindgren Memorial Award, the world's biggest prize for children's literature. He lives in Oxford.

LIBRARY OF WALES

The Library of Wales is a Welsh Assembly Government project designed to ensure that all of the rich and extensive literature of Wales which has been written in English will now be made available to readers in and beyond Wales. Sustaining this wider literary heritage is understood by the Welsh Assembly Government to be a key component in creating and disseminating an ongoing sense of modern Welsh culture and history for the future Wales which is now emerging from contemporary society. Through these texts, until now unavailable, out-of-print or merely forgotten, the Library of Wales brings back into play the voices and actions of the human experience that has made us, in all our complexity, a Welsh people.

The Library of Wales includes prose as well as poetry, essays as well as fiction, anthologies as well as memoirs, drama as well as journalism. It complements the names and texts that are already in the public domain and seeks to include the best of Welsh writing in English, as well as to showcase what has been unjustly neglected. No boundaries limit the ambition of the Library of Wales to open up the borders that have denied some of our best writers a presence in a future Wales. The Library of Wales has been created with that Wales in mind: a young country not afraid to remember what it might yet become.

Dai Smith
Raymond Williams Chair in the Cultural History of Wales,
Swansea University

PARTHIAN

A Carnival of Voices

www.parthianbooks.com

LIBRARY OF WALES

SERIES EDITOR: DAI SMITH

WWW.LIBRARYOFWALES.ORG

LIBRARY OF WALES
titles are available to buy online at:

gwales.com
Llyfrau ar-lein
Books on-line